Making Pretty

Making pretty

COREY ANN HAYDU

KATHERINE TEGEN BOOKS
An Imprint of HarperCollins Publishers

Katherine Tegen Books is an imprint of HarperCollins Publishers.

Making Pretty
Copyright © 2015 by Corey Ann Haydu
All rights reserved. Printed in the United States of America.
No part of this book may be used or reproduced in any manner whatsoever without
written permission except in the case of brief quotations embodied in critical
articles and reviews. For information address HarperCollins Children's Books, a
division of HarperCollins Publishers, 195 Broadway, New York, NY 10007.
www.epicreads.com

Library of Congress Control Number: 2014949410
ISBN 978-0-06-229408-1

Typography by Erin Fitzsimmons
15 16 17 18 19   PC/RRDH   10 9 8 7 6 5 4 3 2 1

First Edition

For two wonders of my world, Anica & Victoria. You are always, always on my List of Things to Be Grateful For.

June 2

The List of Things to Be Grateful For

1 A summer without stepmothers.

2 That I am suddenly and certainly cool enough to hang
out with Karissa.

3 The boy across the park who wears weather-
inappropriate clothes and checks out me instead of my
best friend.

one

I should not be going to a bar.

Karissa and I have matching Elmo T-shirts, but hers is cut to show a lot of skin and mine is layered over a ripped long-sleeved black shirt and under a polka-dot cardigan I stole from my dad's third wife, Natasha.

"Act cool, Montana," Karissa says. "Act twenty-one."

I take my hair down from its ponytail and cock my head to the side and try to look bored.

"Does this look twenty-one?" I ask. We're across the street from Karissa's favorite bar, Dirty Versailles. It's on the Lower East Side of Manhattan and allegedly lives up to its name. Dive meets fancy French palace. It is the opposite of surprising that Karissa likes it.

"You'll need this," she says, handing me a lit cigarette. She lights a new one for herself. "You smoke, right?"

"Yes, ma'am," I say. I like to call Karissa "ma'am" because she's twenty-three and she hates it.

I take a drag on the cig. My best friend, Roxanne, started smoking at college this year so I started too, wanting to be up to speed when she got home for the summer. I don't like the taste but I like how much my older sister, Arizona, hates it and how much my dad would hate it if he were home enough to know.

I like how it compresses the time and space between Roxanne and me. With each dirty drag I can almost pretend I spent the year upstate at Bard splitting cigarettes with Roxanne and her Argentinian roommate, or in Maine with Arizona, making out with boys in white baseball caps.

Karissa moves us across the street so that we're smoking right in front of the bar, where the bouncer can see us.

"Look edgy," she says. "Look sexy. Look like you don't give a crap and could go anywhere but have chosen to grace this bar with your presence."

I'm not convinced I can pull that off, but I don't want this night with Karissa to end. She has on silver leggings and cowboy boots that she spray-painted neon blue, and her hair is so long and wild she could be a mermaid or a lioness. I'm a little bit in love with her, in the way I used to be in love with my cool teenage babysitters when I was like ten years old.

I blow my smoke up instead of out. I thank myself for wearing skinny jeans instead of the ugly shorts Roxanne and Arizona hate. It's impossible not to wonder if I should have done some sort of makeup situation.

Karissa stamps out her cig, so I do the same.

"Pretty K!" the bouncer says when she touches his arm and smiles.

"Hey, buddy," she says. He's a little bit in love with her too. Everyone is. The boys and men in our acting class. Strangers walking from an Italian dinner to a crappy sports bar. The short dude in the sketchy bodega who sold her the cigarettes.

"Come on in," the bouncer says.

"This is Montana," Karissa says, putting an arm around me and kissing my cheek. "She cool?"

The bouncer looks me up and down. It seems like A Moment. I've been asking myself this very same question all year long. Am I cool?

I've had a lot of time to mull it over, in the absence of my sister and my best friend. It's the kind of question I've been working out, listening to stories of dorm parties and gender studies classes and roommates with dreadlocks and how quiet and sweet and full life outside the city can be.

I haven't come up with an answer, and the bouncer looks unconvinced.

"She young?" he says.

"Younger than me!" Karissa says. "But old enough."

"Fine, fine, get her in there," the bouncer says. "But I can't promise she'll fit in."

"Isn't the point to not fit in?" Karissa says. Every word out of her mouth is perfect. Wry and flirty and smart and funny and killer.

Goddamn it I want to be her. But I'll settle for having her take me under her wing for now.

The bar is exactly what it promised to be. Everything is painted gold but also chipping. Chandeliers with fake crystals hang from the ceilings. Half the lightbulbs are out.

It's funny how something sad is automatically more beautiful than something happy.

It applies to people too. Karissa is the sad kind of pretty. Like a very wise Tinker Bell. Tinker Bell's sad too. All wrapped in unrequited love and unbelievability and misery. Karissa, Tinker Bell, and this bar are all lovely for the same reasons.

"Tinker Bell is sort of a tragic literary figure, right?" I say. It seems smart and interesting in my head, like a brilliant thesis I've come up with that Karissa could get behind. Something that will astound and impress her. Make it clear I'm worth the trouble of sneaking into a bar.

"Huh. Maybe," she says. "But I'm an Ophelia girl personally. Crazy and gorgeous and loved and ill-fated. Not that I'm gorgeous. I'm like the opposite of gorgeous." Karissa makes a nervous gesture with her hand running through her hair, and she is completely gorgeous. "But I'm a little crazy, like all the best people are."

She looks at me like I'm supposed to say something, and I want to say something even though I have nothing to say.

"They so are," I say. "I'm, like, bonkers." It's a word Roxanne uses all the time so I am a total fraud, but it works. Karissa beams.

"And Ophelia's about a million times better than Juliet, you know? Juliet had a stupidity to her. Ophelia is all tragedy, all the time," she says. I nod and wonder at talking about Ophelia on a Thursday night at a downtown bar next to a guy with a beard and a green drink and a neon-yellow bow tie.

"Ophelia commits to the tragedy of life," I say, playing with the gold tassel on my bar stool. "She knows how it is."

"Yes!" Karissa says, before turning to the bartender and ordering a bottle of red. He gives us goblets and some kind of French wine and fills everything to the tippy top because he's so distracted by Karissa. It doesn't matter that her teeth are crooked and her chin is a little small and she's even flatter than me. It doesn't matter that she's freckled and that her hair is light brown and not honey blond or platinum blond or champagne blond.

She is charged. And beautiful. And telling me to drink faster, harder, more enthusiastically.

"Let's be drunk," she says. "Let's be drunk best friends who rule the world."

"Best friends?" I say. The music is loud and I wonder if I've misheard her. I've been aching to have a best friend again. Even though Roxanne has been back from college for a few weeks, it hasn't felt the way it did last year or the ten years before that. She talks about people whose names I've never heard. People who have names I didn't even know were names. People who go only by their last names. People who go by shortened versions of their last names: Hertz and Scal and Jav and Gerb. It's hard to keep up.

Arizona gets back tonight. We haven't spoken in over a month, which seems impossible for someone I used to co-parent a stuffed elephant with. She won't even be living at home over the summer. Dad's letting her split a summer sublet with one of her new Colby friends. I hate that the word *sister* has this shifting, changeable definition that doesn't mean two people who share a room and a brain and a speech pattern and a body type anymore.

I'm over it. Over them. Over the things I knew and did and thought. I'm with Karissa now.

"I think we could be best friends, don't you?" Karissa says. She slams down her goblet and fills it up with more wine. Her teeth are insta-purple. "If I find you a cute college guy to hook up with, would you ditch your other best friends and become mine?"

"I'd definitely consider it," I say, but really I'm looking everywhere for the guy I see sometimes in the park. I'm pretty sure we have developed a whole relationship based on continuous, awkward eye contact over the last two months.

"It's rare to have a real connection with someone," Karissa says. She leans in close to me. She smells like baby powder deodorant, and I know from experience, even though I can't hear them now, that her cheap metal earrings are making tiny clanging noises. "You're in high school, so maybe you don't know this, but you'll mostly hate people when you're in your twenties, and you'll be wondering why everyone's trying to be so boring. They're all scared."

I don't tell her that I'm scared.

I do tell her that I've seen a lot of women on a quest to be boring.

My dad's a plastic surgeon. A fancy one who specializes in marrying women, changing everything about them on his operating table, and divorcing them when they're as close to perfect as he can get them.

That's not what's written on his business card or anything. But that's how it goes with Dr. Sean Varren.

"There's a guy for you," Karissa says, pointing across the bar to a dude in a plaid button-up whose mohawk is so tall it almost touches one of the low-hanging chandeliers.

"I think he's for you," I say. He's handsome in the same unknowing, wild, fantastic way that Karissa is beautiful. He doesn't look kissable because he doesn't look knowable.

"For you!" she says. "Be brave. Live big." She shakes her mane and the light catches the glittery blush she wears. Her eye shadow is ironic blue, and it matches not only the boots but also a thin headband she's strapped across her forehead.

I pull my Elmo shirt down so that it covers my stomach. I wave at Mohawk Man. He waves back but doesn't come over. We pound the rest of the bottle of wine. It's a brand-new feeling—I'm used to chugging beer or taking shots of cheap liquor, but I'm not used to wine at all, in any context. It hits all slow and sleepy, and I like that it tastes purple, royal, sweet.

Roxanne favors Malibu rum and kegs of light beer.

If Karissa's my new best friend, everything we do will be different and new and better.

She orders another bottle.

I've made it. I'm here. I'm hers.

When we are drunker and it's later, we end up in a booth in the back. The guy with the mohawk bought us some beers and talked about art for a while, but he must have felt like a third wheel, because Karissa and I have this secret-language way of talking. It doesn't matter that we've only known each other for six months and that there's no real reason for us to be friends now that acting class is over. It doesn't matter that I'm seventeen and she's twenty-three. We're connected. We fit. We're mismatched and cozy in the back booth. We make sense in a weird and wonderful way. Like math except sexy and cool.

I'm getting texts from Arizona asking where I am, saying she got home and ordered us a pizza, saying I was supposed to be there to welcome her home after her post-freshman-year European backpacking trip. She could have returned to New York when her semester ended three weeks ago. She chose even less time with me. She keeps choosing less time with me, over and over.

I don't reply to the texts.

I can't stop swinging my hair around like Karissa does. She makes it look so good, and I'm convinced I could be a little like her, if I tried harder. Arizona texts again, a bunch of question marks instead of words, so I start to feel bad. Punctuation marks make me feel more than words, sometimes.

"I think I need to get home," I say. "My sister's waiting for me. I told her I'd hang out even if she got home late. Start our summer together off right or something. Pizza. Bonding. All that."

"Your sister's back," Karissa says. She doesn't make a move to pay the bill or slide out of the booth. "You must be so happy."

"Mmmm. I miss the way things were with her," I say, and it's the truest thing I've said all night and maybe all month. Karissa hits the bottom of her umpteenth glass of wine. She shakes her head like she's trying to clear it. Wipes her mouth and teeters on the edge of weepiness.

"I need to tell you something about me," Karissa says.

"Anything," I say.

"I'm sort of messed up, okay? Like . . . okay. Okay. This is such a weird thing to announce, but if we're going to be friends, real ones, it's like, we have to know the big things, right? So we need to get all the big things out there, as, like, foundation." Karissa pushes her hair behind her ear in this ballerina way and I am certain she will be famous someday, even if it is simply for that one gesture.

"Let's do it," I say, leaning forward. I wonder if people are listening in on us. I would.

"My whole family is dead. Car accident four years ago. You talking about your sister made my heart—I don't know. I feel like I can't even have a normal conversation if you don't know that about me. Like, you won't understand anything I say if you don't know that, right?"

"Right," I say. Her eyes fill up and mine do too, a mirror image of her. She is Ophelia.

I feel desperately sad for her and a little bit sad for myself that she didn't tell me before. That I've known her all this time without really knowing her. "Are you . . . how are you? About it?" Drunkenness is a blessing right now, because everything I say sounds smooth and deep. I can look right into her green eyes and not blink or blush or get nervous.

"I'm a mess," she says. "I'm not like anyone else." She's

whispering, and little pieces of crystal on the chandeliers above chime whenever the air conditioner clicks onto a higher level.

"That's . . . wow. Wow. I'm sorry. I don't know what to say. It's incredible you, like, get up and walk around every day. Seriously."

Karissa sighs and licks her lips that must taste like wine and lipstick, and she brushes her hair aside again and again.

"I can tell you have something dark in there too," she says. "Something that happened. Or something missing. Or something you want." Even through the beginnings of tears, she sees me. It's a little scary, to be seen.

"All three," I say, thinking of my mother who left us and my father who keeps marrying new women and the emptiness of the house without Arizona and the way three stepmothers in ten years feels less like a surplus of stepmoms and more like a deficit of mothers.

I say some drunk version of this, wondering at the way the words come out wrong and lopsided and unclear, like I can't recite my own biography.

"It's stupid, compared to what you've been through," I say. But Karissa holds my hand across the table. Kisses it. There's a reason books are written about girls who've lost everything.

"Girls without mothers are, like, strong and weak at the same time," Karissa says. "We're all powerful, you know? Like, we have a special secret power and secret pain and they're both more, like, vast than anyone knows."

If anyone else classified me as a girl without a mother, I'd hate them, but with Karissa it seems like a point of pride. Like something

I'm supposed to celebrate with her. Like she's inviting me into a club that I'm not totally qualified for.

Arizona would hate it. She's always saying we have each other and Dad and we don't need anyone else, as if we're made to need less than most people.

"We're going to have champagne to close this night out," Karissa says when I can only manage weepiness and compliments as a reply. She makes the bartender come to us, leaving his post at the bar to bring champagne right to the table, and I know he sees in her what I see. What we all see.

"To everything we don't have," she says, her voice hitching and settling in the single sentence.

We clink and drink, but Karissa stops me before my second sip.

There are enormous, dark portraits of former French kings on the walls, powdered wigs and all. They're in oversize gold frames and decorated with neon graffiti.

"We'll have everything, someday," Karissa says, so sure it sounds like fact. I wonder what it's like to have hope after you've lost everyone that you love. What kind of strength it must take for her to utter that sentence.

"I've never been this drunk," I say, which has nothing to do with anything except it's getting hard to see or think from behind this haze.

"You're freaking adorable," Karissa says. "You remind me of my little sister. She died in the crash too." It aches, hearing her say the words so plainly. Something so large and awful should only be talked about with flowery language and metaphors. Her saying it in such a basic way twists me up inside.

"Oh my God, Karissa, I'm so sorry. I'm so, so sorry," I say. I've never before been this sad about someone else's life.

"We so get each other," she says, her voice all thick and slurry too. "You and me against everything that has sucked in our lives. Two sad girls together. Can we toast to two sad girls?"

I grin. I feel as light and bubbly as the champagne, next to Karissa.

two

I get home all buzzed and beautiful.

Arizona is waiting for me with a finger on her lips.

"Dad just went to bed. You do not want him to see you like this, trust me." She wipes something off my cheek—maybe rogue mascara or sweat or Karissa's peachy lipstick.

"You're here!" I say, and throw myself at her.

"I told you I was coming in tonight." She hugs back lamely. "What the fuck? Who were you even out with? I called Roxanne. She hadn't seen you." I hate the implication that she knows the exact size and shape of my life. That the world paused while she and Roxanne invented new lives in woody college towns.

I hug her again anyway.

Something is different. Everything is different.

I squint at my sister's body. Maybe I'm wasted, but it looks wrong. College has done something to her, even since I last saw her, over spring break. She's fuller on top. More like a Mrs. Varren. Alien, compared to our formerly matching shapes. We have always had matching gaits and proportions—straight and narrow on top, wide on the bottom. We have had matching indignations and resentments, too. Matching long toes and back moles. Matching dirty mouths and a shared best friend.

"You're all wrong" is all I can say, but it's not what I mean. I think I like being this drunk except for the inability to say what I mean. "You feel wrong," I try again.

"I wanted a whole night together," Arizona says. "You and me and catching up and starting the summer together."

"You already started the summer without me," I say, thinking of the one single Eiffel Tower postcard she sent me from her trip. She knows I prefer Notre-Dame and that the Eiffel Tower is what you send to your little cousin or the teacher you're kissing up to or family you used to babysit for. Not your sister. Not your best friend.

I wobble backward when she lets go of me. Our West Village brownstone has always had sloping floors and an almost-obvious crookedness, and it's all bigger and wonkier after all that wine.

"I don't like the way you feel," I say, the effort of words so exhausting I have to find my way to the couch. It's something Janie bought years ago, which means it's stiff and silky and ivory colored. "Fucking Janie," I say, which I always say when I sit on things that Janie decorated our apartment with. The things Tess bought are comfier. The things Natasha bought are flashier. The things Mom bought look like home. Like an idea of home that I have in my head but doesn't exist in real life. "Seriously, what happened to you? What'd they do to you up there?" She's wearing khaki capris, which is lame, but something more substantial has changed. Something bigger than her clothing choices.

She smells a little like the plane, like those ham and cheese sandwiches that they serve in the middle of long flights. Her suitcase is by the front door, a reminder that she's not actually living here this summer.

"Don't freak out," Arizona says. I squint harder at her. Shake my head to make things come into focus. Maybe I can shake off the drunkenness. Unblur the world.

It's her boobs.

I realize it a single moment before she says it.

"I got my boobs done in April. I didn't want to tell you over the phone because I thought it would sound like I got porn-star boobs or something, but I wanted you to see it's like a teeny-tiny upgrade. I'm still smaller than, like, everyone else. I mean, aside from you. So it's not a big deal. Don't be a psycho about it." She's in too many layers for June in New York. A long tee hangs out of her oversize Colby sweatshirt. She wants me to know, but doesn't want me to see them.

"I don't understand," I say. I grab my stomach, since all my feelings about it rush there, and I wish I were either more drunk or more sober. I am in the exact wrong state of mind to be hearing and seeing this.

"I feel more like me now," Arizona says. "Like this is how I'm supposed to look. I never fit in my body."

She's right, her new boobs aren't stripper big or anything, but they fill out the sweatshirt so that the letters of her college rise and fall in a new way. I hate that T-shirts and sundresses and fleece jackets will look different on us now. I won't be able to look at her and see me.

"We don't like boob jobs," I say. My voice breaks; the pressure of a year of hearing about her new Montana-less life, a year of living alone with Dad and Tess and now Dad and his dreamy dating-someone-new look, is too much, and I need her to agree with me.

"I sort of like mine," Arizona says. "But it doesn't have some big, deep meaning, okay? And you look excellent the way you are. Okay?"

"Stop asking me if it's okay," I say. Late-night TV is droning in the background, and I wonder how this conversation would have gone if I hadn't been out with Karissa all night. I wonder if we would have ended up eating prosciutto pizzas and looking at pictures of Europe and rating the Continent's best kissers according to her very scientific data.

I wonder if I have missed something vital, a moment between us I'll never get back.

I'm almost sad, but she turns slightly, enough so that I can see her in profile, and her new silhouette is all wrong and I'm filled with boozy rage again.

"We promised we wouldn't do it," I say. "We promised Mom we wouldn't do it." I hold on to her elbow like that will help steady us both, bring us back to shore together.

She looks like one of them. Like one of the stepmoms. Her clothes are airplane-messy, but her hair is smooth and blonder than I remember, and she has a headband with tiny pink rhinestones.

They glint.

"I don't feel like we owe Mom anything. I'm not sure Mom is the role model of the year," Arizona says.

"You promised me, too. That we wouldn't get any kind of plastic surgery, no matter what Dad said. You don't owe me anything either?"

She hugs me again and I hate it again. We've made a lot of promises over the years about staying away from the stepmoms and never forgiving Natasha and never getting plastic surgery and always being there for each other. These promises are the things that make us work—the levers and gears and mechanics that keep us ticking in sync with each other. They're the things that make us sisters.

It turns out we aren't good at keeping promises or maybe even at being sisters.

"We are going to have an awesome summer together," Arizona says. She feels bad for me. She gets me water and rubs my back and I am a person to be pitied and cared for, but I'm not her best friend anymore. We aren't going to explore Prague and Vienna and Croatia together, because she's already done that with someone else.

"We're not going to be together," I say.

"I'm staying, like, two blocks away. I didn't know Tess would be gone already. You know it has nothing to do with you. It's you and me and Roxanne all summer, okay?"

She's asking me if it's okay again, and I'm too hazy and sleepy to do anything but nod. I pull my feet onto the couch, which is mostly wood and silk, and I rest my forehead on my knees. I think it's going to make the room spin less, but it makes the room spin more and I know so, so little about being messed up. I think I need pizza, but that could be wrong too. Maybe I need more water. Or Advil. Or sleep. Or a new sister.

Arizona crosses her arms over her new chest.

"Dad and I had a really good time tonight," she says. "He's been really supportive of everything."

Everything means the surgery, and that means he knew about it even though I didn't. It makes sense, of course; she would have used the money he offered all those years ago to do it. But it hurts on impact. And the hurt sticks.

I want to tell Karissa. If Arizona has a million people she goes to before me now, I want to have Karissa be my best friend, my sister, my person. I am certain Karissa will agree with how ugly and wrong this all is. I'm sure Karissa will pour us wine and we will toast to never changing and keeping promises and telling each other everything.

"Of course Dad's been supportive," I say. "You're becoming exactly what he wants you to become."

Arizona pretends not to have heard me. She presses on.

"He ate the pizza with me. We watched a movie. He told me he misses me. He said he's proud of how well you're dealing with Tess moving out."

"He actually said Tess's name?" I say. It's not the point, but he never says the wives' names after they're gone. Like if we don't speak of them, they never existed. It means most of my life is erased, whole swaths of time, zillions of tiny and enormous memories deemed unmentionable. Arizona's telling me about her night with Dad to make me feel good, but I'm pissed instead. She missed what happened with Tess, she left me to deal with it, she didn't come home to help deal with the aftermath, she should join Dad in pretending it never happened.

"Yep. No more stepmoms, I think," Arizona says. She finally uncrosses her arms and puts her shoulders back.

Looking at her will never not hurt. That's how I'll open, when I tell Karissa the story of tonight.

Arizona hates the stepmoms. She'd set the apartment on fire to keep them away. And now she's trying to become one. It sounds almost like she thinks her looking like one of them will keep the women away. I want to ask if this is the grand plan, but the crying starts without warning, and I don't get a chance to wonder and hypothesize and calculate.

Apparently, I do a lot of crying when I'm drunk. My eyes hurt from it all.

"We used to be the same," I say in a voice from the part of me that only Arizona knows. It's the sudden, violent kind of teariness, and I grip the edges of the not-sofa and work to keep it in.

I wonder if Karissa will ever see me like this. If Arizona can move on from the world we created together and the secrets we kept, so could I. I don't want her to be the only person who's seen me cry like this. I don't want her to have that part of me.

But it feels good to have her hand around my shoulder and her head close to mine.

"This is a good thing," Arizona says. "And it didn't even really hurt."

But it does hurt, I think. It does.

three

Dad isn't asleep, it turns out.

"Girls?" he says. "Are both my girls here at last?"

I can't help it. I love when he calls us his girls.

He offers to make us popcorn, so I try to stand up straight in the kitchen and talk about going on a nice walk and eating some nice gelato, which is my excuse for where I've been all night, but all I really want to do is eat a whole bunch of Goldfish and un-dizzy myself before bed.

"You were supposed to be here for movie night," Dad says. "I wanted the whole family together."

There it is again, another phrase that zings me, heart-adjacent. The Whole Family. Like we could be all he needs, like the three of us aren't waiting around for that perfect person to fit into the Dad's Wife role. The Whole Family sounds complete. Finished.

"We haven't done that since Tess left," I say. "Family Night was a Tess thing, not an Us thing." Tess instituted monthly movie nights when she and Dad got married. It wasn't the worst. We made it through all of James Bond and about a dozen Jack Nicholson movies and any Pixar movie that came out over the last few years. We ate guac and a lot of cheese, and even after Arizona left for college it was still sort of nice, wrapping ourselves in blankets and turning up the volume whenever sirens screeched or cabs blasted their horns. Tess getting a little tipsy. Dad falling asleep before the best part.

"We still have traditions. Tess wasn't the head of this family. We were here before her and we'll be here after." He looks put together even in pajamas. They're the matching, stripey kind that people in the movies wear, which is fitting because Dad looks like he's from a movie. He touches his perfect head of hair. He used to be balding, but he's not anymore. He used to be graying, but he's not anymore.

I want what he's saying to be true so badly it nearly sobers me up.

Then I catch sight of the ceiling fan and I'm drunk again.

Being drunk is a little like running a race against your last drink, and mine has officially caught up with me. I was pretty gone before, and now I am officially trashed. Nothing feels particularly real, and that makes me sputter-laugh.

It is not subtle.

"You're drunk," Dad says.

"Well, that didn't take any see-rus, see-yus, *serious* detectiving work," I say, struggling to get my mouth around the words.

"You're acting out because I've made mistakes," Dad says. Arizona grins like she's proving a point, and I dig into the popcorn. It's hot and on the cusp of being burned. I try not to care and just crunch.

"I understand that and I'm ready to earn back your trust."

Arizona mouths *I told you* and tucks her hair behind her ears and juts out a hip.

"Dad feels bad about how hard this year was for you," she says. "So do I." They share a look, and I know I missed some kind of bonding situation, but I'm pretty sure half my buzz is from simply being around Karissa, so I don't care the way I should.

"You need water, Montana. And to never do this again, okay? Or to make sure you have adult supervision if you do." He nods, agreeing with himself. It's something he does.

"I had adult supervision," I say.

It must come out like mush, because neither Dad nor Arizona replies, and there's no look of wonder or confusion on their faces. I'm not sure who they think I was with—maybe the mysterious friends I pretend to have so that I can stay at Natasha's apartment from time to time.

My dad would hate me being there, but Arizona would hate it even more. We are supposed to have a united front on all stepmoms and girlfriends. We are supposed to forget all about them once they've moved out and moved on.

It's not as easy as they make it look. I tend to hang on. And with Natasha I've hung on for a long, long time.

"I want you to know things are different," Dad says. He seems relaxed, and he pulls a slab of cheddar out of the fridge and starts grating it over the popcorn. "Trust me, this is excellent," he says. I believe him. Cheddar is the key to happiness. "A friend taught me to do this."

A friend always means a girlfriend.

"I don't want to have a whole big talk right now," I say. "Are those new slippers?"

He has zebra-striped slippers on. They look ridiculous and comfortable. Those are two things my father is not.

"Your old man can still surprise you sometimes," he says with a laugh. He kicks one off his foot, like a Rockette with a joint problem, and I try to imitate the movement, but slip and bump into the counter.

"I'll put her to bed," Arizona says. She's so sober it hurts.

"I don't need bed! I'm rocking out! I'm a whole new girl too! Wait until you see all the things I'm gonna be and do!" I stand up on one of the kitchen chairs. It seems like one of the greatest ideas I've ever had. "I'm gonna dance it out. I'm not gonna be one of you." I point at Dad and then Arizona's chest. I am on a freaking roll. "I'm not gonna be who you want me to be!" I sing to the tune of nothing.

"You know I want you to be you and only you," Dad says, even though we have cold, hard evidence that that isn't true.

"You and only you," I sing to the tune of a Frank Sinatra song that may or may not actually exist.

I don't fall off the chair, exactly, but I slip and end up on my butt, hysterical on the ground. It feels so good to laugh this hard and be this wasted.

"Montana. You're going to hate yourself in about six hours," Arizona says. Dad nods.

"Look. What I wanted to tell both my girls is that things are going to change around here. I know me and Tess splitting up was hard on everyone, and I'm finally ready to settle down and make a stable environment for all of us."

He looks very proud of himself. He has said this exact sentence so many times I hear it in my dreams. The optimistic part of my father forgets the past so easily, so fully, that we have entirely different experiences of our lives together.

"I've met someone special," he says. And I know that at least at this moment, Arizona and I have hearts and bodies and breath working in sync. Hearts drop. Bodies tense up. Breath stops. "I wanted to let you girls into this journey so we can go through it together and emerge together." I think he memorized that last part when he was at his support group. He says it too fast and too proud.

Dad started going to support groups after Mom left. Divorced men in random churches all over the city sipping coffee and handing one another tissues with as much masculinity as they can muster for that particular gesture. That's what I imagine, at least. They tell themselves they are making the right decisions. They use words like *journey* and *codependency* and *positive energy* and *staying in the present*.

I sort of hate these guys, who are on their first divorces, not their fourth, like my father. They don't know us, and whenever he's spending a lot of time in the group sessions, he makes grand pronouncements like this and feels very good about himself.

I'd have to hate any group of people who make my dad feel that happily announcing another girlfriend at this point is a good idea or some "change."

"I'm sorry?" Arizona says. Arizona is polite until she isn't. She has excellent manners, but pushed too far she'll eventually explode. She's broken more than one cell phone from throwing it on the ground.

"All I want is for you girls to have what I had growing up," he says. "That's what I've finally realized." His parents live on a farm in Vermont. We are never going to have that. On cue, an ambulance rushes by outside, the whining sirens growing and shrinking in volume.

"I'm good with things the way they are right now," I say. It's not a lie. I prefer things the way they've been since Tess left to the way they'll be if he's dating someone new. I like making my dad coffee in the mornings and going to Reggio with him on weekday nights. Splitting prosciutto sandwiches and the world's best lattes. Listening in on old men and first dates and disgruntled waitstaff. I like that he tells me about his day, instead of telling whatever wife is waiting for him at the kitchen counter. I like knowing the nurses' names and how many procedures he's done and what the worst part of paperwork is.

If I was not full-on wasted, I'd tell him.

But I am full-on wasted.

The kitchen twists and turns, checkerboard tiles shifting around on top of one another and making me motion sick.

"I thought you were taking time off from dating," Arizona says. Her arms are back over her chest and her face is contorting to stop itself from crying.

I can't stop moving my head from side to side. It won't stay up all the way, and it feels good to let it give in to its own weight. I'm trying to catch the conversation in my mind, but it keeps slipping through the cracks the champagne caused. I can't quite keep it straight.

"What's this now?" I say. Arizona sighs and Dad pours me more water.

"It's different this time," Dad says before I fall asleep on the kitchen floor. The words are like a fairy tale—something I've heard over and over, so many times, that it can lull me to sleep.

When I wake up in the morning, I'm at the bottom end of my bed and I have lines all over my face from sleeping so hard and for so long on a textured blanket I keep there.

I don't remember how I got here, but I remember enough of the night to know Dad has a new girlfriend and Arizona has a new body and Roxanne has a new life and I only really have Karissa to keep me sane and happy.

I wake up with this ache I get sometimes after I think about my stepmothers too much. It's like missing them, but it hurts more because I also sort of hate them. Nostalgia meets rage. The kind of combination that can make you throw up, like orange juice and milk mixed together. All wrong.

Roxanne texts that she's on her way over, and I tell her what to bring. Coffee. Cigarettes. Hair dye.

June 3

The List of Things to Be Grateful For

1 The rubber-stamped poodle still on my wrist, declaring
I'm twenty-one and Karissa's friend and old and cool
enough to go to Dirty Versailles.

2 An Elmo shirt that smells like smoked cigarettes and rain.

3 The summer ahead with Roxanne and Arizona and
getting back to the life we used to all have together.

four

I am cooler today than I was yesterday.

Arizona is bustier and sadder, things that go hand in hand in my opinion.

I'm cooler not only because of Karissa's special attention on me last night, but also because Roxanne has dyed my hair pink. We didn't bleach it or anything. I wanted it to look dirty and vague. I wanted it to look beachy and sort of mine but sort of not. So the pink floats on top of my dark blond like a punk-rock veil, and I can't stop looking at myself in window reflections as we walk to Washington Square Park.

"Remember when you wanted to be pretty?" Arizona says, wrinkling her nose.

"I thought you were all into changing ourselves," I say. Her breasts are fully out today. Tank topped and pushed up and making me depressed. We used to sneak into each other's beds every night and put water balloons under our shirts when we were feeling silly, pretending to be Janie or Natasha.

"It's not the worst thing in the world," she says, "to try to be happy."

I wonder if she hears herself.

I try to share a look with Roxanne, but she stabs her straw into her iced coffee until the tension lifts.

"You both look great," she says.

"You should have run it by us," I say to Arizona. "Like I asked you this morning what you thought about pink hair."

"And I said I thought it would look weird on you," Arizona says. "Besides, I ran it by Roxanne. So chill."

Roxanne's face matches my new hair.

"You told Roxanne?" I say. It's not like I don't know that they talk without me. We have group emails and texts and three-way phone calls and video chats, but of course they talk about college crap on their own.

I didn't know they talked about things that mattered without me there.

The sun is suddenly too bright. It's funny how I waited all winter for the summer, and now I have a sweaty back and my eyes are watery from the intensity of the light and I'm hating how my legs look in shorts.

"I knew Roxanne wouldn't judge me," Arizona says.

"It's not judgment to, like, question your choices and wonder why you're going against everything that's ever mattered to us," I say.

"I can do something for me and it can have nothing to do with you or Dad or whoever," Arizona says.

"Not when it's plastic surgery!" I say too loudly.

When we sit on our favorite benches, Roxanne plays some song on her phone, turning up the volume and singing along. It's dirty and seems like the kind of song that isn't popular yet but will be soon.

I distract myself with someone else's conversation. Two middle-aged women on the bench across from us complaining about their sons' girlfriends. I want to enter their conversation and leave this one behind.

What I really want is to ask Arizona and Roxanne how often they talk without me and whether they prefer it to talking with me. I want a map of the exact distance apart we've grown this year, so I can find my way back.

"It's off the table," Arizona says, which is what we always say when we've decided something is no longer up for group discussion. Like when Roxanne started hooking up with her TA or when I skipped their graduation last year.

"Let's talk about the bags under your eyes and the sudden need to have cool hair," Roxanne says to me.

"Girl was out of control last night," Arizona says.

"You didn't invite me?" Roxanne pouts, and I think maybe against all odds our first day back together is going to be a good day in the park. The kind where we laugh and tease and buy ice cream from the truck and feel both five and twenty-five at the same time.

"I was out with Karissa. From acting class," I say. They've both heard me talk about her perfectly wavy hair and the way everyone falls over themselves trying to get her attention. They've heard about her jangling bracelets and every color of cowboy boots and neon lacy bras peeking out under all manner of T-shirt and tank top and reconstructed sweatshirt.

"Ah. She tell you to dye your hair?" Roxanne says. I blush. I don't want that to be the case, and it isn't exactly, but I'm not a true original like Roxanne. I am trying to be cool, which isn't the same thing as actually being cool, and I know it.

"Trying to be more like you," I snark back. I know compared to Roxanne's spirit and Arizona's smartness I'm nothing special. But to Karissa I'm something more. Trying to explain it makes me sound even lamer, though.

Arizona sighs and brushes her fingers through her hair. She is practicing different looks. Sexy. Sultry. Kitten-y. Aloof. I want to call her on it, but I think everything Arizona-related is off the table today.

"We were at a bar," I say. "Dirty Versailles. Lower East Side. Near that hairdresser you go to. Sluts and Posers?"

"Pimps and Pinups," Roxanne says, laughing like a maniac.

"Exactly."

It's so sunny we're all squinting. The air smells like roasting nuts and dog urine and New York, a not-terrible combination that grows more pungent in the summer.

"You still smell sort of alcohol-y, now that you mention it," Roxanne says.

"You said I couldn't shower before you dyed my hair!"

"I said you couldn't wash your hair! Gross! You're gross!" Roxanne says too loudly. Arizona hides her eyes. Anyone walking by would now wonder if she's part of our group or on her own. She doesn't fit. I shift away from her and watch the dude juggling by the fountain. Roxanne lights a cigarette and we share it, passing it back and forth, tilting our chins to the sky as we exhale.

"Montana show you the guy yet?" Roxanne says. We've been coming to the park every day since she got home, so she's had several sightings of Bernardo, who sits on the bench across from us.

Arizona scans the park and points at a guy in a sleeveless tank. "Him?" she says.

I think she's joking, so I scoff before realizing she was making a legitimate guess. "Oh. He's cute, sort of. But no. Him." I nod my head in Bernardo's direction.

We're all looking at him pretty intensely and I'm preening, running fingers through my almost pink hair and wondering if day-after wine smells good or bad on my skin. Truth be told, I didn't want to let go of last night, and that's why I didn't shower. Why I had to keep that poodle stamp on my hand and the little bit of Karissa's fruity perfume hanging on my skin.

Bernardo smiles. Points to his own head, then to my head, and gives a thumbs-up.

Swoon.

The boy across the park: he wears a man-scarf and has thick glasses with dark frames and cool sneakers, and sometimes he reads books in Spanish and sometimes he reads books in English, and when I found out from a little detective work that his name is Bernardo, I started writing that name all over my Lists of Things to Be Grateful

For. I don't know him, but he seems like someone to be grateful for.

I'm always grateful for dimples, after all.

He and his group of friends sit on the benches across from mine. We eye-flirted with each other for the first month. Nothing more. I noticed he was reading the same book as me. *The Great Gatsby*. I figured his school was probably doing a unit on it too.

Then it was the Stephen King novel I was chilling out with.

Then *Catcher in the Rye*.

Then *The Hunger Games*.

Then *Valley of the Dolls*.

After *Valley of the Dolls* we started nodding at each other. Then waving. Then holding the books up so they covered most of our faces and peering over the tops. It's been the best, weirdest, quietest flirtation.

Arizona thinks it sounds creepy, but ever since she started at Colby she thinks everything I do sounds sort of lame or weird or creepy. Roxanne and I think it's hot as hell. I can't stop thinking about the messiness of his hair and the warmth of his eyes and the relaxed way he leans back when he's sitting on the bench, how his body says *I'm all good* with his arms stretched out on either side of him, his elbows pointing behind him.

"There's a guy like him on my floor at Bard," Roxanne says. "But, like, a way druggier version of him. We made out at this party. Good kisser. Bodes well for your boy." I don't want to hear about Bard, but I try to smile and nod like I'm supposed to do.

"You colleged better than me," Arizona says. "You need to teach me your ways so I can college better next year." Roxanne says something about guys you meet in class versus ones you meet at parties and the differing hookup potentials of both and I tune out.

He gets up from the bench and doesn't break eye contact with me as he walks over. He nearly trips over mariachi players and a kid on a motorized scooter that should be outlawed. It's happening.

I don't think Bernardo is walking toward me because of the almost pink hair. But I hope it's made him realize I'm not the kind of girl who will wait forever for the cute guy on the other side of the park to say hello. And I've already been waiting two months. Since the moment it got warm enough to reasonably sit on a park bench for two hours every day after school. It's what I used to do with Arizona and Roxanne, so it's what I continued to do this year. I couldn't think of how to do spring and summer any differently.

"He's on the move," Roxanne says.

"He wants to ask what the hell you have done to your beautiful hair," Arizona says.

"My hair's never been beautiful," I say. But I so badly want him to think it's beautiful. Then and now. Always. "Maybe I should text Karissa and ask her what to do." I'm sort of showing off. I want them to know she's the kind of friend I could text in the middle of the day. I want them to know what level I'm at. "Guys seriously love her." I take my phone out and start tapping away, something about *how can I get a cute guy in the park to talk to me?* I hit send and remember her saying we should be best friends. Hopefully she remembers that too.

Bernardo is closer than he's ever been. In a few more strides he'll be at our bench, and I'll know the sound of his voice and the exact shade of his eyes. "Make eye contact! Eye contact is key!" Roxanne says under her breath. I keep my gaze on him. It's nice to have someone who can help me figure out what to do. I probably should have made new friends this year, but I didn't really bother.

"You look the same but different," Bernardo says. He stands right in front of me, and I have no idea if I should stand up or stay seated. I grip my own thighs and squeeze, hoping I can keep all the nervousness there and not in my face or my voice. I feel all sixth-grade-ish. In a good way.

He's wearing a navy T-shirt with some band name I've never heard of on the front in big white block lettering. His hair is messier than usual, poking out every which way. Thick and black and chaotic. There's a gap between his front teeth and his nose is crooked. He is unkempt and imperfect and staring at my almost pink hair.

"I'd say thank you, but that's not exactly a compliment," I say. I twirl my hair between two fingers. I wish it were even pinker.

"I'm Bernardo," he says.

"I know. I'm Montana," I say. We're smiling at each other and it's the greatest. Like we already have a secret and the rest of the world is left out.

My father says that sometimes not knowing someone is even better than knowing them. I try to un-hear those words and un-feel the truth of them right now. Taking relationship advice from my divorced-four-times father isn't wise.

"You should do the pink hair too," I say. I don't know why that comes out, except I'm so hyperaware of my new look that I'm having trouble thinking of anything else to talk about.

I want him to know I can talk about other things: favorite street performers in Washington Square Park, least favorite books from school this year, whether beer tastes like urine or like wheat, what kind of music the band on his T-shirt plays and if he prefers to listen to them on his headphones when he's walking around the Village or if he'd rather blast them on speakers at home. But all I can talk about is the shade of pink now adorning my head.

"You think I could pull it off?" Bernardo says. He reaches for my hair, picks a clump up, and puts it against his face like we're going to really check and see how he'd look with pink hair. Almost pink.

"Are you too scared?" I say. Roxanne giggles. She and Arizona are staying quiet but focused. Bernardo's friends watch us from their bench. Someone near the fountain is playing terrible accordion. Bernardo gives me a long look.

"I'm scared, but also awesome," he says. I can feel Arizona rolling her eyes next to me. It doesn't matter that I can't see her. She's my sister; I know what sentences she'll love and which ones she'll hate. I know her opinions before she tells them to me. That hasn't changed.

She's gone from finding him sweet to finding him lame. I can feel it. She has her Stepmothers Look on her face. Judge-y and sure. I'd bet money on it.

"I don't know what scared but awesome means," I say.

"It means let's do it. Let's dye my hair pink." He winks but doesn't smile. The accordion player is attempting a version of "Happy

Birthday" to no one and Arizona is shaking her head *no, no, no*. I think he might be serious.

"Right now?" I say.

"Oh my God yes right now yes!" Roxanne says, a flurry of words and breathiness. She rushes forward like a puppy let off leash at last.

"You don't have to do this. I was pretty much joking." I'm shy around him, even though the guy has been watching me all spring and is now willing to dye his hair for me. I don't know him; he's still a stranger and a cute boy, and now that he's seen fun Roxanne and Arizona's new body, I don't know why he likes me.

"It seems like you might be worth it," he says.

I laugh. More or less. It's mostly a snorting cough of embarrassment and surprise, but I'm smiling, so it vaguely resembles a laugh. He has an accent I can't quite place except that I assume it means he's lived in New York his whole life and probably has a parent or two who speaks Spanish.

Bernardo sort of salutes his friends across the path and shakes hands with Arizona and Roxanne. They introduce themselves, and he raises his eyebrows at Arizona's name.

"Arizona and Montana," he says. "This a joke?"

"Sisters," I say. I touch Arizona's elbow on the word and want to exchange a smile with her, give one of those we-love-being-sisters looks, but she's not having it. She is too busy wrinkling her nose and adjusting the straps of her tank top and probably planning her escape route.

"Our mom was a hippie. So our dad was briefly a hippie too. He's like that," Arizona says. For someone who doesn't want to talk, she's saying way too much.

"And now?" Bernardo says, which is sort of the million-dollar question, to be honest.

"Our dad sort of dates a lot. And sort of changes a lot when he dates. But he's a good guy," I say. There's a break in conversation where I'm supposed to say what's up with my mom too, but I don't.

"We don't really have a mom," Arizona says for me.

"We're over it," I say, and it feels true.

"You don't look too much like sisters," Bernardo says. It's the first time anyone's ever said that, and it aches. Until right now, everyone's always been able to guess. We've had the same dark-blond hair and blue eyes and wide hips and flat chests our whole lives. We've had matching pale skin and T-shirt collections and side ponytails. "I mean, I can see it now that I know," he says. "But at first glance I'd have no idea."

I look at her. I've been avoiding taking her in. She doesn't even look like a New Yorker anymore, let alone like a family member. My throat closes up, recognizing the sudden distance between us. If we were walking down the street, no one would think we were sisters. It's the huge kind of loss that is impossible to swallow all at once, so I look away again.

"They're like twins!" Roxanne says, because she hasn't looked at Arizona yet either.

"Arizona's older," I say. "She's in college." It is a useless sentence that explains nothing.

It's weird, how a new set of breasts can feel like a betrayal. It sounds stupid and I know I can never say it out loud.

"We have the same eyes. And nose," Arizona says. I want to gauge what amount of pain she's feeling. I hope it measures up.

Bernardo looks at Arizona's face, then mine, twisting his head all around to see every angle, looking for similarities. He shrugs, like it doesn't really matter.

"Yeah, no, I see it."

Arizona grins, thinking he's really seen our sisterliness at last, but I can tell he hasn't. He doesn't. He won't. It's gone.

five

We pick up hair dye at the Duane Reade on the way to my place and after we squeeze, all four of us, into our bathroom.

"It should be pretty bright for, like, six weeks," Roxanne says. "Then it's gonna sort of fade over time. Especially in the sun. Okay?" She's an expert. Today her hair is brown with purple stripes, but who knows what it will be next week. She's been growing it long, so it hangs heavy and thick past her shoulders, a certain kind of beautiful that I think she doesn't get enough credit for.

Roxanne is always this person for Arizona and me—creating magic where there was nothing, manufacturing ease where there was tension. On our last day together last summer she dragged us to Coney Island to sit on the beach in bikinis and eat Nathan's hot dogs. They were good. We forgot to be sad about the fact they were leaving. After their graduation, the one I skipped, we painted stars and hearts on our cheeks with face paint and played our recorders in Washington Square Park. We made ten dollars and bought pizza.

"Six weeks of pink hair, huh?" Bernardo says. He doesn't seem nervous. But he doesn't seem exactly happy either. He shrugs. Gets a look on his face like he's doing the math on how many days six weeks means. I get a wave of loneliness at how little I actually know about him. How unfamiliar and unpredictable his moods are to me. He looks my way with raised eyebrows and shining eyes. "Can we handle that? That's some serious commitment. You've gotta hang out with me for at least as long as I have this crazy hair."

"Six weeks is a long time, dude," I say while Arizona washes her hands in the sink and Roxanne runs out to the kitchen to find some rubber gloves. "You might hate me. Then you'll have pink hair and nowhere to sit in the park and some serious disappointment."

"I thought this was all about being some über-individual," Arizona says. "Maybe this dude should go with a different color. Or shave it all off instead." It's like she's joking but she's not.

"My name's Bernardo," he says. He sounds nice but firm.

I give Arizona a pleading look. She knows how long I've had my eye on him and how few guys I've ever had my eye on.

Bernardo shrugs again. I guess it's a thing he does. I take note. When my dad meets someone and "falls in love" and marries her, he doesn't know anything about her. Except for the way she makes him feel and how pretty she is and how pretty she will turn out to be. How pretty he will make her.

Our apartment, decorated by years of wives and girlfriends, is something I have chronicled extensively in my head. I know which toothbrush holder, throw blanket, overpriced vase, chaise lounge is from which wife. It's obvious, the objects perfectly matching up alongside their personalities.

Dad has no idea.

He could easily confuse a Natasha couch with a Mom one, or a Tess piece of art with Janie's taste. As if he never knew them at all.

I'm not my father. I notice the drawings on Bernardo's sneakers, little stick figures near the soles, etched into rubber that used to be white but is now gray from the grimy New York streets. I want to notice everything about him, and like him because of it. I don't want to extract or shift or mold. I don't want to love the way my father loves.

Bernardo is a guy who shrugs and doesn't smile all the time and draws stick figures on his shoes and likes crazy adventures with strange girls. Bernardo is unafraid.

I'll look up the band on his shirt later. I'll listen to no fewer than five songs. I will learn something about him from the lyrics and the rhythm and whether the guitars are loud and electric or cooing and acoustic.

"Montana has to do the honors," Roxanne says when she's back in the bathroom. With all four of us in the tiny space, we can barely move. Bernardo sits on the closed toilet and Arizona perches on the ancient standing tub. Roxanne slips rubber gloves over my hands and holds her nose while showing me how to do the bleach and then the dye.

I can't feel the texture of his hair through the gloves, but it's intimate anyway, pulling at the strands, covering them in thick paste, making sure I haven't missed a spot.

"Too late to change my mind?" he says halfway through.

"This is the weirdest day of my life," Arizona says.

"That's A, not true and B, really sad if it is true," Roxanne says.

Standing over Bernardo feels right. And when he winces from the way the cheap dye burns his scalp, I laugh instead of apologize, and that feels right too. "I have a good feeling about this," I say.

"Me too," Bernardo says. I don't think he's talking about the hair.

"You smoke?" I say as we wait to wash the dye out of Bernardo's hair. We haven't moved from the cramped bathroom, although I can't really say why. It smells like the kind of chemicals that will kill you, and it's deathly hot. Arizona has shifted from the edge of the tub into the tub itself, where she can stretch her legs out and lean back. Her shoes are off. Her hair's in a high, frizzy ponytail. If it weren't for the French manicure and khaki shorts and C cups and pink polo, she could be my old sister. I wonder if Bernardo sees it now too. If the fact of our being sisters has clicked into place as soon as Arizona chilled a little.

I wonder if this side of her came out in hostels in Austria and France last week. I don't think the dorms at Colby even have bathtubs.

Arizona asks for a cigarette too, but she hates smoking. Used to hate smoking. I should know exactly how she feels about smoking these days, but I don't.

"I could smoke," Bernardo says. "I don't really do it, but it's one of those days, I guess, right?"

Bernardo is a guy who doesn't smoke but sometimes smokes.

Bernardo is a guy who starts to look tired when he has been adventurous and free-spirited for over two hours. His eyelids look heavier and his voice has a new grumble in it, on the edges.

I grin at him and he half smiles back.

Bernardo is a guy who never grins.

"On it," Roxanne says. She has a pack in her purse; she picked them up with the hair dye because she knows how to have the best possible afternoon. We each light a cigarette and I open the window wide so that the four of us can gather around it and blow smoke out onto West 12th Street. Arizona gives up after half a cig, so I stand in between Roxanne and Bernardo and thrill at Bernardo's shoulder against mine and how quickly I've mastered the art of casual smoking. I still hate the taste, but right now I'm enjoying the shape my lips make when I exhale and the grace of bringing my fingers to my mouth. It's like a ballet move.

"Dad's gonna kill you, he's gonna smell it all over you," Arizona says. She coughs but doesn't leave.

"Dad's gonna kill me anyway," I say. I shake my almost pink hair in her general direction and take another puff. "Besides, his new girlfriend smokes." I know this is true because when he's been out with her, he comes back with the smell of someone else's cigarettes clinging to his blazer.

"Sounds like none of us are going to make it out of today unscathed," Bernardo says, a little more gravel in his voice.

Bernardo is a guy who says funny things but doesn't know they're funny. Bernardo is a guy who doesn't laugh but watches me when I laugh.

I really like a guy named Bernardo, I text Karissa even though she hasn't replied to my first text and I'm paranoid that we didn't actually bond like I thought we did. *I didn't think Bernardos could be hot.*

Is there anything better than liking someone you never thought you could like? Karissa says, and it's perfect and I'm left wondering why I can't say these things to my sister anymore.

Bernardo's hair ends up being way brighter than mine. My dirty blond is still partially visible under the veil of color. Bernardo's hair, on the other hand, is a brilliant, deep pink, since we stripped it of all color before re-creating him. He is all neon insanity. Mine is a brown-blond-pink-beachy-messy color, but his is a statement.

"Yes," I say, in answer to nothing, because there's no other word for how it feels to look at him.

He doesn't cry or anything, looking at himself in the mirror. He doesn't gasp. He doesn't blush.

"Well, here we go," he says.

June 6

The List of Things to Be Grateful For

1 When Tess moved out three months ago, she left her blender, three pairs of silver shoes, a fancy Pilates machine, and the so-ugly-it's-pretty painting of roses hanging in the living room. These will be placed, as always, into the Closet of Forgotten Things.

2 Knowing that the pizza at Ben's on MacDougal has the perfect ratio of melty cheese to doughy crust. The ratio being: mostly melted cheese, minimal sauce, thin crust.

3 Boys with pink hair. Boys with pink hair. Boys with pink hair. (Boys who dye their hair pink because of me.)

six

A couple of days later, getting a bagel, I'm on high Bernardo alert. It's summer in the way it's only ever summer in New York for about three days a year, so everyone's in the park. I slow to a stroll and hope he appears. I'm expecting him and his buddies, draping themselves over their bench. One of the guys always has a harmonica. The other talks so loudly that people walking by get uncomfortable. So they'd be hard to miss if they were here. I could text and ask him if he's in the park.

I have Bernardo's number, but he doesn't have mine.

"I dyed my hair pink," he said before he left my place. "So you know where I stand. Text me when you want, okay?"

I haven't texted yet. Karissa said to wait a few days, but I don't think my fingers will let me hold out much longer.

I start up at a normal gait again and think about words I could text him. I come up with *hi* and pretty much short out after that. I could ask him how his hair's holding up. Or if he's liking the weather. I make a pact with myself to say something by the end of the day.

Preferably something not about the weather, because I'm not fifty and I'm not boring.

When I'm past the benches, on the far side of the park near the arch, I see a flash of neon pink.

It's him.

He's far enough away that he won't be able to see me, especially since my hair isn't so spectacular. I don't stand out like him.

I don't call out. I watch him from here.

He's running. In circles. Like a pink dog. His striped scarf flies out behind him, and man, Arizona would hate that he's wearing a scarf on such a warm day.

Then there's what he's running from: little kids. Little Bernardo look-alikes, two boys and two girls who I assume are his siblings. They scramble and kick up grass and cigarette butts and pant behind him. They screech and swat at his torso.

When Janie lived with us, she brought her two tiny sons, Frank and Andy. Arizona and I taught them to play Chutes and Ladders and how to speak in pig Latin. Bernardo's family looks like that but better. More real. Something that lasts.

Whatever Arizona and I get never lasts. We have it for a few years and then are asked to adjust to something else. And at the end of the day, even Arizona and I didn't last. Not the way I thought we would.

There's a woman with dark hair and a kind smile watching. His mother, I'm sure. I almost can't bear the sweetness. She has probably never gone anywhere, never changed anything. Her shirt looks like it is from ten years ago. Her haircut too.

I wonder what it would be like to have the same family your whole life. Or to even have one person who is always yours. Always close and connected and familiar.

Today Arizona is going to something called Pure Barre class with a girl named Esther, and afterward they're going to make dinner together. Every bit of that sentence sounds strange and imaginary. We've never made dinner together. We order dinner. The only things we make are sandwiches.

I'd assumed Bernardo was like me—lost and from something off and unsettled.

I don't send a text. I don't linger to watch the whole perfect family summer scene or wonder whether he's already regretting his hair. It's obvious, when he pulls a ski hat out of his pocket and puts it on, that he is. It's June, after all. And he already has a scarf on. Weirdo.

I try Natasha, because a few hours with her makes me feel like I'm not as messed up as I feel when I'm at our apartment with Dad and all the things his ex-wives left behind. She doesn't answer. She's out with her real family and I'm not part of it, no matter what she says, no matter how vehemently she insists I am always going to be her stepdaughter.

No one wants to always be a stepdaughter.

Roxanne is with her parents for the day, so that leaves Karissa. I probably should have started with Karissa.

She gets back to me right away and tells me to meet her for pickles and wine at her place.

* * *

I run home to change at my apartment, and by the time I'm ready to head over to hers, my hair's in knots, pink and blond wrestling in and out of lazy curls. I throw on blue leggings and a black T-shirt and enough deodorant to not have to shower. I wonder what Karissa will think of the new look.

Before I get to Karissa's place, I give in and text Bernardo.

I'm texting you. So you know where I stand too. ☺

Karissa's all over me when I get to her place. A few drug-skinny friends are sitting on her big pink couches, and there are bottles of wine open on every spare surface. I try to look more like twenty and less like seventeen, and I don't know if the hair is helping or hurting. I try not to care.

"Look what you've done! You are hands down the coolest, least bullshit person I've ever met in my life." Her hands go to my hair, twisting and pulling the strands. Her own hair is in messy waves that crash all the way down her back, practically to her butt.

"I call it summer pink," I say, which I only came up with this very moment. Five too-cool twentysomethings make noises that sound almost like laughter.

"If I could get cast in commercials with summer-pink hair, I'd absolutely join you," she says. "But I don't have the face to pull that off. Or the skin. Man, if I looked like you, my agent would like me about a billion times more." She has this list of things she hates about herself and that agents and casting directors supposedly hate about her. It would sound negative and bitter coming out of my mouth, but Karissa makes insecurity look almost appealing. Open and comfortable and raw. "I look like ass today, compared to you," she goes on. "You need to stop showing me up." Karissa is approximately the greatest person I've ever met. It would be impossible to show her up. She pours me a plastic cup of wine. "This is Montana!" she announces to the room. I expect bored nods or total shunning, but with the mention of my name, they all brighten a little. Two of them actually smile.

"Montana!" a girl with short dark hair says. She gets up and shakes my hand. She looks from me to Karissa and back again. "It is so nice to meet you finally."

"Yep. At long last," I say like it's all a joke.

"They're being weird," Karissa says. "Don't be weird, guys. Montana is my friend. From that acting class I did. She's an old soul." She overemphasizes the word *friend*, like they might think I'm something else, but I don't know what that something else might be, so I'm sweating with nerves.

"Oh, okay. I see. Right," a guy with shaggy blond hair says. "She drinks?"

"I drink," I say, and Karissa smiles. "I smoke too." Karissa freaking beams. I'm as cool as she'd told them I would be.

I pour a little more into my cup and wonder at a world where Karissa is bragging to her friends about me.

"These people are, like, my created family. Taking care of me ever since mine died," Karissa says. I'm not used to people speaking at full volume about things like death, so my heart leaps a little at its mention.

"That's awesome. I'm so sorry about your family, by the way. I don't know if I got that across the other night. But I'm so, so sorry," I say. I hope it's right. Her pain makes me feel a little panicked. Like I'm supposed to help but I have no idea how.

"Lady, I don't even remember the end of the night, honestly. Which is the best, right? When it, like, fades? Little bits and pieces bubble up, but most of it exists in some, like, twilight zone?"

"You make blackout drunk sound beautiful," I say, even though I've never actually been blackout drunk.

"I have a secret," Karissa says. She has three pickles and a glass of wine in her hand, and the smell is odd and perfect. I'm used to women who all look the same and smell the same and eat the same sad foods—nuts and berries and lean meats and so much spinach I sometimes wonder if it's a requirement of being my dad's wife. Karissa is someone else. She doesn't remind me of anything or anyone.

I think I could be unusual like her. An original.

I steal one of the pickles from her and dig in like we do this all the time—share food and drinks and moments. And secrets.

"I bet you have a million secrets," I say. Karissa laughs and gives me a little shove.

"You're too cool for us," she says. Obviously the exact opposite is true, but I shrug like I totally know, and throw my summer-pink hair back over my shoulders and sip wine and for that second I am the girl she says I am.

But when I look at Karissa, I know I'm not in her league. Not even close. She's wearing a white dress that I'm pretty sure is actually lingerie and a strand of pearls that I'm pretty sure are plastic and a big pink shawl that I'm positive only she could pull off. Patches of freckles cluster around all the best parts of her: her nose and cheeks, her shoulders, her knees and thighs, the back of her neck, hidden except for when she occasionally pulls her mess of hair into a ropy ponytail.

We're so close we're touching. My phone buzzes and I almost don't check it, but even with Karissa next to me, I still want it to be Bernardo. I wasn't expecting that. I thought she was big and bright enough to eclipse him completely.

I sneak a peek. It's him. Asking when he can see me next. Saying he was excited to hear from me. I have a surge of adoration for both Bernardo and Roxanne. I try to keep it under wraps, but the smiling happens without me being able to control it. Too big and too sloppy.

I'm all kinds of fluttery.

I text back that he'll see me soon.

"Looks like you've got a secret too," Karissa says.

Then we're stupidly grinning at each other, and I think maybe we really are going to be mismatched best friends.

"Enough about me, you're the one wanting to share secrets," I say. "So spill."

"I can't tell you yet," Karissa says. "It's good. I think it's good. I want you to think it's good. Promise you'll try to think it's good?" She's the kind of person who wants you to promise the impossible without asking any questions.

And when I'm around her, I'm the kind of person who makes promises I can't keep.

"I promise," I say.

* * *

We split a cigarette on the sidewalk outside Karissa's building. The girl with the short black hair and her date, who has a ridiculous hat and an even more ridiculous beard, come down too. I work on fitting in with them.

"Could you guys, like, get arrested for this?" I say. I'm too drunk now to pretend to be old enough to be doing any of this.

"Whatever, no, who cares," the girl with black hair says, which isn't an answer at all.

"You're not thirteen, are you?" her friend says.

"She's practically an adult," Karissa says. "We don't need to baby her. She's a whole person." She nods very seriously, and I want to tell Bernardo about it. I want him to know there's a beautiful mysterious perfect weirdo probably soon-to-be-famous actress who thinks I'm Real.

"She's right. I barely even have parents." It's not the kind of thing I'd say if I weren't pretty fuzzy on the Manhattan sidewalk.

"Not true, you have a dad," Karissa says. She winks. It's something she used to overuse in acting class. Her one flaw as an actress. Which makes her even more perfect, having a funny little flaw.

"My dad's a mess," I explain to her friend who isn't asking questions, because I am oversharing to an insane degree and probably she wants me to stop, but I won't. "He's been married four times. And, like, a thousand girlfriends in between. And he thinks we should all get nose jobs and tummy tucks the second we turn eighteen, you know? Like, not because he's evil but he actually thinks that's the key to womanhood happiness or something."

"I didn't know all that," the friend says, like she didn't just meet me two hours ago.

"It's a wonder I turned out so cool, trust me," I say. "My sister Arizona almost became cool too, but she changed her mind while she was at college and decided to be not cool instead."

"Your dad must be pretty hot, with all these ladies all over him," Karissa says, winking again. I hit her arm and she giggles like I'm tickling her and it's all very Montana Has Arrived.

There's a long pause. Pauses on New York sidewalks aren't quiet, exactly, because they are full of cars honking and strangers talking as they walk by and other people's television sets. But in some ways the noise makes it even quieter.

"What's that thing they say in Greek myths or whatever? About truth in wine?" I say. I shouldn't drink during the day. I shouldn't drink at all, probably. I don't know how to do it right. I keep ending up like this: too open and vertigo-ed and rubbing my eyes to regain my balance. None of that magical in-between that Karissa talked about.

"You can tell us anything," Karissa says. "That's how we do it, at wine and pickles parties." She giggles again and her friend laughs too, and I feel like I'm getting inducted into something wonderful and cozy. Like a cult but good.

"Don't feel bad for me or anything. I'll probably have a new mom soon, anyway!" I say, and Karissa's eyebrows spike. "I mean, not really. That'd be fast even for him. But he sounds all smitten. And this one's *different*." I scoff so they know exactly how seriously I take that description.

"Sounds like love to me," Karissa says. "Maybe this one really is different." She almost sings it, and I wonder when she was last in love. Probably constantly or never at all. However she does love is how I should do it. Cool and calm or crazy and fearless. She has a necklace with a metal heart hanging from her neck, and I decide it's enough evidence that Karissa knows things about romance that I need to learn. Things my dad or my mostly gone mother or my uninspiring ex-sort-of boyfriends can't teach me. "Do you want him to be in love?" she asks. And the answer is somewhere deep down far away inside me.

"Yes," I say. "Like, real love. Not this. I don't want to watch the same movie play out over and over forever."

"Things don't change until they do," Karissa says.

"My dad's not like you and me," I say, which is mostly wishful thinking, that anyone but me thinks I could be like Karissa at all, even a little. "But if you say I should have hope, I will. Again."

Arizona would call me an asshole, remind me we're stuck in an endless cycle that's never going to get better. Roxanne would laugh. Maybe that's why I need Karissa. For the whole hope thing.

"You're a rock star. Let's do this forever, okay?" She kisses my cheek with the side of her pink-painted mouth and squeezes my shoulder. I am the luckiest person in the world, for one moment.

June 9

The List of Things to Be Grateful For

1 The mysterious and imperfect beauty of Karissa's
freckles.

2 Texting so late into the night with Bernardo that we both
start typing nonsense: **Him:** *hi&vgh(.* **Me:** *5555ght.* **Him:**
@;)rhuo. **Me:** *** ** **.* The hidden meanings therein. The
one million possibilities of what that nonsense means.

3 The possibility that my father could be in real love, if I'm
to believe Karissa and believe in real love, which I think
I have to. The Post-it on the counter that says we have
a reservation to meet the new girlfriend tomorrow night.
The fact that I don't rip it up and miraculously Arizona
doesn't either.

seven

When Dad sees my hair almost a week after I dyed it, he changes our reservation from his favorite fancy restaurant, Le Cirque, to this Italian place on the Lower East Side. People with almost pink hair can't sit in a place like Le Cirque—there is a domed ceiling and silver platters and little one-bite appetizers or sorbets in between every course. People with almost pink hair have to stay below 14th Street where they belong.

"You had to do this tonight of all nights?" he says.

"I did it last week, but you haven't been around to see it," I say. "So let's make sure we're directing our anger correctly." To Dad's credit, he doesn't tell me to cut my attitude. Instead he nods, swallows, and agrees.

"Well. You have a point there," he says. Roxanne used to wonder why Arizona and I have never stopped loving my father. Then she witnessed the measured way he admits to screwing up and his serious head nods and the way he laughs at my meanest jokes, and she got it.

"You know, my new friend might just like your crazy ways," Dad says. He winks and I almost text Karissa to tell her that her signature wink is taking over the world, but I decide texting her and Bernardo will be my reward for getting through this night with a half-pleasant smile on my face.

"Call her your girlfriend, dude," Arizona says. Dad laughs. His stubble is growing out, and he has this new tie that is purple and striped and a little too hip. He's wearing it with a blue-and-white-striped shirt, and I have never seen my father unmatched. His fancy gold watch is gone and his hair is a little mussed.

"Okay, dude," he says, like he's been practicing saying the word *dude* lately, in general.

"Tell your sister she'll never get a job or a boyfriend with that whole punk look she's rocking," Dad says to Arizona, and the tone is all joking, but there's something under it that hurts, and I know that thing is that it's his truth.

Also, my dad can't really pull off the word *rocking* even with his fuzzy face and power-clashing outfit.

"Actually, the color's growing on me," Arizona says. I know this probably isn't exactly true, but when it comes to Dad's comments on how we look or how in love he is, we're automatically on the same team no matter what. Even if we haven't been talking much the past few days or months and even if her new boobs are squarely between us, changing everything. "Better than if she'd gone all goth-black or something."

"Fair enough," Dad says. "Can't blame a guy for wanting to show off his beautiful girls, though." The word *beautiful* is another thing that should feel good but hurts, because I know he doesn't really mean it. But Arizona is in a yellow sundress and heels, and at least Dad has one good, pretty daughter with enhanced boobs.

Dad's never talked to us about what happened with Natasha and our thirteenth birthdays, but it sits between us, this awful truth that dirties up every nice thing he says about Arizona and me.

I'm weak, so I weave a messy braid and hang it over my shoulder. I love how long and wild my hair has gotten. Arizona's is shiny and shoulder length and parted down the middle. It reminds me of Tess's. Natasha wears hers in a low bun, and Janie teased it out and never tucked it behind her ears.

I don't remember Mom's hair very well, except that it was dark blond and wavy like mine.

None of the wives have had pink hair. One of the girlfriends—before Tess but after Natasha—had a silver streak. It didn't make her cool, but it was a nice change of pace.

"She's going to meet us here, and we'll take a cab to CucinaCucina together," Dad says, sighing at my jeans and probably the wide set of my hips. I could have worn more than a T-shirt, but I hate anything more than a T-shirt and this one is at least of the *Mona Lisa*, which has to make it classy. I am not in proportion. I am not symmetrical. Like Mona Lisa. "She's special," Dad goes on. "I promise. You'll see. She's not like any of . . . anyone else. Anyone else I've ever met."

"Where'd you find her?" Arizona says. I laugh, because it's the perfect word for what Dad does. He finds girlfriends and wives, he doesn't really meet them.

Dad doesn't answer her question. He looks sheepish and puts his hands in his pockets, and I don't know that I've ever seen my father nervous before, but this is what it looks like on him.

And without meaning to, I have hope again.

"Cell phones off tonight," Dad says. "Even mine, okay? Everyone I want to hear from will be at that table."

The hope nudges forward. Dad never turns off his phone. Maybe the new woman *will* be different. I smooth down my flyaway hairs and ask Arizona for lip gloss. I don't know exactly why, but if Dad can move a little in one direction, I guess I can too. Because who knows. Because maybe.

Dad answers the door, and I hear the laugh.

Her laugh.

Shit.

Arizona and I push our way onto the stoop.

"What are you doing here?" I say, even though I already know and definitely don't want it confirmed.

Karissa smiles and blushes. "You promised you'd be open-minded about my secret," she says.

"What the fuck are you doing here?" I say because the blush tells me everything.

"Hey now," Dad says. My whole body is beating with anger. Like my heartbeat has taken up residence in every joint and bone and muscle.

"I know how much you love Karissa," he continues. "And I want you to know that I do too." He's nervous but measured, and it makes me even angrier.

She is all legs and giggles and shakiness.

"Hi?" Arizona says, trying to navigate the moment without any sort of road map.

"I'm Karissa."

"I'm Arizona."

"You can probably tell I know your sister," Karissa says, reaching for me and then changing her mind. Instead she hooks her hand into a tiny, nonfunctional, finger-size pocket right below her hip. "We were in acting class together. So."

"So," Arizona says. I'm unable to speak, and I have a feeling this is the last syllable Arizona will be able to get out for a while too. Karissa is only a few years older than us. She looks like she could still be in high school. She wears dresses with fake pockets and gives me cigarettes and wine and a special brand of attention. She's mine. She cannot belong to my father.

"Absolutely one hundred percent no," I say. I won't look Karissa in the eye, but I have no trouble staring down my father.

"I didn't approach her until your class was over," Dad says, like it's a good enough excuse. My class with Karissa finished up two months ago. I wonder if he knows about the bars and the boys and the pickle-and-wine parties and the cigarettes and the way she tells me I'm adult and special and her best friend.

"You know I think you're the greatest," Karissa says. Her voice is low, as if it's a private moment between her and me, but with all four of us on the stoop, there's no room for secrets. "And I honestly believe this could be something . . . magnificent."

Loneliness jabs at me. All the time I spent with her, I thought I was finding my Person. It's unbearable. And embarrassing. And so terribly sad.

"This isn't happening," I say. If I could think of the right words to yell at her, I'd do that, but there's a screeching in my mind, a banshee of fury, and it's hard to think with that going on.

"We're still best friends. I don't want that to change," she says, in the exact moment that everything is changing. I can't stop thinking of her skinny friends and their bemused expressions. The way they said my name, like it meant something. They knew. Of course they knew.

It seems stupid to want to be the most important person in someone's life. But other people have that. So I don't see why I can't want it too.

"What if this made us all super happy?" Karissa says "Like, just, what if?" She has her crooked smile and her hair in her eyes and the same energy as my father, caught in between naive positivity and crazy-making denial.

"This is my family," I whisper back, but the word hurts to say.

For a moment it is only me and her. We aren't blinking or moving or speaking. "We both deserve everything. Remember?" she says.

"But this is *mine*," I say. "And you said you wanted *me*. Not my father." My hands go to my throat, the universal sign for choking. I'm not actually in need of a Heimlich or anything, but I need them to know I can't breathe, something's stuck in my throat, I might pass out.

"Can we get the cab, please?" Arizona says, shifting the moment into something else, something looser and more okay. "I swear to God someone forgot to pick up after their dog, and I cannot do this in the presence of puppy crap, okay?"

She makes me laugh. A totally involuntary laugh, a really small one, but it's there and it feels good so I appreciate it, and take a mental note that it may go on my gratitude list tomorrow morning. So, so much about Arizona has changed, but at the end of the day she is completely not going to stand for anything as undignified as a dog-shit-flavored conversation about the newest of Dad's soon-to-be-failed relationships.

With a twenty-three-year-old.

With my friend.

I give it, like, a month. And if it's one of his monthlong girlfriends, there's no need for Arizona and me to be involved.

Because, come on.

They all get in the cab. I stand there like I'm getting in last, but then don't.

"I can't," I say.

"Get in," Dad says. He's not kidding. He wants me to squeeze in the back with Arizona and Karissa and sign off on this mess of a situation.

Not this time.

"You can have anyone else," I whisper, getting close to his face in the window. "You don't even know her. She doesn't even matter to you. In two years you won't remember her favorite color or what she wanted to be when she grew up. But she matters to me." I think maybe he'll hear the truth in that.

"Montana. Don't be a teenager about it," Dad says. It's a thing he says that used to make me laugh, but not today. I'm going to be Montana about it. I'm going to stay here and smoke cigarettes and Google the names of my stepmothers and some of the ex-girlfriends I remember and call Natasha, the stepmother I've semi-adopted as still mine, and try to warm the chill in my chest from seeing Karissa on my father's arm.

"You can't make me sign off on this," I say. The cabdriver starts the meter, and I know my dad won't let it run too long.

"Totally," Karissa says. "You need some time. Eat some ice cream. Chill. We can talk after dinner. Your dad and I understand." She reaches to the front seat and puts a hand on Dad's shoulder. My body convulses.

"What if I don't want to talk to you later?" I say. I curl my toes and stand my ground as best as I can.

"We'll bring you back some pasta. You will eat it," Dad says. He rolls up the window and stares ahead. Arizona watches me from the backseat, and I know I'm supposed to do this with her, but I can't. She started it, the making-our-own-choices thing. She changed everything. So she can't expect me to do everything with her anymore. She made the first crack in our impenetrable united front.

I call Natasha.

"You need to come over?" she says. "Our couch is your couch. You know that."

"I hate my father," I say.

"We'll adopt you," she says. I still can't believe she is the same person she was when they got married seven years ago. It doesn't seem possible. She changed so much after my father and she split up.

"Can't you marry him again?" I say. "Wouldn't that be easiest?" I want the family in my head, the one that doesn't make me feel alternately claustrophobic and untethered. The completely nonexistent one.

"Come over, sweetheart. Help me make dinner. We can talk about your dad being the worst," Natasha says. That doesn't sound right either. I don't want to hate on my father with his ex-wife. It is impossible to decipher what the fuck I want, to be honest.

"That's okay. Thanks. I'll come over this week for sure. It's okay. I'm okay." I don't sound believable, but Natasha believes me.

When I hang up, I decide that what I really need, what will really help, is seeing Bernardo after I have it out with Karissa. I tell him to come by later.

That feels good and all, but I miss the other day and Karissa's party and the way the world was opening up, because now it is closing back in.

eight

When I first met Karissa, she had on a pink camisole, a brown leather vest, and no bra. She did a monologue from the play *No Exit*, and everyone in class watched her with the jaw-open, wet-eyed look of people realizing they aren't good enough.

"Amazing job," our teacher said. "Now do it again, but remember that your whole life all anyone's wanted from you is sex. And you love it, but you're tired of it too. Right? Don't apologize halfway through. It's not okay, what they've done to you. How they've treated you. And you know that, but you also know it's your only power. You understand what I'm saying, Karissa?"

Karissa teared up. She scratched her thighs with her silver fingernails and looked at the ceiling for too long a moment. Donna didn't like when we tried to escape a difficult part of a scene by sighing or looking away or diffusing it in any way.

"No, no, leap right in! Get in there!" the teacher said.

This time, Karissa got choked up halfway through the monologue.

The class nodded in unison at the perfection. When she got to the last line, she was on her knees. She was crying, but not wiping away the tears. Not choking them back.

No one from the outside was supposed to watch class. It was supposed to be a safe, private space. And I guess it mostly was, but the day that Karissa nailed her monologue, my father was at the door, peering in through the tiny window, watching the way her mascara tears made a spiderweb over her face. On someone else it might have looked messy and ugly, but on Karissa, with her brunette waves and unlined, practically translucent face, it was romantic. The mascara made a paisley pattern, black on white, and she looked masked rather than destroyed.

"Who was that?" Dad said after we walked in silence through Washington Square Park to our favorite place in the village, Caffe Reggio.

"Who?" I said.

"The beautiful one. Without the bra," Dad said.

Karissa is not the kind of woman my dad usually calls beautiful.

The wife he was just about to divorce, Tess, has D cups and platinum hair and an impossibly flat stomach. My father likes impossibly perfect women. He likes them because he makes them possible.

That's why when he tells me I'm beautiful, it reeks of lies. I know better. I know what he really sees when he looks at me.

"Please do not talk about my classmates' bras," I said. "Or better yet, please do not say 'bra' to me. Ever. Please extract the word from your vocabulary." I dropped my voice on the word *bra* because the café was cramped and the table of seventy-year-old men playing cards over by the window were all wearing hearing aids, so I was pretty sure they were listening in.

"Well, don't call her your classmate, then," Dad said. "That makes her sound like a teenager. And that girl is not a teenager."

"She's, like, a few years older than Arizona."

"She's hot."

I sighed, because *hot* should be banned the way the word *bra* is banned, but my dad cannot be stopped, especially when he's all hopped up on a soup-bowl-size cup of cappuccino.

With his third wife, Natasha, he always used to say, "Now that's an ass!" whenever she walked away from him in her tight black jeans. When he was with his second wife, Janie, I would catch them making out, his hand either up her shirt or down her pants. I was, like, eight. I don't remember much about him being with my mother. I was only five when she left us for the West Coast and then India and communism or Buddhism or one of those, but I'm sure he didn't hold back with her either. He gave her liposuction and a new nose, but, as she tells me once a year on my birthday, she regrets both of them and hopes I don't take that route.

The point being, my dad can be exceedingly gross about women.

Even then, at Reggio, he was doodling on one of the postcards on the table. It was a Renoir, I think. A painting I'd seen a million times of a woman in a red hat with a little girl. My father drew lines on the woman's face, places he could fix, if she were his client. He did it absently, not knowing it was happening. The doodles are all over the house, too—on magazine covers and friends' Christmas cards. He can't leave work, not ever. His mind looks for flaws to fix, always.

"Her name is Karissa," I said. "She's the best in the class. Do you want to split the prosciutto sandwich?" I held the menu in front of his face so that he would forget everything about Karissa. It did not work. She had green eyes after all. And a dozen silver bracelets on her right hand that clanked against one another if she moved at all, making everyone hyperaware of her movements. She had long eyelashes and red lips and that cool combination of camisole with leather vest that means she's good in bed, I think.

She wasn't perfect. But that's why she was so goddamn beautiful. My dad has never understood that. He sees a field of wildflowers, thinks it's really great, but also thinks pulling out all the weeds and manicuring it into a perfect garden will make it better. Then he's disappointed at the result.

With her freckles and softly frizzing brown hair and crazy outfits, Karissa is totally a field of wildflowers.

"Do you like her?" he said.

"She's talented." I added more sugar to my latte. After one day in her presence I wanted her to be my friend. Or my new sister. "She smokes."

"People give up smoking," Dad said.

And I guess maybe I should have known then what was coming.

nine

Natasha is the wife who taught me about gratitude.

She is the wife I wish was still our mom. More than I wish our actual mom was still our mom, because our actual mom chose to leave us, whereas Natasha chose to make things right with me a year after she left.

She taught me about writing the List of Things to Be Grateful For. She writes ten a day. I try for three.

I work really effing hard to find things to be grateful for on days like today.

For instance, I am grateful for the stoop and the perfect temperature of the evening and the fact that I can pretend planes flying up above are stars in the sky.

Arizona comes home from dinner to find me on the stoop and shoves takeout pasta into my hands like it's a grenade. Orecchiette. Little ears. My favorite, only because of the name.

"I needed you there," she says. I almost forget about her boobs, her face is that sad.

"You don't get it," I say. "That's Karissa. That's the girl I've been talking about all spring. That's her. You know how much she matters to me."

"Not fair," she says. "I'm supposed to matter to you." Karissa comes up from behind in her own cab with Dad. I guess they couldn't even all stand to come home together in one car. Dad kisses Karissa on the lips, a smacking sound that will echo in my head forever, and blows by me on his way into the apartment and up to bed.

Karissa lingers a few feet away for a moment, then heads inside, where I can feel her waiting for me and Arizona to finish up so she can come outside and chat too.

"We can't let this happen," I say.

"Is she, like, unstable?" Arizona says. "She was a little erratic at dinner."

I almost tell her about Karissa's impressive grief and story-like past. But I keep it for myself. I guess I have a habit of keeping things from Arizona, a reality I don't want to look at too squarely.

"Also, that woman can drink. No wonder you were such a disaster the other night," Arizona says. "She's staying over. Do you want to stay at my place so you don't have to deal with that?" She almost forgives me already, and that's what I love about my sister. Her anger has a sharp peak and a deep valley. It's enough to make me think I could tell her about Natasha, at last, after all these years, and that she'd forgive me for being close with the one person we're supposed to hate the most. "And I'm sorry, I want to be supportive, but for the love of God, you look like a cartoon character." She pulls at my hair and raises her eyebrows. We're sisters again, just like that.

"Pot calling the kettle black," I say, even though I'm the one still in the doghouse and should definitely shut up.

"They look natural," Arizona says. "Don't even try to tell me they don't. And it sounds stupid to you, I guess, but he's not totally wrong. I do feel sort of great. And sure. I walk around the Village and feel like . . . a woman. Like, in control. I don't know. Can we shut down this topic? Like, permanently? I want to feel good with what I did." She looks down at her own cleavage. We both do. "I don't know," she says. "Anyway. Eat up. I'll hate you less tomorrow." She digs a plastic fork out of her pocket, because Arizona is nothing if not prepared to take care of me, so I sit on the stoop and dig in. There's nothing quite like eating fancy food on your stoop. It's cheese and oil perfection, so for a glorious moment I'm okay. Cheese can make me forget about anything for the length of time of one bite.

Arizona catches a cab, and the cheese and I watch her go.

Karissa sits down next to me only a minute later. She must have been watching us from the front door's window this whole time. I'm nervous to be near her. We're in some weird space between what we were three days ago and what we are about to become. It feels like wearing jeans that used to fit and still technically button up, but might rip at the seams if you kick your leg in the air.

"You okay?" she says.

"Shit, dude," I say.

Janie is the wife who taught me swear words, and Tess taught me about family dinners. My real mom taught me that anyone can leave, even mothers who smell like brownie mix and soap.

Karissa was supposed to be my friend who would teach me about the correct ratio of cigarettes to liquor and maybe making the most out of small boobs and a sizable ass and how to make the city seem new every day.

Instead she's going to be girlfriend number eight hundred fifty-seven, and I'll be learning about betrayal and whether or not I'm good at denial. I'll learn how quickly something can be taken from me, which is a lesson I was already pretty knowledgeable about, to be honest.

"Don't freak out," Karissa says. I stare at the potted flowers Tess put out here. They're dying, and I want to replace them. I liked the way she put different kinds on every step, like a mini botany lesson on the way into the apartment.

"Not possible."

It's funny that we're talking in tiny sentences. The situation is enormous, but we are being stingy with actual words.

I relax a little. I can't help it. My orecchiette is perfection in a cardboard box and the moon is bright and strange above the buildings and it's nice to have someone to sit with at the end of the night in the middle of the big city.

"You take after your dad, you know?" Karissa extends the word *dad* so that it's a word with a melody. "Like, the things I like about you are the same things I like about him."

It takes everything in me to not scream at her, but I can't stop thinking about the fact that she has no family, that they're gone and she's the brilliant sparkle that's left. It's hard to imagine lashing out at someone like that. I sit on my hands like that will somehow keep my volume and tone in check. Take a deep breath.

"I take after my mom," I say. There's a series of horns, a domino effect of sound moving down the street. Cacophony. I don't even know that the things I'm saying are true. One phone call a year is not enough to get to know my mother.

"Me too," Karissa says. "I mean, my mom. I take after her. It's nice, right? Helps? To have something to share with someone who's gone?"

I'm being tug-of-warred between rage and compassion. I can't even form a response.

"What if this was really good for both of us?" she says. "My mom always used to say that the best things come from the most unexpected places." She takes a piece of pasta right from the box, no fork. And another without asking.

"I feel like Sean Varren is all new to you. But we've been here before. This isn't new for me." I give her a heavy look. I shift the box of pasta a little so that she'd have to reach across me to get another piece of it. It's mine. I don't want to share.

"But I'm new," Karissa says.

We listen to someone playing classical music a few floors above us. It's probably my father, who likes to fall asleep listening to the radio. I look at her face to see if she knows that about him.

I hate her and love her.

I want to yell at her about finding her own family, not stealing mine. That dating my dad is disgusting. That she's a liar and a fake and an awful person who I wish I'd never met. Those things are all swimming inside me.

But mostly I want to tell her that I'm worried about her.

"He's going to hurt you," I say. "This isn't whatever you think it is. Whatever he's saying it is." I don't like how it feels, talking about my father like he's the douche football star that I'm worried is cheating on my friend or something. But it's a true thing I can say. And I want to say a true thing out here on the stoop tonight.

"We both deserve something great," she says, but this isn't something great, so I don't really have a reply. "I think we could all be really happy. Like, together."

Karissa is not a Sean Varren wife. I don't know how to explain that to her without a comprehensive history of the last ten years of my life, so I don't say anything.

My skin itches. I poke as many tiny pasta ears onto my fork as possible and shove them into my mouth, like that will dull the urge to stand up for myself. Karissa takes something out of her purse. It's a hunk of parmesan cheese wrapped in the restaurant's cloth napkin. She pulls out a silver cheese knife too, and a small plate.

"Cheese," she says. "We did cheese for dessert." She puts the napkin on my lap and cuts bites of parmesan for both of us, and it's impossible to hate someone who makes every tiny moment so fucking beautiful.

The cheese is exceptional. Nutty and buttery and the tiniest bit sweet.

Karissa grabs my cheeks, a weird, hard gesture like she might press with too much force and smush my face entirely. Her hands are cool despite the wicked humidity, and I'm always shocked by her ease with intimacy. "Let's be magnificent," she says. She's grinning and her eyes are wild but warm. If there is a feeling that is smack-dab in the middle of scared and elated, I'm there. "We're still us, okay? We're Montana and Karissa. We eat cheese on stolen plates in the middle of the night on the stoop. We are spectacular."

She stares at me until I nod.

ten

I wait for Bernardo outside after Karissa goes upstairs. If I work at it, I can pretend she's not in my father's bedroom.

"You're still pink," I say, when he's halfway down the block. He has his scarf and combat boots on, and I wonder if this guy ever dresses for summertime.

Bernardo laughs, the best kind of chuckle that comes from surprise and not obligation. He is not a guy who laughs often, so his laughter is especially awesome.

"You're still pretty," he says. We have matching laughs now. Matching darting eyes. Matching pink hair.

We've texted so much over the past week that I can almost forget we haven't actually been together. He doesn't know much about me, except it feels like he knows the most important things about me. Who I am, rather than anything about my day-to-day life. I probably look like a distraught mess and smell like garlic and repressed rage.

I care but don't care. I feel the same rush of closeness with him that I felt when I first met Karissa. Like we have something vital in common.

Or maybe I'm simply becoming a person so desperate for connection that I feel it with randoms all the time. I don't know. That's what Arizona would say. That ever since Arizona and Roxanne left for college and Tess moved out, I'm all kinds of unstable and overeager and emotionally wonky. That I'm a little bit like my dad.

But I'm not pretending I'm in love and I'm not counting things I could change about Bernardo, so I can't be that Sean Varren–esque.

I give Bernardo a hug despite Arizona's voice in my head. His arms are strong, something that matters to me.

Bernardo's someone who translates well from real life to text messages. Still, it's nice to see him and smell him and remember that his glasses get foggy in the humidity and that his nose is straight and his teeth whiter than white. The fun of pink hair makes the rest of him more serious, those dark eyebrows underlining his solemn steadiness.

"So it's you and me," I say, sitting back down on the stoop. I don't really do coy. "Real life. No friends around. I like it." I smile and hope he likes it too. He doesn't return the smile, but I still get the sense that he does.

"You don't need to go get your groupies?" he says.

"If anything, I'm Roxanne's groupie," I say. The idea of me being the ringleader is preposterous. I keep trying to be my own person, but it seems like all the options are taken already.

"I don't think you'd pull off groupie very well," he says. Nothing that comes out of his mouth is light or flirtatious. It's all so real. Words with weight. "Groupies have to be background noise, right? You're melody. You're like a strong melody. Get-stuck-in-your-head melody. The Beatles. You're the Beatles."

I am pretty sure my body falls through the stoop and down into the depths of Manhattan. With the mole people and the rats and the subway. I have been stuck all year between trying to be unique and trying to still fit in with my friends or Karissa. The idea that I'm actually solid and verifiable on my own feels good. Makes me fuller than the pasta and cheese feast did.

"You can't think I'm that great already," I say. But it's a lie, because I sort of think he's that great already.

"Don't be self-deprecating," he says. It's beautiful and unnerving not to be able to make everything into a joke.

"I'm not sure I can stand up," I say. "All the sweetness is making me sort of shaky." We've skipped some normal part of the dating experience. Right from nervous first meeting to swoony falling in love.

"I want to see you in the streetlights," he says, and pulls me off the stoop and onto the sidewalk. I want to ask about his perfect hint of accent, but I don't know how. I want to know everything about where his voice, his tone, his pronunciation of the word *streetlights* comes from.

It's cool enough outside, the humidity letting up or maybe not yet sinking in. The streets are lit by streetlights and signs and still-awake apartments, but more than that, they're lit by the passing cars' headlights.

"You've always lived here?" he says. I don't know if he means the city or the West Village, but I nod because the answer to both is yes. I've only lived here. The structure of my family is always changing, but the brownstone, the red bricks, the crumbling stoop, the yellow paint in my bedroom, the view of the Italian restaurant across the street from our building all stay the same.

"Where do you live?" I ask. I can't believe I don't know the answer to this yet. I know what he ate for dinner last night (a turkey sandwich) and his favorite song ("Romeo and Juliet" by Dire Straits, which I downloaded and fell in love with). I know what he thought of all the books we read while silently flirting in the park last semester. But I don't know the basics of his life.

"I'm in Brooklyn. Clinton Hill. My parents have lived there forever so they'll never leave, but my school's around here. That going to be okay with you?"

"I love Brooklyn," I say, but I don't really know if I like it or not. I basically never leave my little corner of New York. Bernardo grabs my hand and brings it to his mouth. "Do you have siblings in Brooklyn?" I say, but I know the answer. I saw them running around him at the park. I know he has a full life with lots of ease. That's stuff you can see even from a great distance, like how I'm sure my particular fucked-up-ness shines across the park at everyone too. Strangers pass me and know I'm from a crazy world.

"Four. Two of each. All younger," Bernardo says, and I blush at how badly I want to fold myself into his life.

I'm jealous and a little scared I can't compete with all that.

A year or two ago I would have bragged about Arizona and the way we operated like two parts of one brain. I would have thought maybe Tess was going to be The Stepmom, the one who was lasting. I would have explained that Roxanne is like a sister, so I almost had two sisters and almost had a mother.

I don't know how to explain anything anymore.

"Sorry this is totally like an interview, but I want to know more about you," I say. I think it's that I want to know more, and not that I want him to know less.

"I don't mind being interviewed by a cute girl," Bernardo says with a straight face and a squeeze of my shoulder.

"Do you speak Spanish?" I say, even though it sounds awkward and weird and like I'm curious about the wrong things.

"I can," he says. "Sort of. Badly. But I don't. Sometimes with my dad. Terms of endearment and swears mostly."

I smile. Bernardo puts a hand on my back, rubs for a moment, and keeps walking. He doesn't smile, but not in a bad way.

I take note in my head: Bernardo is a boy who doesn't depend on smiles. Bernardo is a boy who swears and loves in Spanish.

"I had a crap night until right now," I say. He hasn't asked, but I feel like it must be obvious, from my messy, lipstick-less face.

"I had a crap year until I saw you in the park a few months ago," he says, turning the conversation into something sweet and large again.

"I'm the worst, seriously. Or, like, not the best."

"I said no self-deprecation!" he says, but his eyes glint. "Look, I want to fall in love with a girl who reads and does weird stuff and has crap days and sends funny texts and sits at park benches drinking hot coffee when everyone else is drinking iced."

"We're not in love," I say, leaning toward his ear and whispering into it. I smile when I pull back, and my body is trying to hold too many feelings for one single night.

"Wouldn't it be nice, though?" Bernardo says. I smile and look down and try to stop the happy laughter from bubbling up like a water fountain. It would be nice. "I don't know. I'm a romantic. Call me crazy, but being in love is the best."

"Have you been?" I say. It feels like it would take something away for him to say yes, but I can't put my finger on why. I want one big love, and only one. The exact opposite of my dad.

"Yeah," he says, and my stomach drops. "That's how I know I want it again."

"It was good?" I say, so that he knows I haven't been there.

"It was great until it was gone," he says. He winces, like the pain is physical and still sore.

"I'm sorry," I say. An ambulance rushes by, all sirens and whooping and so loud we have to stop talking for a moment. "That it hurt. Not that it's over."

Bernardo nods.

"It's not the worst thing, being hurt," he says. I want to ask what that means, exactly, but he takes my hand and squeezes and I think that is as much as he wants to say right now.

We end up at our park. I don't know that either of us made the decision to come here, but feet followed feet and the park is lit up by people smoking and checking their phones, little dots of bluish and orange light, so it feels safe and the strangest kind of romantic.

Bernardo sits on his bench. I try to follow, but he nods at the bench I usually share with Roxanne and Arizona, so I sit over there. He's at his bench, I'm at mine, it smells like weed and someone's McDonald's, and that is when Bernardo finally smiles at me. He watches me from there for a moment before joining me on my bench.

"You're weird," I say. It's the most flirtatious I know how to be.

"Well, yeah," he says. "It's even more fun to watch you from over there when I know I can do this after." I don't have time to ask *do what?* And I don't have a chance to pull back and worry about how it will be. I don't have a chance to think about before and after.

He kisses me and there's only now.

eleven

Karissa is downstairs the next morning. She is sitting on the counter. Not on one of the bar stools next to the counter, but actually on the counter. She's got a face-size to-go cup of coffee and she's glowing in the general direction of Arizona, who has her legs crossed and her own enormous coffee and is at her normal stool, the one closest to the fridge that she claimed when we were little kids.

"Finally!" Karissa says. I'm in an extra-large Knicks shirt and gym shorts and I'm not at all ready for contact with humans.

"You're all here," I say. "For breakfast?"

"Karissa called me. Told me to bring coffee and pastries. She's making French toast. With the pastries." Arizona is giving me a look that usually means she hasn't had enough coffee to deal with whatever is going down, but in this case must mean something else, because she has literally the most amount of coffee possible in her hands.

"I have no idea what you're talking about," I say. I can't tell if it's sleepiness or all the kissing that's got me hazy and confused this morning. I had no idea the aftereffects of a great night with a cute guy were so close to exhaustion.

"It's something I made up when I was little. I know it sounds insane, but it's delicious," Karissa says. She's whisking eggs, so I guess she's serious, she's actually going to slather the pastries in eggs and fry them up like normal people do with challah bread. "I want to share with you two what my sister and I shared."

"Oh," Arizona says. Karissa wipes away a tear, and this is probably why Arizona asked if she was unstable.

"My sister died not long ago," Karissa says. "My whole family did. So I get a little sentimental. Especially in the mornings. That's something you should know about me."

Arizona has no idea how to respond. She raises her eyebrows at me, but I don't know how she should respond either. I thought that information was something I had earned the other night, something secret and special and hard to get to. I'm surprised to hear it slip out of Karissa so easily in front of Arizona. Surprised and something else too. Jealous.

"I want us to know each other. Like Montana and I know each other. Like your dad and I—" Karissa stops herself, hearing the sentence before she says it aloud.

This all came out easier when she was drinking with me. Drunk people are more prepared for heavy topics. The morning is time for magazine reading and risk-free conversations about pizza toppings or Sunday-night television.

"I'm so sorry. Losing your family must be . . ." Arizona can't finish the sentence, so now we are in a sea of broken sentences. She looks at me, and I know she feels a little of what I feel toward Karissa. If only for a moment.

"We're all just trying to survive the last terrible thing that happened to us, right?" Karissa says. She jumps off the counter and takes an apple fritter from the box Arizona brought over, starts coating it in egg. She trips a little over her extra-long bright-purple silky pajama pants.

There's silence, and it's the not the kind I had with Bernardo last night.

"What's the last terrible thing that happened to you?" Karissa asks.

"I'm sorry?" Arizona says. She keeps grabbing different things on the counter—a spoon, a Post-it note that my father doodled body parts on when he was talking on the phone the other day, her cell, an almost-bad banana.

My mind does a little jump, and I try to remember what I have told Karissa over the last six months about my sister. And about my father. And about my life, of which she is now a part in a wholly new and unexpected way.

I told her that the guy Arizona liked didn't call her back after they hooked up at some party. I told her all the terrible things Arizona had said about her roommate. I told her that Arizona got crappy grades this last semester and lied about it to Dad. I told her about Dad's other wives. I told her way too much.

"My family dying is the last terrible thing that happened to me. The thing I'm still trying to survive. What about you? A breakup maybe?

Or something with school?" I can't quite tell if Karissa remembers everything I told her about Arizona, or if this is coincidence. I can't seem to interpret any part of this moment.

"I'm pretty much fine," Arizona says.

The kitchen fills with a cinnamony smell. Bliss.

"I wish I was that kind of strong," Karissa says, and Arizona rolls her eyes. Karissa catches the tail end of it, and her face breaks a little. Her eyes well up, and I want this to be going more smoothly. I want Arizona to see what I love about Karissa and for Karissa to see why she should not be in our kitchen cooking breakfast. I want everything to reset.

"So, I kissed Bernardo," I say. I wait for it to fix everything, to make us all friends or something. Arizona clears her throat and drinks more coffee and touches more things on the counter: a glass of water, Dad's business cards, the set of knives in their wooden stand.

"You kissed him or he kissed you?" Karissa says. Arizona's run out of random objects to touch, so she starts picking at the French toast chocolate croissant Karissa drops in front of her and is doing this rabbit thing with her mouth and nose.

If I concentrate, I can pretend Karissa is here because I invited her over to meet my sister. I try to telepathically communicate that plan to my sister, but it doesn't go through.

"Both?" I say. I will Karissa to leave my father. If she left him today or this week, it would still be soon enough to salvage our friendship. If she left him this summer, even, we could maybe someday go back to the way things were and the way they were going to someday be.

"He's one of those . . . big gesture people," Arizona says. She sounds exhausted, but I love her staying here when I know she wants to run out the door. A part of me wants to run out the door too, or fight with Karissa, but I think I don't know how. "He's like sappy, sort of. Stylish and sappy and intense."

"I'm gonna count those all as positive qualities," Karissa says. She's fried up two halves of a muffin, a doughnut, and a half a bagel in this round. The kitchen reeks of nearly burned egg and powdered sugar and simmering butter. Sort of delicious and foreign and a little bit awful. It's not the way our home has ever smelled. "I want to meet him!"

"Montana's barely met him," Arizona says. "I've barely met him. I don't think you'll be top of the list." It comes out calm and cruel. Karissa jangles her bracelets around her wrists, like silver and gold hula hoops, and my heart jingles and jangles too.

"Everyone needs to meet him! But, like, after I've kissed him more," I say, and it's a thing I would have said at Dirty Versailles with Karissa before, so it almost sounds right.

"We could do a start-of-the-summer party!" Karissa says. "Next weekend! Bet I could convince your dad—"

"No. No, thank you," Arizona says with a sour look on her face. "I don't think we need that, right, Montana?" She wants me to choose her, strongly and positively in this moment, and I do. Of course I do. But I also can't. Because even if Karissa is with my dad, Karissa is still Karissa.

"Maybe for the, like, the Fourth of July or something. Maybe later," I say. In my head, in the stupid part of my head, I think maybe it will be over by the Fourth of July. Maybe on the Fourth we can have wine and pickles and fireworks and "The Star-Spangled Banner" at Karissa's cozy apartment and laugh about how she used to have a thing for my dad.

But for now I'm here and it's June and my sister hates me and Karissa has house keys and knows where our spatulas are kept.

"Even better!" Karissa says, not catching the moment. Or catching it and dismissing it and trying to make it something new. "Fourth of July was my parents' favorite holiday. It was a whole thing. With sparklers and flags and booze and tiny hot dogs."

Arizona and I go silent. We nod and look serious, because apparently we both deal with someone else's grief the same way. Solemn muteness.

I try some fried muffin. It's buttery and beautiful. I love it.

Arizona scratches her nose, which I'm sure isn't itchy, and starts playing with the magnets on the fridge. Most of them are from medical conferences or pharmaceutical reps.

It's hard to keep hearing about these people who aren't in the world anymore. When we were in acting class for all those months, Karissa said nothing about them, and now it seems like they're always in the room with us.

"I'm sorry, guys. I'm really sorry. I don't mean to keep talking about them. Being with your dad is bringing up all these old feelings, and it's making me a weirdo. So. I'm sorry for all this." She gestures at her tears. She's a pretty crier, with delicate wet eyelashes and eyes that get even greener and ocean-ier when they're filled with tears.

"Breakfast is great," I say. "And obviously you can always talk to me. Cry in front of me." I mean it, even though I have to force my mind to forget the thing she said about being with my father. I have to pretend that sentence didn't exist.

Karissa hugs me, tightly, bringing me in close to her, and she doesn't let go right away. I pull away the tiniest bit, not wanting Arizona to get any madder at me, but Karissa hugs even harder before releasing.

"I really need to go," Arizona says. Her face is red, and when she stands up, I think again how much she looks like Tess and Natasha and Janie now. I swear she's wearing Tess's pale-pink flats. "Park tomorrow, Montana. Karissa, please, please do not make me try this again. I'm sorry, I know you're probably very quirky and cool and my heart breaks for what you've been through, but I can't pretend that's enough for me to want you to be in my house. With my father. Trying to be my friend or something. I'm sorry. I'm an awful, terrible person. But we want our dad. Not you."

I don't agree or disagree with the word *we*.

"You don't have to leave," I say to the counter. I am saying it to Arizona and Karissa both. I don't want this moment to be happening at all.

"You feel the same way I do," Arizona says.

I shake my head but only when Arizona is gone.

"We'll be okay," Karissa says. "We'll win her over."

They both seem to be positive I'm on their side. But no one's really asked.

Maybe we will be okay, when Karissa and my dad are done. Maybe I'm this wonderful type of person who can forgive things and move on but also be strong and principled. I'd like to think I have that fair, kind, excellent person inside of me.

A month ago Karissa took me out for Vietnamese sandwiches, which I'd never had before. They are delicious and vinegary. She laughed in a horsey way at everything I said. She told me about her first kiss when she was twelve and talked me through her first time when she was fifteen with some pointers on positioning. I'm pretty sure other patrons heard us or at least saw me laugh so hard I spit up a sip of water.

Which is all to say, I want Karissa and my dad. I want them both. Just not together.

Karissa pours orange juice and I smile a lot, so she knows I like her weird breakfast that is partly a memorial to her sister and also that I still like her. I feel a little sick, maybe from the crazy French toast or maybe from the things Arizona said or the circumstance we've all somehow ended up in.

"I'm not one of them. The evil stepmoms or whatever. I'm different. I promise," Karissa says.

I don't reply. I don't know how to, but I know to keep my eyes on the counter so that she can't do one of her forceful stares that convince me to agree with her.

"Tell me everything about the boy," she says. And I do. Because my sister left and Karissa's right here.

twelve

Arizona turned thirteen almost two years before me, but she didn't tell me about the thirteenth birthday gift until mine was presented by my dad and wrapped in fancy gold paper with a silver bow and a fake rose taped to the middle as extra decoration. I was pretty sure it was something shiny, like a necklace with my birthstone or the tiara I'd seen when I was out shopping with Natasha that Dad told me was ridiculous but I insisted was perfect for all kinds of events.

I used to like things like diamonds and glitter and princess costumes. I used to believe in things like birthdays and stepmoms.

The present was a slip of paper.

Dad's office stationery, and a promise that I could get any procedure I wanted when I turned eighteen.

"For confidence," he said.

"I don't get it," I said. I looked to Arizona for a translation, and she shrugged. Arizona was not very sociable when she was fifteen.

"When I was thirteen, all I wanted to know was that I would be prettier when I was older," Natasha said, trying to explain away the confusion all over my face. She had a bad habit of saying things that were definitely insulting but that she didn't spend any time thinking about, so were therefore somehow "not meant to be mean."

"Oh," I said, because there is very little else to say to a gift certificate for future plastic surgery.

"You can get anything done!" Dad said. "Like, if you don't grow into your nose. Or, you know, breast enhancement, if that's what you'd like. I can't imagine you'd need lipo, but that would be fine too."

Dad had been talking about me growing into my nose for years. It had never seemed that big to me.

I thought of the random doodles he drew on magazine covers and spare slips of paper. Fixes he could make to the models' faces, arms, thighs, boobs. Idle illustrations of perfect and imperfect bodies and noses and chins. There was a magazine on the coffee table with Gwyneth Paltrow in a bikini on the cover. He'd drawn dotted lines around her eyes and near her hips. It shouldn't have been a surprise that he assumed I'd be imperfect too.

"Your ears are pretty close to your head, so pinning them back won't be necessary," he went on. I was tearing up. But if he saw the tears, he'd be insulted. He liked to deal with facts, and the facts, the literal facts of numbers and symmetry and measurement, said that my nose was too big and my chin a little too small. It wasn't something to be sad about. Especially when he was promising to fix it. "But your chin we could add a little something to. When you're eighteen, of course. I would never do any of this on someone your age. But to know it's there, like a safety net, Natasha and I thought it might help. With adolescence. With confidence. I want you to know we get how hard it is to be your age and that we're here for you and you'll get through it." Dad smiled. "We're so lucky to have Natasha around to help me understand you girls." He put his arm around her and beamed like a victor of some contest for Dad of the Year.

I wondered if maybe it was me. If I was the weird one who didn't like the gift. He and Natasha seemed so sure that it was a full-on winner, I assumed I must be somehow off. I knew I was supposed to reflect back Dad's happiness, but I felt the panicked sadness of waking up from a too-close-to-reality nightmare.

"I got you a pet chameleon!" Arizona exclaimed, right at the moment I thought all my insides were going to start pouring out of my eyes and nose. I thought I could maybe cry so hard and so long that I'd turn hollow, eventually.

"You—you did?" I said. Arizona was giving me our patented *don't cry* look, which we had perfected long, long ago when I was five and she was seven and Mom left.

"I did," she said. "That's what you wanted, right?" She ran to her bedroom, where I guess she'd been storing the little guy, and brought him down in a glass cage with a book of instructions for feeding and cleaning and general chameleon care.

"Yes," I said, staring at his scaly face, "this is what I wanted." If Mom had been around, maybe she would have remembered the chameleon too, but it didn't matter. I had Arizona for that. Dad was good at being around and not leaving and finding random women to live with us, and asking us one million times a month if we were happy, even if he never explained quite what that meant. Arizona was good at filling in all the gaps that were left. And Mom was good at birthday cards and not much else.

I loved that chameleon hard and named him Lester. I stopped wanting anything that glinted in the sun or was meant to make me prettier. I stopped wanting Natasha around. Until after she and my dad broke up a couple of years later.

I keep my plastic surgery gift certificate in my desk drawer. I am positive I'll never use it, but I keep it as a reminder of something. I'm not sure what.

I thought Arizona was doing the same thing. It's uneasy, to be suddenly different from the person you thought you were exactly like.

Dad's never mentioned it again, but I'm sure he's wondering how I'm going to use it, checking my face to catalog the ugliest parts and make suggestions.

Meanwhile, my chameleon Lester died two years ago. They don't have very long life spans, as it turns out. Changing themselves that often, to fit every possible circumstance perfectly, exhausts them, I guess.

thirteen

These days Natasha lives in a big apartment on the Upper East Side with some burly lawyer guy and twin daughters, Victoria and Veronica.

And sometimes me.

Once every few weeks, I manage to convince my father I'm with some friends from school who don't exist and convince Arizona I'm on some adventure and convince Roxanne I'm in for the night, and I stay at Natasha's. Like it's my home. It's been easier this year, of course, without Roxanne and Arizona watching and caring.

I'd tell Roxanne, but I know she'd tell Arizona. In the hierarchy of friendships that everyone pretends doesn't exist but everyone also knows does exist, Arizona loves me most and I love Arizona most but Roxanne loves Arizona most. It's a thing I always suspected but am now sure about.

Sometimes I think Arizona loves me most but likes Roxanne better. That stings too. To be unchosen. To not be anyone's favorite person.

So I stay sometimes on Natasha's white leather couch under Victoria's gray cashmere blanket. Natasha has a tiny white dog named Oscar and more shoes than any of the other wives, and as soon as she and my dad were over, she got nice.

We started with coffee.

I went to her wedding.

I babysit her kids.

She cooks me dinner and gives me hand-me-downs and punks them up with me when they're too prissy.

She apologized for the gift certificate, for the things she didn't understand.

She is making plans to take out her implants.

She says she made a lot of mistakes and she is trying to unmake them or at least not make any more.

When she hugs me, she means it.

She is my big, unspeakable secret.

Once or twice a year I consider telling Arizona and letting her into the fold, but I can't seem to bring myself to admit I've broken one of our sister-promises. Or maybe I can't stand the thought that Natasha would like her better too. That there would be no one left who was mine.

I like to think it's the first thing. That I'm a girl ashamed to have broken a promise, and not that other girl who's all lame and selfish and needs more than I'm supposed to.

After too much of everyone else, I find myself at her place, where I'm safe. It's like hiding out when you're little. Under the table or in the closet or whatever. No one knows I'm here, and they'd never think to look for me at Natasha's.

We sit on her couch, side by side, and share our Lists of Things to Be Grateful For.

"Victoria's wonderful spirit," she says.

"The stoop," I say.

"The Starbucks barista who told me I look like Denise Richards."

"Coffee after nine p.m."

"The way we change over time and become better and worse, in tandem," Natasha says. She always has one thing on her list that blows my mind a little.

"Karissa. That she exists, but not what she's doing," I say, because I've never not read something on my list. It's a weird intimacy between us. We don't hold back.

"New friend?" Natasha says.

"Sort of." I kind of can't believe she hasn't been on any other lists I've read to Natasha, but sometimes it takes a while to admit you are grateful for something or someone. Sometimes I'll write about a great dinner with my father three months later. Like I can't appreciate it from up close, the way some paintings are better from a distance.

"New mom?"

"No. She's not the stepmom type. She's one of the in-betweeners."

It feels mean to talk about Karissa that way, in the old lingo that I've always used about Dad's wives and girlfriends.

"I can live with it. I have love in my life. I'm filled with gratitude. I'd like those things for your father even though he is incapable of that reality." Natasha says all these yoga things that would sound like total bull coming from most people, but she is legitimately serene. I've seen the change, and that's even better than meeting someone who's always been sweet and kind and wise. I like Natasha even more because she used to be so heinous. "I want your dad to be happy. And you. I want you to have what you want." She knows but doesn't say that what I want is to have had a mother. Wanting a mom is not the kind of thing you say out loud. Not unless you're five and have a boo-boo. "And Arizona," Natasha says, with a sigh. She always says Arizona's name with a sigh, because she can't fix what went wrong there and it twists her up inside.

There was only one time that I actually tried to tell Arizona about my relationship with Natasha. I floated the idea that Natasha had changed. Said I saw her walking down the street, pregnant and looking all cherubic. Arizona scoffed and said *that poor baby* and stomped instead of walked the rest of the day.

I wonder if it would be different, now that Arizona has actually used the gift certificate. It's the thing that made Natasha worse than the others. The thing that made her unforgivable. I wonder if Arizona actually using the thing makes her hate Natasha less. Or, I guess, more.

Maybe more, since no matter what happiness crap she's spouting, I think Arizona did it to get closer to my father, to be the daughter he wants in the hopes that that would make him stop finding new women in his life.

And now that she's met Karissa, she must know she failed.

"Monanana!" Victoria calls out, waking up from her nap. Veronica doesn't have as many words as Victoria, but she's every bit as loving. She hugs my legs and gurgles in my direction.

"They love you," Natasha says. "Their big sister."

"Except not," I say. I love-hate when Natasha calls me their sister. I even love-hate it that Victoria knows my name. It's light and heavy, right and wrong. I lift Veronica in the air. She has brown eyes and her mother's old nose. I remember Natasha's old nose from when she was first with my father, and seeing it on Victoria feels right.

I wish I shared something like that with them. Something tangible to tie me to this family, like a nose or an eye color or a last name. And I wonder if Natasha regrets changing her nose every time she sees it on her daughter's face.

"So. What's this new girl look like?" Natasha says. She's looking over my list again. She's the only person who's allowed to do that. She flips back in time, to older entries she missed, and I love watching her smile at the things I've written. "Goddamn it you are a writer, lady," she says, reading back a few of my entries in this awe-filled voice that hurts from how good it feels.

"Karissa's like a fairy," I say. "Like . . . hipster Tinker Bell. Or punk ballerina. She's perfect, sort of."

"Well, don't rub it in. I'm not that evolved," Natasha says. But we both know she pretty much is.

"Whatever, she's not about to be a wife or anything," I say. "I'm still rooting for you to get him back. We can adopt the girls. You liked the brownstone."

It's a nice dream to have, but I could never wish that on Natasha for real. Her new husband is kind, and they have this incredible marriage.

He reads her gratitude journals too. I was a little devastated when she first told me, since I thought I was the only one who got that privilege. But really it's good to see solid proof that closeness, the way I imagine it, exists, even if it doesn't happen exactly when you want it to.

"We're a forever thing," Natasha says all the time. "You and me."

But I have to let go of the dream, since she's a forever thing with her husband too. I'm not her daughter. I'm not her best friend or her wife or her sister. I'm not even her stepdaughter anymore.

Other dreams: joining a commune of motherless girls with Arizona. Running away with Bernardo. Moving permanently into Natasha's apartment. Making a weird sort of family with Karissa where we go to bars and live in her apartment and throw our own pickle-and-wine parties. I'd accept anything, as long as it feels like it will last and be mine.

Anything but Karissa being the next temporary moving part in our nonfamily.

If Karissa hadn't turned everything on its head, I could see myself sharing the List of Things to Be Grateful For with her too. I ache for how badly I want her to be mine again. I was so close.

"I'm gonna tell you about a boy," I say to Natasha, testing it out with her the way I did with my sister and Karissa.

"You better," she says, and pours me more tea and brings me another cookie, and if I didn't have a pack of cigarettes in my purse and the memory of a bunch of drunk nights in my head, I'd think this was my real life.

"You're falling in love?" Natasha asks, and I shake my head and say of course not, but the things Bernardo said ring in my ear like a premonition, and I wonder if I could be. Falling, of course. Not fully in. I don't believe in falling in love too quickly or with someone I don't know. I don't believe in anything my father does.

But I like the idea that Natasha can see the beginnings of it, like it's a scent on me or etched onto my skin, and not the fleeting, ephemeral thing I've always thought it was.

Love, as something stable and real and tangible.

I can't really imagine.

I stay over at Natasha's, and the girls keep me up most of the night by calling out for me and their mom and dad from their cribs.

I feel like I'm in the CIA, like I have a secret identity where I live part-time as a good girl with a mother.

Natasha didn't even comment on my hair. Maybe in this light it isn't noticeable. Maybe her apartment is that transformative.

Between nights out with Karissa, and days in the park with Roxanne, and the memories of the school year spent in a cloud of invisibility and vague friendliness, and Bernardo on my mind, and trying to fall asleep on Natasha's couch, it's like I'm living seventy-five different lives and don't feel fully comfortable in any of them. Arizona digs her heels in on the life she wants, and I'm out here dipping my toes in everything to see if any of it could fit.

It gives me a miniature panic attack. Something stuck in my heart and throat that doesn't ever bloom but festers and hurts.

I don't fit anywhere.

I am a mess, I text Bernardo when I'm half-asleep on the couch and too drowsy to stop myself. The leather keeps sticking to my legs, and the girls have lullabies playing too loudly on their baby sound system. Natasha turned it back on when they woke her up a half hour ago, and it hasn't turned itself off yet.

That's why I like you so freaking much, he texts back.

I love that he doesn't try to tell me I'm not a mess.

I want to tell you everything, I say. It's funny. When someone is romantic and strange and too big to be real, you learn to match them, at least a little. *And I want you to tell me everything*. I'm thinking of the girl he used to love, and I think I could even handle knowing about that.

Then that's what we'll have to do, Bernardo writes back.

I could melt into this thing between us.

June 13

The List of Things to Be Grateful For

1 Oscar licking my hand to wake me up.

2 The type of sleep that comes with anticipation. Reckless dreams and lots of rolling back and forth all night and waking up so early the rest of the house is still asleep. Little baby snores from the next room.

3 Wide hips. My wide hips. The swing of them. The undeniability of them. The way they fill out my ugly jean shorts.

fourteen

I learn very quickly that Bernardo looks as good on the Lower East Side of Manhattan as he does on the West Side. He buys me my very own winter scarf to wear in the summer at a stand on St. Mark's that is probably the only place in the entire city selling knit scarves in June.

"What if I get sweaty?" I say when he wraps it around me and declares it sexy.

"Sweaty is sexy," he says.

We eat french fries from the Belgian fry place and I introduce him to garlic mayo, so if he wasn't falling for me before, he definitely is by the time we've finished a whole cone of the things.

"Next time we'll go to Brooklyn," he says.

"Next time?" I flutter my eyelashes, but I'm not as uncertain as I'm pretending. When something's solid, you don't have to worry about it being a liquid. We are a solid. Sometime in the last few hours, walking around the city, or maybe texting late last night, we became one.

"Do you like guacamole?" he says. It sounds dangerous in my ear, in a way I never thought avocados could be.

"To a kind of scary degree," I say. "Guac and cheese are pretty much all I need."

"You're in luck. My father makes the world's greatest guacamole."

"You want me in your home? Me? You've seen me, right? Mothers don't love me." I could change out of my cutoffs for a meet-the-parents moment. I could get real shoes instead of flip-flops and borrow a blouse from Karissa instead of a T-shirt, I guess. It must be serious if I'm willing to give up T-shirts. But I won't give up my pink hair.

Our pink hair.

Or the scarf, I guess.

"I want it all," he says. "And she'll like you because I like you."

"You don't know me," I say. It's more Arizona's voice than my own coming out. It feels like he knows me and that I know him. It feels like all that time spent staring at each other in the park counted as getting to know each other.

But Arizona and I got coffee this morning in the park, and she kept shaking her head when I talked about Bernardo, like I was wrong about my own feelings.

"You can't like someone all at once," she said before adding another packet of sugar to her iced latte. She was wearing a straw hat that would look elegant on a model but looked out of place in the park.

"It's not all at once," I said. "A lot can happen in a short amount of time, though. And a lot can happen without speaking. And a lot can happen while you're kissing."

"You sound like Dad," Arizona said, and I almost canceled on

Bernardo because nothing would be worse and I am so used to trusting whatever Arizona says. I think she expected me to cancel on him too.

"We going to go to that place with the cute crappy cheap dresses in SoHo?" she said. They sell flimsy things in trendy patterns with lots of wood and metal embellishments at the chest and waist. Arizona thinks they'll have sundresses, but they won't. Not the kind she likes now.

"I told you I'm going out with Bernardo," I said.

"And I said I think you're moving too fast and being a little too girlfriend-y with him," she said. She might as well have been wagging her finger at me.

"I don't know what to tell you," I said. "I guess I disagree?" Arizona and I must have disagreed a thousand times before she went to college. More, I'm sure. But now we disagree about things that matter. Like we are fighting about the shape of the earth. Whether it goes around and around or reaches an end point that we could all fall off of.

Arizona thinks we could fall off some cliff at the end of the earth, and I know that's not the shape of things.

Bernardo and I are outside a thrift store in the East Village, and I pull him in.

"Tell me what you like in here," I say. "That will help me understand you in a way nothing else could."

Bernardo picks out a fringed leather vest. "This," he says. "What does this tell you about me?"

"You don't want to know," I say.

I try on a hat with a veil, and Bernardo pulls down a retro airline messenger bag situation. He finds a red studded belt and buckles it around his waist. It looks fucking good on him, and I tell him so.

I find an enormous cashmere coat and wrap myself in it. It's a ridiculous thing to wear in June, but I'm learning from Bernardo that that's a stupid reason to resist something. Seasons and time don't mean anything.

With the coat and hat on and the music in the thrift store playing too loud, I ask him to tell me about his ex-girlfriend.

"Casey?"

"Sure. Casey," I say, hating her already. Casey. She sounds peppy and pretty. She sounds brown-eyed and busty.

"I'm over her, first of all," Bernardo says, like it's a question he gets asked a lot. I wrap another coat around myself. I need layers for this. What I really need is armor. "So don't freak out."

"I'm not freaking out," I say, freaking out.

"She was older. In college. Kind of a partyer. Really smart."

Kind of a partyer means sex. And smart means really pretty. I should not have asked about her. Older means sex too. And older means better. And older means he'll never be over her.

I take a deep breath and tell those thoughts to go away. Natasha would remind me that being open is good, I think, and Karissa would tell me to trust in my awesomeness.

Karissa always wants me to trust in my awesomeness.

I take off the coats and try to trust in my awesomeness.

"You loved her," I say. It's a statement. I already know it's true, and I am desperate to be okay with it. A sad look comes over his face, and I know he loved her a lot and I also know that he needs me to be there for him while he talks about it.

So I do something I don't think I'm capable of, because he's worth it. I decide to support him. I decide to be okay with it.

"That must have been hard, when it ended," I say. I start hunting through the store's box of jewelry. Necklaces and bracelets are all tangled up with one another, but if you look closely, you can find beautiful things. As long as you're willing to spend some time untangling them, righting them, making them yours.

"It was sort of bad. I don't know. We were really, really together. Then she changed her mind. Said I was too young and immature, and I think she started seeing someone old. Like twenty-five." Bernardo shakes his head, trying to rid himself of the image he's created. "It happened fast. I was pretty unprepared."

"That sounds terrible," I say. I've pulled out a strand of gray pearls. I'm sure they're fake, but they're beautiful anyway. I put them around my neck and look at myself in the mirror. Do I look like the sort of girl who could inspire that kind of heartbreak?

"I sort of thought she was it," Bernardo says. "My parents thought I was insane. But when you love someone . . . I don't know."

"When you love someone what?" I ask. No one tells me much about what it's like to really love someone. I take off my hat and put on red-framed cat-eyed glasses with no lenses. Bernardo kisses my nose. I didn't know that I wanted to be kissed there. That I would feel small and sweet and adored.

I wrinkle my nose.

"Damn that's a cute nose," he says. I cover it up. It hurts. Being complimented hurts sometimes.

"When you love someone what?" I ask again. "What were you going to say?"

"When you love someone, you want to be with them. You want that to be it. You don't want it to end. When you love someone and you're seventeen, you want to be thirty, you know?"

I don't know.

Bernardo's the kind of guy who wants to skip ahead fifteen years, to get to the boring part.

"That sounds intense," I say. I grab a tie from the rack and throw it around his neck. It's green and paisley and wide. I show off my skill at tying ties. It's the kind of thing you become an expert in when your dad is sometimes single.

"You say intense like you really mean crazy," Bernardo says. "Partly she was just really hot and liked watching baseball with me and my dad, and made paper cranes and origami and stuff, and I thought that was weird and cool and hot. Should I not say hot? It's bad to say hot about my ex, right?"

The store owner is giving us a look that means we either need to buy something or leave, so we leave.

I've taken the gray not-pearls by accident. I could go in and return them but they didn't notice, and the pearls are probably, like, a dollar, and there's something sort of wonderful about being dangerous and not myself. So I keep them on. Twist them around my fingers.

"You are an intense dude," I say.

"You're still saying it like it means crazy," he says.

"It does, a little," I say. I bump his hip with mine. I kiss his neck. I haven't kissed him anywhere but his lips, so the smell and taste and feel are all brand-new. "I'm a little crazy too," I say, and it sounds flirtier than I meant it to. Like an invitation for something.

"I loved Casey," he says, a sentence I didn't need to hear. "Because she made me feel like I could be someone else. Someone new." He shrugs. "Casey, loving Casey, was hopeful, like I could change. But that meant she wanted me to change. Wanted me to be someone else. And, I don't know, it's like . . . you can grow, but you can't really change. Or something."

We look at each other on the sidewalk, which is not an easy thing to do in New York. People have to bump and maneuver and sigh around us. Sidestepping our little moment.

"Intense," I say for a third time, grinning and squinting from the way the sun sometimes hits a window and becomes a burst of blinding light. "Intense," I say, and this time I do mean crazy, but I also mean wonderful.

"Thanks for asking about her," Bernardo says as we walk, slipping an arm over my shoulders and pulling me close before we both realize it's too hot and humid to be stuck together like that for too long.

"I used to sort of think I could have that with my sister. That closeness. But I think we have too many weird things between us now," I say. I wasn't thinking about Arizona, but now I can't help it. It's that word—*mine*. It makes me think of the way we used to hold hands on subway rides with my father, when he left us in the hospital day care on summer days when he couldn't find a babysitter. We'd read books to each other in the corner of the room and not give anyone else the time of day. It reminds me of Roxanne too, and the way she ate breakfast at our house before school instead of hers. That the three of us could fit in one bed and I didn't feel younger or smaller or anything.

"Weird things?" Bernardo says.

He told me so much and it feels like I should tell him something real, so I tell him my one big secret.

"Like, this one ex-stepmom, Natasha? I still hang out with her. A lot. All the time. My sister would kill me," I say. It feels new to say it out loud.

"Is she great?" he asks. Bernardo asks perfect questions.

"She is the greatest. She's family. Except not. She's family and she's also the terrible thing I'm doing to my family. It's strange."

"It sounds like you need her," Bernardo says. His glasses are getting a little foggy from the thickness of the air, and I take them off so I can rub them down for him. Make things clear again.

"I don't know what I need," I say.

"What about all the other stepmoms? There were a few, right?"

"What about them?" I say. It's hard to explain how Tess and Janie and the other girlfriends are all variations on a theme, or else wildly inappropriate deviations. My dad's love life is a long, complicated pattern that I still haven't completely worked out.

We're making turns every single street, bringing us farther east, then farther north. The farther away from the center we go, the fewer people there are, until it's almost possible to imagine a moment alone.

"What are they all doing these days?" Bernardo says. "Or I guess, do you think about them? Or what were they like? I don't know what I'm asking."

"I think about them," I say. I don't know how to answer the rest of it. "I think about seeing them. I think about what if they'd stayed with us."

"Like, alternate lives?" Bernardo says. He's trying to put words to something that I've never even thought through. A little place in my mind I've been avoiding. "Like how you are with Natasha?"

Something about the way he phrases it hits me weirdly. Not the wrong way exactly, but askew.

"Natasha isn't an alternate life," I say, "she's part of my actual life."

"Totally. Of course. I'm sorry. I meant . . . maybe you don't want to have to leave them all behind."

There's this complex at the top of the East Village, Stuyvesant Town, and we've somehow found our way there, by accident. Dad dated a woman for a few months who lived here, so I know the playgrounds and the funny little car-less labyrinth inside. I lead him in. There's nowhere to actually go in there—no cafés or pretty views or anything—but it's a funny pocket of Manhattan that I haven't seen for five or six years probably.

It's comforting, that I still know my way.

"I guess I would like them to be more than . . . apparitions. Or blips. Or whatever. At one time or another I really tried to make each of them feel like an actual mom, you know? Or at least like an aunt."

"Maybe someday you'll meet them again," Bernardo says. He adjusts his glasses and we leave Stuyvesant Town as quickly as we came. Back out on the street I'm happy not to have grown up there, no matter how cute and village-y and cozy it seems. I like the wildness of the rest of New York better.

"I guess I have no idea what's going to happen next," I say, "even if it seems like I do."

Bernardo pulls me in again, and we walk like that, his arm around me, our skin sticking together from the heat and sweat.

Sweating together makes me think of being naked together, and that's not the worst thing to think about while we look at the sky and the buildings and the city and each other.

"You make things make sense," I say on the sidewalk, looking up at someone's rooftop, filled with bushes and potted plants and all the things we New Yorkers do to make the city look more like the country, to have the best of both worlds.

fifteen

"I'm coming home with you. Today can't be over yet," Bernardo says at the end of the day.

It's past dinnertime but instead of eating we kiss on the cab ride home, and the driver grunts about teenagers and being underage and the authorities, whoever they are. Bernardo pulls on my scarf while we kiss.

Maybe I don't need anything else but this.

When we get to my place, the driver has to honk his horn to get us to stop making out. We get out of the cab and almost start up again on the street, but Karissa is on the stoop, smoking. She throws her arms in the air, a mini celebration.

"You're home!" she cries. She pulls me into a hug, and I'm shaky from the kissing so I collapse into it a little. "I'm having a really hard day," she says. "It would be my mom's birthday." She says it right into my ear so Bernardo can't hear it, but every part of me sure can.

Her hair looks blonder than usual. Still mostly brown, but with a sunlit layer on top. She's dyed it, for sure. I think they call that color Sean Varren blond. She's in gold leggings and a long white top, loose and linen-y.

"I'm sorry," I say, working hard to push down the anger that rushes out of me from seeing her so comfortable on my stoop. Drinking coffee out of my dad's favorite mug. The conflicting feelings give me a headache. I love her gold leggings and the way she looks happy to see me. I hate everything else.

"I'm Karissa. Are you Bernardo?" She sticks her hand out to Bernardo when he's done paying the cabbie. Those jangling bracelets of hers make a full-on racket.

"I am," he says. He squints, maybe trying to put together the idea of Karissa, who I'd told him about, with the reality in front of him.

"Well, great. Come on in, guys. Your dad's heading out, and I could use some company."

I guess she is now at the level where she stays at our place even if Dad isn't here. And I guess, since it's her dead mom's birthday, I have to be okay with that.

Dad's by the door, definitely suited up and on his way out, and he does a double take when he sees Bernardo. Maybe because I'm never with boys or maybe because of how Bernardo looks. How we look together. Pink and scarved and sweaty. Matched and odd.

"I'm Sean," he says, but doesn't even wait for Bernardo to answer with his name before he's out the door. "Take care of my girl!" he calls out from the sidewalk. I don't know if he's talking to Karissa about me or to me about Karissa. I hate both options, actually.

"So that's my dad," I say. Bernardo nods and looks around the apartment, maybe trying to pick up clues that he couldn't catch from those three seconds with my father.

"He forgot about today," Karissa says in that whisper again. Bernardo checks out the gold-framed full-length mirror in the hallway. Old-school Natasha.

"He forgets everything," I say. "It actually means he cares more, not less." Bernardo does hear this, and he looks at me with concern. Clears his throat, and I know I've said some weird truth about my dad that normal people find heartbreaking. It happens from time to time.

"He also forgets that I'm allergic to peanuts and that Arizona's birthday is in April. It's nothing personal," I say.

I am definitely making it worse, because Karissa bites her lip and Bernardo rubs my arm as if I've said something deep and tragic.

"Well, I guess that's helpful to know," Karissa finally says, and Bernardo excuses himself to go to the bathroom, but not before kissing my forehead.

The second he's out of sight, but probably not totally out of earshot, she grabs my arms and sings into my ear.

"Boyfriend! Only boyfriends kiss foreheads!"

If I squint, I can pretend our gold-framed mirror is chipped and adorned with cherubs and set up behind the bar at Dirty Versailles. If I work really hard, this whole moment can be something else entirely.

"He's affectionate. It doesn't mean he's my boyfriend," I say, but I sort of think he is. "He's too cute to be my boyfriend."

"You're smitten!" Karissa's eyes light up. They are approximately the brightness of traffic lights stuck on *go*. "I love first love! I love smitten!"

She's a whole new person from the one who was two seconds ago talking about her mom's birthday. She is light and whirring. She goes for her iPod, which is already in Dad's dock, and starts playing oldies. The Crystals. She swings her hips with the song. I can't help doing the same.

"I met him, like, five minutes ago, okay? It's not what you're thinking." But I am smiling and hip swinging and a little happy she's here, to do this with me.

"You have to let me hang out with you," Karissa says. I start to say no. Arizona will hate it, and I'm not sure how long I can go on pretending she's not my dad's latest girlfriend.

Her face shifts a little. "Today sucks. I need a pick-me-up," she says. "I'll make it epic, I promise."

"I feel uncomfortable—," I try to say, but Karissa cuts me off.

"Can you wait until tomorrow to feel uncomfortable?" she says. Her eyes look a little like a stormy sea, and there's sadness there, under all the dancing and shiny clothing and bright smiles. I can feel her missing her mother, and I can't say no to it.

"As long as you let me feel not okay about all this tomorrow," I say, and she meant it as a joke, but I mean it as a reality. I am eventually going to need more permission to feel not okay.

Bernardo comes back smelling of the brand of soap Tess had us stocked up on.

"So what do we think? Board games?" Karissa says when Bernardo's back. "Drunk board games! For me at least. I can be drunk. You guys, I'm not so sure. I should probably wait before I become your official beer buyer or whatever. I bet you have Taboo, don't you? Scattergories? I bet you have Scattergories and I bet your dad has Scrabble and I bet Arizona has Monopoly. I'm so right, aren't I?"

I nod and feel like I'm betraying Arizona for about the millionth time today. She would hate Karissa guessing something about her, pretending to know her. I should hate it too.

"I'm totally kidding about only me being drunk! I'll chaperone. It's cool. We're all cool," she says, smiling so hard the freckles on her face shift around. I hate how much I still love her.

"Drunk board games it is," Bernardo says in the flurry of Karissa's words.

"Thank you," she says, squeezing my hand. "Seriously. Thank you. I know this is still sticky, but I need you and it means so much to me that you get that." I smell all of Karissa's smell—cigarettes and baby powder and musky perfume and supersweet hair spray. A combination that is oddly perfect. I grow a little, from her nice words and the way she is acting like I matter and like she gets it, and I think of things I could do to make her feel better—get a cake in honor of her mother, toast her mother, tell her about the day my mother left.

She winks at Bernardo and sneaks into the kitchen to go liquor hunting. I press myself against him the second she's out of the room, because this might get awkward and I want him to remember what our bodies feel like together, before the situation scares him off.

"She's a lot," I say.

"You're being good to her," he says. "You're really good to peo-ple, even when it's hard for you. Like with talking to me about Casey today. I noticed."

Sometimes compliments cause these heart palpitations. For me, at least.

Sometimes they hit and make me feel like I might be about to die, until I realize no, that's a good feeling, not a bad one.

That compliment hits and sparks and practically explodes in my chest. I've been spending so much time wondering what's wrong with me, wondering why I'm not a good enough sister or friend or daughter or person, that the idea of me being good is a little unbearable.

Compliments don't always sound true, but today, right now, that one does.

Once we are in the basement, Karissa takes a sloppy drink from the bot-tle of wine and hands it to me, like some ancient family-making ritual.

I take a sip and pass it on to Bernardo.

"So we're doing this?" he says. I guess it's a question I should have asked before going down this rabbit hole, where we don't give up our friendship even though she's also something else. It's dangerous, to be two things at once, to be blurry and undefined and weird. We are entering into messiness without asking enough questions.

So it's my fault, in some ways.

I jump right in.

"Might as well," I say with this shrug and smile like it's all so, so cool.

sixteen

Karissa, Bernardo, and I end up on the couch in the basement playing charades because I don't feel like hunting around for board games, and I don't want to have any kind of deep conversation either.

Karissa is the world's best charades player. It is the opposite of a surprise. I'm into it for about a minute, but the wine hits me fast and I'm drowsy quickly.

"You need to commit," she says, when I try to act out *Moby-Dick*. I blow up my cheeks and point to a pretend hole in the center of my back and wiggle my fingers around to represent water spouting out of it. "I mean, come on. The word 'dick' is right in the title. What are you doing not acting out the word 'dick'? That's, like, a gift from the charades gods."

I shake my head, but there aren't words to respond to that.

"Very creative," Bernardo says. "I wouldn't have thought of that either." He takes another sip of wine. He eyes the vodka. Dude is drunk. He reaches for my hip bone, a place that has been dying for his touch. He purses his lips into a kissing face and strains toward my cheek, but I'm too far away and he's too off balance, so he ends up kissing the air.

It seems impossible that we've been hanging out for such a short amount of time. Maybe because Bernardo is all mine and everyone else in my life is someone I have to share, but I feel closer to him than anyone else right now. When Arizona and I were more like the same person, I felt closer to her. Like we shared cells. That's gone, but I feel some version of it with Bernardo already.

Maybe it's the pink hair. Or the way we kiss. The perfect fitting together of lips. Or the way we listen to each other.

"Should I make cocktails?" Karissa says when there's a lull in charades and conversation and energy. "Have you guys had martinis before? I could introduce you to martinis!"

I don't want to be drunk like I was at Dirty Versailles with Karissa. But there's a full bar down here, and Karissa starts clattering away with bottles and glasses and a metal shaker. I like the way the martinis sound, getting made. I like the way Karissa adds olive juice and speared olives and the way Bernardo has to lap at the top of his like a cat. I almost say no to my own precarious glass, but I reconsider the smell, the coolness of the glass, the lightness of the laughter coming out of Karissa and Bernardo. The way it felt to be Karissa's best friend at Dirty Versailles. I consider the phone call Karissa must have gotten a few years ago when she found out her whole family was gone. I consider the darkness of the night. The fact that streetlights don't reach the basement. I consider the Swedish pop Bernardo is playing from his phone and the tinny, two-dimensional sound of music without real speakers.

I consider it all, and sip from the splashy top.

It tastes like rubbing alcohol and olives.

"Is this what it's supposed to taste like?" I ask.

"Need more olive juice?" Karissa asks.

"Needs less . . . everything," I say.

"I guess I'm not a great bartender," Karissa says, and Bernardo and I nod and cringe at our drinks, and I wonder at the way she is imperfect and still somehow perfect.

"You guys are so comfortable with each other for having just met," Karissa says, slurring and spilling some martini down her shirt. "It's so much like me and Sean."

I put down my drink. It's disgusting, and I won't be able to stomach it if we talk about him. About that. About it.

"I don't want to talk about my dad." I take the bottle of wine back from her. It should go to Bernardo next, but he's getting all particular about which Swedish pop band is the best Swedish pop band for late night in the Village while drunk on white wine and having an awkward relationship talk. Turns out, it's the musical stylings of Club 8.

"Right. Of course," Karissa says. "Let's talk about Bernardo's dad!" When Karissa's drunk, she's good at sliding between topics, at finding hidden doorways into new conversational spaces.

So we talk about his dad for a while instead. How he loves poetry and the History Channel and didn't get mad when Bernardo said he didn't want to play any sports, even though his dad loves baseball.

"He's Mexican from Mexico?" Karissa says. She asks questions that I don't know how to ask.

"Yeah. Met my mom when he was visiting here. Couldn't bring himself to leave her. Or the city. They're stupid in love."

He talks a lot about love, for a guy.

He's all lit up. He's beautiful. Holy shit.

We play more charades and drink more wine until I'm even drunker than either of them. I want to text Arizona and tell her about the night. She'd hate that Karissa is here, but I want some part of her to know I have a life, that I can move forward too. That if she can become a whole new person, so can I.

I drink martinis now, for instance. And think about having sex with a boy with pink hair. I can even wonder about love, in this state. I can be less afraid of it.

"You guys totally saved this night," Karissa says. "I needed that." She starts dancing, like it's reason to celebrate.

"Maybe I'm drunk, but I want to say something to you," Bernardo says, leaning over to my shoulder, which he kisses. "I needed this too. You. I needed you. At this particular moment in time."

I blush. It's a little too much, but in the good way. Like being stuffed from a delicious meal. Overdone but for all the right reasons.

"Okay, good," I say. I smile at both of them. It's cozy down here, wine-drunk and love-happy. "I think I sort of love you so far," I say to Bernardo, words plucked from some part of my brain I didn't know was there. I mean to say it in my head, but the wine makes me say it out loud and in a bedroom-y voice that isn't my own.

I count the number of days I have actually known Bernardo. I multiply that by the number of days I spent watching him. I divide that all by the things he's said that fit perfectly into what I need. It's some kind of crazy relationship math so I can ignore the voice in my head that says loving someone this early on is insane.

I have my hand on his chest and I swear his heart stops beneath it.

"I like that. I love you so far too," he says. I somehow hadn't realized I said it first.

"Did I just see the first time? Was I a witness?" Karissa says. She hasn't stopped dancing since she started. She's tripping a little now, her dance more a series of stumbling steps and sloppy hand movements.

"So far!" I say, too loudly. "I said so far!" I'm giggling in the best way. Loose and sloppy and giddy. Saying *I love you* feels effing good and I had no idea. It's like a drug. It's better than wine.

I can be a girl who says I love you first and fast to a boy who deserves it! I can!

I wonder if everyone feels like a superhero after a few sips of martini and a ton of wine.

Bernardo keeps looking at me like I matter, like I'm his. And Karissa does too.

"Guys? I like wine," I say when we're all dozing off. It doesn't really sum up everything I'm feeling but will suffice. Everything seems okay. For this one drunken moment. Even Karissa and my dad being together. Even that.

The room fills with the sounds of deep breathing. I'm too full to sleep. Full of wine and feelings and anticipation and giggles and mistakes.

"We have to get you home," I whisper in Bernardo's ear, giving him a little shake. Karissa's hand falls from her stomach to the ground with a thump. She doesn't make a sound, she's that far gone. She looks younger than me, and sad in her sleep. It moves me, the things she's survived. I have to tell Arizona and reach for my phone to text her immediately, but I'm just un-drunk enough to think better of it.

"No, we have to sleep here. On the floor. Together," Bernardo says. He keeps touching my face. With only his fingertips. He traces every feature like he can't believe how lucky he is to see them all up close and personal, and it feels even better than the wine.

I try to push him to his feet, but it's so tiring and he is radiator-warm and comfortable and my legs are already all wrapped up in his, so I rest my head on his chest for a moment and fold into him. He wraps his arms around me.

"It's a lot," I say.

"Can you use more words?" Bernardo says, and I sigh, because the whole point is that sometimes a few words are enough to sum up something very large and unmanageable. Tonight is large and unmanageable. I don't answer but instead let Bernardo fall asleep, and before I can stop myself, I fall asleep on top of him.

I wake up a few hours later and manage to carry Bernardo out to the street and pile him into a cab. He is heavier than I had imagined. He smells sweet, though. Sweet and a little sour, too. An exciting smell. A smell that means he is living.

I smell the same way.

seventeen

I don't remember much about Mom, except that she dressed me and Arizona in matching outfits and told us how jealous she was that we would get to be best friends forever. She's also the one who introduced us to Washington Square Park and people watching and sticking our feet in the dirty fountain water, picking up pennies with our toes.

On my fifth birthday, a few weeks before she left, Mom bought us a dozen cupcakes and said we had to try each of them. We sat on the edge of the fountain, balancing on the curved stone surface. I kept kicking water at Arizona and she kept laughing. Cupcake crumbs fell into the fountain, but I didn't care.

"I love that you don't get mad at your sister. You respond with joy," Mom said. I didn't understand at the time, but I memorized the words, loving the singsongy way Mom said them and the seriousness with which Arizona nodded her head in response.

"She likes splashing," Arizona said with a shrug.

"You'll be an amazing mom someday," Mom said. She sounded

sad. She'd been sounding sad more and more often.

"Can I be Montana's mom?" Arizona said. Even at seven, her voice had a deep, adult quality. Grounded. Mom took her seriously. I kept splashing water and licking icing off my fingers and the sides of my mouth. I couldn't get a single bite in without a huge mess.

I guess I never really tried to eat it neatly. Licking it up was half the fun.

"What about me?" Mom said. Arizona shrugged and put her hands in the fountain. Her cupcake floated for a moment, then sank. She used her hands to splash the water at my face, and I laughed so hard that cupcake sputtered out everywhere.

"Can we go to the pet store today?" I said, like I did every time Arizona and Mom and I were having fun. I was sure that someday Mom and Dad would agree that I could get a puppy or a kitten or even a hamster or lizard. It didn't occur to me that it might never happen. I was positive that if I found the right moment, I'd get what I wanted.

"We can go inside, but we're not getting anything. But if you'd like to pet some puppies, we could do that," Mom said. She didn't let me pet the puppies all the time, but on special occasions I could convince her. "Is that what you want to do with your birthday?"

Arizona sighed. She didn't like puppies or kittens. She didn't like the ruckus of the pet store or the smells: pet food, feathers, dog breath, and kitty litter. But for me, she'd go. She'd even help me pick out the cutest puppy to snuggle.

"What if we find a really nice one? A special one? The best dog ever? Then can we get him?" I could barely control the words as they tumbled out. I wanted to ask the question one hundred times, over and over until I got the answer I wanted. I needed Mom to understand how desperate the need was, and how logical too.

For some reason, that day, on my fifth birthday, Mom seemed to really hear me. She looked at me with a brand-new smile, one I hadn't seen before, and gave a half nod.

"I'd like you to have a puppy," she said. "It helps, to have a puppy."

Looking back, I have to assume she already knew she was leaving. Like a puppy is a consolation prize for a mother.

I thrilled at her not-no response and started jumping up and down in the fountain. The water was past my knees, and when it splashed it had enough force to cover my hair, my arms, my sister. I couldn't stop smiling. I looked right at Mom, to thank her.

"Your eyes are weird," I said. Something was different about them. I should have noticed it earlier, but my birthday and cupcakes and puppies and fountains full of water made it hard to spend much time looking at the details of my mother's face.

"My eyes?" Mom touched her eyelids, touched the delicate lashes, the soft skin around the edges. She looked like she was about to cry. I felt like I was going to cry too, either from seeing her so upset or from the unrecognizable shape and texture of her face. What I would later come to easily recognize as a face-lift.

"Make them go back to normal," I said. All of her looked different, but especially the stretched, smooth skin around her eyes.

The cry started then. An unstoppable thing. Rocky and young and raging.

"Shhhhh," Arizona said, part sympathy, part terror.

"I want Daddy!" I wailed while Arizona patted my back and Mom looked around like she might get in trouble for having a crying child.

"Can you walk your sister home?" Mom said to Arizona. She put on big sunglasses to cover her eyes, and I felt immediately calmer. I wiped away tears and snot, but it was too late to save the day. Arizona took my hand and gave a big, solemn nod.

"Yes. Take a left on Christopher. I know the way," Arizona said.

"Will Arizona take me to the pet store?" I said. "Will Daddy?" I wanted to apologize, but also make sure she kept her sunglasses on. I wanted a puppy and my mother and the safety of knowing my mother's face wouldn't change day to day. I wanted it all.

"Another day," she said. "We'll do it very, very soon."

Arizona held my hand all the way back to the apartment, like she was supposed to, but I still felt scared of the blinking orange DON'T WALK signs and the strangers who asked if we were lost and even the familiar sound of traffic. We'd never been alone on the street before, and we both knew it was wrong.

"I messed up," I said. I didn't know how or why, but I knew I'd changed the afternoon, I'd made it bad when it was supposed to be good.

"No way," Arizona said. I had never loved her more.

Mom came home with more cupcakes, and I was sick of them by then, but we ate them anyway. Dad, me, Arizona, and Mom in the kitchen, singing *Happy birthday to Montana* so many times I couldn't get it out of my head for days after.

She left us not long after. I don't eat cupcakes anymore, not even on my birthday.

June 14

The List of Things to Be Grateful For

1 The dreaminess of a white-wine-and-half-a-martini hangover when it is accompanied by French toast and *Breakfast at Tiffany's* and a king-size bed and Karissa.

2 Kissing after sleeping, and the fact that unbrushed teeth can be romantic because they mean you are close to someone.

3 The soreness of your back after sleeping on the floor. The fact that it means you did something strange and uncalled-for and ridiculous.

June 18

The List of Things to Be Grateful For

1 The way Roxanne will listen to every detail of every kiss without judgment and the knowledge of how rare that is.

2 Arizona's summer apartment. Not the fact of it existing, but that it is downright wallpapered with pictures of the two of us together.

3 The photo Natasha texted me of Victoria and Veronica in toddler bikinis, dipping their feet in the ocean for the first time.

eighteen

Dad takes us to the diner, which is a terrible sign, because diners are where we go for difficult conversations.

"Get grilled cheese!" he says, and that means it is extra bad and we should jump ship immediately, because shit's about to go down in a serious way. Grilled cheese is code for total drama.

"Mom's coming back," Arizona says. This is what Arizona always says. It is absolutely never true and Mom probably never will come back, but for some reason Arizona lives in a state of fear that Mom will come back and a slightly greater fear that she never will. So anytime Something's Going On, that's her first thought.

"Mom?" Dad says like he's never heard of her.

The waitress comes by and I take his advice and order grilled cheese and a milk shake, because I don't like the look on his face. A combination of nervousness and sappy happiness that I've seen before. The look he gets when he knows he's doing something I will hate, but it's making him happy so he's going to try to justify it.

"Yeah. Our mom. Is she coming back or something?" Arizona says.

"Of course not," Dad says. "Did she say something? That's extremely not true. Unless she's coming back without telling me? Did she say she's moving to New York?" Something about my mother unnerves my father too. We are all disasters from even the mention of her.

"I haven't heard from her since my birthday," Arizona says. "You know that. We have a birthday mother. The end." She looks shaky, my sister. Mom would hate the way Arizona looks now. I know almost nothing about the woman except that she thinks plastic surgery was the biggest mistake of her life. That it ruined her and ruined her marriage and that she thinks it will ruin us.

It's hard to take advice from a mother who left you.

I almost get it. Almost.

"This isn't about your mother. This is about Karissa," Dad says. The waitress brings our food out, and Arizona starts scarfing her sandwich and sucking down the milk shake. I can't bring myself to eat yet.

"She's twelve," Arizona says.

"You don't ever like the women I date," Dad says. He has this calm way of speaking that makes it impossible to fight, even though that's all Arizona wants to do.

"They're not really worth having any feelings about," Arizona says. Dad clears his throat, which is his version of yelling at us.

The red seats are stickier than Natasha's leather couch. They're not real leather, for one, and they're gross from whatever jam and syrup and ketchup has landed on them in the last day.

"You're breaking up?" I say, because he usually takes us to the diner when he's either breaking up with a woman or deciding to marry her, and I know, I *know* he is not deciding to marry Karissa.

She is practically my age. She lets her hair air-dry. She wears cheap jewelry and makes terrible martinis. She never had braces. Her chin is a little like mine. She makes me feel like I'm important and wild.

"Karissa means a lot to me," he says.

Fuck.

He tries to say these speeches differently every time, but they're so stale and familiar that they physically hurt. Muscle memory or Pavlov's dog or whatever. I hear the words and start to ache in all the familiar places.

Except worse this time.

"And Montana, I'm so glad you and she have such a strong relationship already. I think that makes this very new. And very unique."

I have been hearing some version of these exact sentences my whole life. Everything is always new and unique in my father's head. But in reality it is monotonous and the worst kind of boring. Recurring-nightmare boring.

Except this time with a twist.

Arizona grips my knee under the table and is already scraping the bottom of the milk shake, slurping at the last few sips. We both stare at the salt and pepper shakers.

Something terrible is happening right now, I text Bernardo under the table, and I'm elated to have him to report to, a way to escape the moment a little. I let my mind remember that there will be a whole life with him outside of this.

I take a huge bite of grilled cheese at last, and it's perfection, but there is not enough grilled cheese in the world to make what Dad's about to do less painful. He reaches into his jacket pocket. He's the only person wearing a suit in the crowded diner.

"You are not serious," Arizona says. "If you take a ring out of your pocket right now, I am going to lose my fucking mind." Her voice is cut up and jagged. She sounds like an animal, not like herself.

My throat's dry and I close my eyes, willing the diner and the milk shakes and my dad's earnest face and the velvet box away.

Inside my head I'm screaming. Actually screaming. But on the outside I'm straight-faced and mute.

He brings it out even after Arizona's threat. He looks sheepish but determined.

"Don't make a mountain," Dad says. He is known for saying one half of famous phrases without saying the other half. "In group we talk about moving forward, and it can be hard for the kids, but you girls move forward too. Arizona, you don't even live here. And soon Montana won't either. And I need someone to share my life with."

It sounds so reasonable, except when you factor in how many times he's been married and how young Karissa is and how they only just met and that she is my friend and not meant to be his wife.

She cannot be my stepmom.

Cannot.

The black velvet box flips open with a practiced flick of his wrist. Personally I'd never marry someone who looks so comfortable proposing. The ring inside is enormous, like the rest of them. It glints even under crappy diner lights, and I swear some of the customers nearby are straining to catch a glimpse.

I scarf down french fries and pickles and the delicious remains of melted cheese still stuck to the plate. I decide not to cry.

"You can't do this," I say. I put my shoulders back and my head up, like if I can posture myself correctly, he'll change his mind. "This is not okay. You know this is so absolutely not okay on any level."

"You'll understand when you're older," Dad says. "I know this is hard." He smiles all wise and kind and insane. Arizona's whole body tenses up. She rubs her temples and can't stop fidgeting. She sips the last of her water since the milk shake is gone. Even the water is mostly ice now—we are vacuums when we're upset about Dad.

"This isn't a normal situation," Arizona says. "Your friends at your support group thing are talking about normal situations. This is a fucking shitshow."

"Please don't swear in public," Dad says. It's the *in public* that kills me.

"Why are you doing this?" I say. I want to say *why are you doing this to me*, but I stop myself before the last part comes out. I know it will only make me sound young and difficult and whiny.

"Come on, Montana," he says. It is the worst possible answer.

"Why are you doing this now?" Arizona says. We are in a competition for who can be the first to get Dad to say something real.

"The thing about love," Dad says, starting a sentence I don't even want him to finish, "is that you don't answer those kinds of questions about it. It's unanswerable. It simply is."

I am feeling so, so sick.

"Can you wait? Please? Wait a few months? Or a year?" Arizona says.

"I'm ready now," he says. Defensiveness is creeping in, and his voice is rising and people are listening to us. New Yorkers have a knack for knowing when an interesting conversation is happening. I'm sure once the ring came out, most of the diner started only half listening to their companions so that they could mostly listen to us.

"I need to get out of here," I say, and Arizona nods and we start sliding out of the booth, but Dad stops us.

"I'm doing it next weekend," he says. "Washington Square Park. I expect you to be there."

Arizona laughs. "Dude, come on," she says. "You have got to be kidding. You are not proposing to a teenager this weekend." She says it loudly on purpose. She wants everyone to hear, to judge, to know.

Dad clears his throat again, and I bet he's wishing we had more grilled cheese and milk shakes to fill the awkwardness.

"Do not say things like that," he says. "That's inappropriate."

Arizona laughs again. She can't stop laughing. She is grabbing her stomach and having trouble breathing. There are tears running down her face. She's officially lost it.

"You are inappropriate!" she says, so loud the waiters jump to attention and start printing our check. "You! You!" There's this edge to her voice that I've never heard before, and even her perfect outfit can't save her from seeming unhinged.

"That is enough," Dad says, in one of those yell-whispers that parents are so excellent at. "This is happening. And you're going to get behind it or at least act civil. And it is not up for discussion. I expect support from my girls. The end."

My father thinks he's going to marry K, I text to Bernardo.

I can't stop thinking about Karissa drunkenly dancing on the basement couch or flirting with the bartender or handing a lit cigarette to me. She will never be my mother.

I'm sure she'll say no.

I'm sure none of this is real.

I'm sure in a few months he will be with a new woman with a big shoe collection and lots of makeup and a love of furs and dinner parties and French toile. Karissa is not marrying my father.

"Dad. Seriously. We're not coming," I say. "Don't make us come."

"It would mean a lot to me," he says. "I need my girls there. We're a team. The three of us." It breaks us both, when he says *my girls*. And *need*. And *team*. When someone leaves a family, the ones left behind pull together and form a thing—a strong, necessary, desperate thing—and even in the worst moments, it exists. Because no moment is worse than the moment when we were all left behind.

The worst thing that happened to us keeps us together in this overwhelming way.

"Please, Dad. Don't say that," Arizona says. She's still laughing, but it's the terrible kind that comes from her ribs and the pit of her stomach.

"You're my girls," Dad says. He has tiny tears in the corners of his eyes. They probably won't ever come out, but they sparkle there, much smaller than any ring my father would ever buy for anyone, and make it impossible for us to say no.

"Wanna come to my place tonight?" Arizona says. Dad's left us on the sidewalk so that he can go and meet up with Karissa at some swanky bar that is probably the opposite of Dirty Versailles.

There's need written all over her face. We would usually spend all night together after Dad's done something messed up. We like to make lists of women who would be more appropriate than whoever he's picked. Mary Poppins. Hillary Clinton. The mom from the Berenstain Bears. That therapist he made us go to when Mom left. My sixth-grade teacher. We can do it all night long. It's one of our rituals.

But Bernardo is texting back and asking me to meet up at this fondue place he knows, where we can dip pretzels in chocolate and bread in melted cheese and we can play footsie under the table and make out by the bathrooms. Or, he says, we can go to his friend's place and play video games and drink beer and be a Couple in that capital *C* kind of way. Or we can make out in my basement.

"Oh, I think maybe not tonight?" I say. I know she knows I'm probably going to see Bernardo, but she doesn't ask about it.

"Right. Got it," Arizona says. She swallows, and I watch the nothing that she swallowed travel down her throat.

"Tomorrow maybe?" I say.

"Yeah, I don't know, probably not. I have plans, I think." Arizona starts applying lip gloss and looking at the archway across the park.

The funny thing is, I'd love to spend the night with Arizona being Arizona and Montana, doing the things we used to do. But doing something new is less painful than trying to do something old and familiar and having it feel all wrong and foreign.

Bernardo doesn't remind me of all the things I miss or wish I had.

"This is messed up, right?" I say, trying to do a compressed kind of rehashing of the night, like we'd usually do. We aren't so far from what we used to be that I can't see it anymore, but far enough that I don't know quite how to get back there. Like sometimes walking around Manhattan I can see the Empire State Building, and I know it's north of where I am, but I can't be sure if it's four blocks away or fifteen. I'll try walking there from where I am and end up unable to find the actual entrance. It's tricky.

"I mean, whatever. I give up," Arizona says. "You've obviously checked out of this whole thing."

She keeps shrugging and rolling her eyes. It reminds me of Arizona at cleven, when she was really into passive aggression.

"I don't know what that means," I say. "You chose not to be around this summer. You chose . . . all the things you chose. I'm following your lead. And whatever. It's not like I want Dad to marry my friend. I'm not exactly psyched here."

"But you have Bernardo. So."

"You'll meet someone."

It's the wrong thing to say. I know it immediately, even though I can't put my finger on why.

"You're so much like him," Arizona says. She sounds sad more than angry, but she walks away without hugging me, and I don't call after her.

Later that night Bernardo and I dip things in chocolate over a white-tableclothed table, and I feel like I'm in some idea of a romance that I should hate but it feels so, so good. I even forget about the diner and the way Arizona looked at the archway instead of at me and that more and more things are shifting, making this summer a kind of earthquake instead of a vacation.

It doesn't matter as much, when I'm so busy falling in love with him.

Besides, Arizona left me first.

nineteen

Dad wasn't that sad after Mom left.

"It's for the best," he said when I curled up next to him in bed the first few nights after. I hated the way that sounded, like I was never meant to have a mother at all. I'm pretty sure he'd already met Janie, because she was on the scene pretty quickly. Her dark hair curled perfectly at the ends. Her nose was so small I was worried she wouldn't be able to breathe through it. Her body shifted so much in the first year of their marriage that I believed Arizona when she said Janie was an evil monster and not a real person. That her magic power was changing shapes and that we had to be careful.

So I was very, very careful around Janie.

But when Janie started getting melancholy and strange a few years later, Dad freaked out.

"I did it again," he said to Arizona and me late one night, in the basement. I was eight and Arizona was ten, and we were watching movies and eating popcorn and asking to call Mom, which we still did once a month even three years after she left.

"Daddy? Are you okay?" Arizona said.

"I wanted Janie to be around forever," he said. "I wanted her boys to be your brothers." Dad leaned his head back so that it rested on the top of the couch and he stared at the ceiling.

"She's gone?" I asked. Dad wasn't very good in those days at telling us when things were ending. We'd learn in abrupt moments like this. We'd learn by accident. We'd learn by eavesdropping.

"She's gone," Dad said. "She left. I can't seem to keep anyone." I was pretty sure dads weren't supposed to be this sad in front of daughters. Something felt bruised and wrong, but I couldn't identify what. I hid my face in a couch cushion.

Arizona was better than me, even then.

"We won't leave you!" she said.

"I hope not," Dad said. "You're my girls. I need you."

He pulled us in for hugs, each of us under one of his arms. I brought the couch cushion with me. I liked the title. His girls. Arizona did too, I could tell from the way she hugged Dad back, so forceful he coughed a little, her arm too strong around his middle.

We'd been wondering who we were, I guess. Trying to piece together all the strange bits of our lives and not liking the results. Kids at school made fun of my dad's job. Said it was gross and creepy. Counselors at school felt bad for us. We weren't sure who was right.

Being his girls, being needed, watching movies from the crook of his arm in a room that smelled like popcorn and aftershave felt right.

"Do you want to live with your mom?" Dad said then. His

forehead never really wrinkles, but there were lines that wanted to pop out at that moment. His eyes were sad. I wished he could have lines around them. I wished his face moved like other daddies'.

Arizona and I didn't answer.

"You look so much like her. Both of you." I took the cushion away from my face then and wondered what I could do to look less like her. Dad sounded sad when he said it, and I didn't want any more things making Dad upset. "You must miss her," he said.

We still didn't reply. Even Arizona couldn't come up with a perfect thing to say. We knew we weren't supposed to lie, and saying we didn't miss her or didn't sometimes want to live with her in the house with the big tire swing that she sent us pictures of the year before would be a lie.

"Girls?" Dad said. His voice was so small. The little tears in the corners of his eyes that never came out were streaming down his face. "Would you rather be with her? Sometimes she thinks she wants you back. And if you hate it here, if you want to be with her, I can make that happen for you. I can try." He sniffed. It was awful. Worse than Mom leaving and the side of the closet without her clothes in it. Worse than the sad birthday cards that came in the mail, the kind that were from CVS and not even a nice stationery store. The fact that she wrote our names and her name and let the Hallmark message in the middle be her note to us, instead of writing her own.

"You're my girls," he choked out, the words making us nod with recognition. *Yes! Yes, we are! That's who we are!* "You know how lucky I feel that I got to keep you."

Arizona and I looked at each other over his stomach. We'd talked before about running away to find our mother.

It's terrible and strong, the pull toward a mother, even if she's not the mother you deserve. Even if she's across the country or across the world or telling people you don't exist. Even if you have a father with strong arms and soft pajamas and an easiness with the words *I love you*.

"You still want her more," Dad said. "Even though I'm right here." He stopped asking it as a question. And that's when we both snapped to it and realized we had to answer him.

"No!" Arizona said. I mimicked her.

"No, no!" I said.

"We're in it together," Arizona said. She sounded twelve. She sounded eighteen. She sounded a hundred.

"I don't know what I'd do without you two," Dad said, coming back to life. "You're everything to me. You are. We can do this. We can survive this together, okay?"

We nodded, and I was unsure of what exactly we were agreeing to.

Dad wiped his eyes and cleared his throat, and we tried not to ask questions about Mom maybe wanting us back. We tried not to care about that.

Later that night, Arizona snuck into my bed.

"We made Dad cry," she said.

"We can't ever do that again," I said. We gripped pinkies. We kissed our fists. We slept in the same bed and tried and tried and tried not to miss our mother.

June 20

The List of Things to Be Grateful For: The What Love Is
Edition

1 When everything seems small because love is the
biggest word there is.

2 Knowing that Bernardo likes things that are serious and
strange. Foreign films. Big books. Unlikely statements.
Veiled hats from vintage stores. Me.

3 The sensation of holding in laughter, which is not unlike
the sensation of holding in the words *I love you* or other
things that seem like they should be secrets but aren't
meant to be secrets. Both start in my stomach and flutter
around and come out all at once when I have no more
muscles to tense up as defense.

twenty

As promised, I'm invited to Brooklyn to meet the parents.

"I'm scared," I say on the phone. I hate the phone. It reminds me of claustrophobic conversations with my mother on my birthdays, and I don't want to associate Bernardo with anything like that.

"Well, what would make you less scared?" he says. Bernardo is a guy who likes to solve problems. Or at least likes to solve my problems.

"Don't know."

"When are you least scared?"

"When Roxanne and Arizona are in charge," I say. What I mean is that I'm least scared when I'm barely there, when I'm background noise.

"Well, bring them," he says. "We're a 'the more the merrier' kind of family."

"If you mean that, you're my hero."

"Then I guess I'm your hero," he says.

* * *

Arizona says no.

Arizona says she is reaching her capacity for crazy requests from people, and she's going to get a tan in the park instead.

Arizona says I've known this guy for a week and there's no reason to bring the whole crew to some crazy Brooklyn dinner.

Arizona says I have no idea what I'm doing.

Roxanne says okay because Roxanne is down for adventures. Plus, she likes the idea of Bernardo, or at least the idea of me getting wilder and dreamier and sexier.

Roxanne also says okay because she's bored in New York this summer. She misses Bard. She misses her roommate. She misses college.

I try not to hear her when she says it. I want to be enough.

Roxanne and I wear dresses that seem like the kind of dresses parents would like. I think Dad's annoyed when he sees me flounce downstairs. He wishes I'd wear something like this for his dinners, for meeting Karissa, for the diner even.

He's doing work at the kitchen counter. There are pictures of women's faces and he's drawing on them and it's depressing. He has manila folders with before and after photos from old cases, and he brings them too close to his face, making a *humph* noise every few seconds.

When he looks up at us, he still has his doctor glasses on and a face-lifted "after" picture in one of his hands. If I had a couch cushion I could use like I did back when I was little, I'd hide my face in it now, not wanting to be seen by him.

"Wear that Friday, to the park," he says, envisioning a perfect proposal where not only does Karissa say yes, but his youngest daughter has her hair back with a headband covering the pinkest parts and a navy polka-dot sundress flaring out over her hips and making her look almost like she has curves on top too. "Don't you feel good and confident all dressed up like that?" he says. I don't answer. "It makes me happy to see you so happy. This is what I've always wanted for you."

I know what he's always wanted for me. If I were a different girl from a different home, I'd ask him about the gift certificate right now. I'd take the opening and make him apologize for it or at least acknowledge its existence.

I am not that girl. I shrug.

"Such a pretty girl," he says. It should sound nice and complete, but as usual I hear everything that's wrong with me too. I hear *such a pretty girl, but*. I hear *wouldn't you like to use that gift certificate as soon as you turn eighteen in a few months?* I wonder if he'll ask, on my birthday, what I plan on changing about myself. "You and Arizona. Both so pretty," he says, and I hate that too.

It's possible I would hate anything he said right now. We haven't made up since the day at the diner. We haven't even spoken about it.

"I'm meeting my boyfriend's parents," I say, ignoring the rest. "It's a whole thing." I grab his coffee mug from him and take a few sips.

"That should be interesting," Dad says. He doesn't ask follow-up questions. He traces the jawline of one woman's picture. She's not old or young. She's not pretty or ugly. He adjusts his glasses before drawing a line near her ears. "You want Karissa to do your makeup?"

"I'll do it!" Roxanne says. Dad likes that she sits around our house like it's part hers. He pours her a coffee too and offers to make her some toast.

"But don't you dare put that crazy stuff on my daughter's face," he says, pointing at Roxanne's thick eyeliner and the little star sticker on her cheek.

"I'm good. No makeup necessary," I say. Dad laughs like that is a great joke I've made.

"Well, it's up to you, I suppose. Will you bring him to the park Friday?" Dad says. He is officially obsessed with the park Friday. He tells Roxanne to come too, and to bring any boys she might be dating. "Or girls!" he says, because he is nothing if not accepting of people who are not his children.

"I'll be there, Dr. Varren," Roxanne says. And I very nearly hate her for pretending it's fine, but she'd never let me down like that. "I'd hate to miss one of your epic proposals." Dad hears and reddens but doesn't drop his mug or fight back or anything.

"I freaking love you," I say when we're out the door.

"For so many reasons," she says, leading us to the subway. She's a subway wizard, so she gets us to Bernardo's little pocket of Brooklyn quickly. It's all trees and brownstones out there. The dogs are bigger, too. I don't see Duane Reade or any banks for a bunch of blocks in a row. It's a whole new world.

Bernardo meets us outside his apartment building. It's a cute little walk-up and they have two floors of it, but it feels small with all five kids and two parents and now me and Roxanne here too.

"Montana!" his mother says when she sees us. Her eyes flit back and forth between Roxanne and me, and I wonder which one of us she is hoping belongs to her son.

"That's me," I say, stepping forward. She's small and solid. She has an apron and curly brown hair that's graying at the roots.

"Of course it's you," she says, gesturing to my hair.

"Oh," I say, self-conscious so quickly I can barely stop myself from stuttering. I've never met a boy's parents before. I don't know why I didn't think of that earlier, but this is a big first. "I'm sorry about this. About his—"

"Of course he did it for a pretty girl," his dad interrupts, lumbering over. He's tall and dark, with a heavy beard and unreadable eyes. His accent is so strong I almost don't hear what he's saying, and I'm not sure whether to laugh or nod or look over at Bernardo, so I sort of do all three.

"Our Bernardo, always impulsive," his mother says. Bernardo cringes so hard I mistake it for a seizure for a moment.

"Thank you for having me. This is Roxanne, my best friend." There's all kinds of hand shaking, and I wish I looked like Arizona, only for today. Bernardo's brothers and sisters swarm around us and show us sock puppets they made and drawings they're working on and their mom's purse and the family gerbil.

I don't fit in, in the deepest way. I wonder if Casey did.

"This is the girl," Bernardo says, when one of his sisters asks him why I'm having dinner there.

Bernardo's parents make a Mexican feast, with homemade tortillas and very hot chicken and the most excellent guacamole I've ever had. There's some kind of spicy mac and cheese that's green and decadent and so eatable I almost forget I'm trying to impress people.

"Honey, be careful with the spice," Bernardo's mother says to him after he's put extra sauce on his chicken and scooped a few jalapeños onto his pasta. "You know it upsets your tummy if you have too much."

Bernardo goes red.

"I know how to eat," he mumbles. His shoulders slump, and behind his head I can see a picture of him when he was little. He doesn't look very different.

"How do you like the food?" his dad says. He's beaming over his work. My mouth's full and so is Roxanne's, so we both nod enthusiastically, and Roxanne squeezes my thigh under the table, telling me she's happy for me and this new bit of life I'm getting to have.

"Good. That Casey girl hated Mexican food. Bernardo tell you that? What kind of person doesn't like spice? Or cheese? Or cilantro?" He shakes his head, and I wonder how many times Casey ate here and how well she knew the kids. Whether she brought them presents on Christmas. What exactly he loved about her. "She was a little uptight. Bernardo doesn't need any more uptight in his life. You uptight?"

"She is super not!" Roxanne says. She beams and takes a huge bite of chicken.

"I guess not," I say.

"I'm so sorry," Bernardo says. "My parents get a little—"

"We're your parents," his mother says. "We have a say."

It's one of those conversation-stopping sentences.

"Not really," Bernardo says. The words sound tired, and I'm sure he has said them so many times before that they are reflex more than argument. I don't know where I fit into this conversation, so I smile and try to seem agreeable and not uptight and into the food.

"Sorry," he whispers to me while his parents ask Roxanne about college. "They think I'm seven still."

"You're not, right?" I say, and Roxanne overhears and laughs. Everyone loosens up.

We spend the afternoon at the table. No one moves to get to work or to vanish into their rooms. The kids sometimes grab toys from their bedrooms or chase one another around in a precarious indoor tag situation. But otherwise there's the feeling that this could go on forever. There's simply the changing of light as afternoon moves to evening moves to night.

"You should bring your family here sometime soon," Bernardo's mother says. No one so normal has ever liked me so quickly. She keeps asking if anything is too spicy and refilling my water glass, which I'm really only drinking because I'm nervous.

"Maybe!" I say. I want to get off this topic as quickly as possible. I'm not sure what Bernardo's told them. Hopefully not too much.

"What do they do, your folks?" his dad says. He keeps rubbing Bernardo's mom's back, and she doesn't stop smiling. They are happy in this easy way. Maybe that's what it looks like to be together for decades. Maybe that's what it looks like to stay with someone.

Bernardo cringes.

"Don't interview her, Dad," he says. I wonder if maybe I'm not supposed to answer.

"It's a normal question that we'd ask anyone," his dad says, looking at me with eyebrows raised. "We talked to Roxanne about her teacher parents. Sound like lovely people."

"Oh, my dad's a, um, plastic surgeon?" I say. I find if I say it like a question, as if maybe they won't even know what a plastic surgeon is, I hate myself less.

"Huh. Interesting," Bernardo's dad says. He nods seriously, and I try to see how much he's judging me. "A doctor, then!"

"Yes!" I forget I could say doctor and be done with it.

"There was a very nice plastic surgeon down the street who worked with kids who'd been burned. Very important work," Bernardo's mom says. She wants this to be where I come from. I hate lying, but nodding isn't the same thing as lying. So I nod.

"Totally!" Bernardo says. His face is a mess of emotions I haven't seen on him before. I'm so used to him one way, it pinches to see him this other way. It's the first time I realize he hates something about me.

He doesn't look my way.

"Montana's father is really respected," he says. Every extra word that comes out of him hurts me more. I'm allowed to be embarrassed by my father, but I'm not ready for my boyfriend to be covering for him too. Covering for me. Making sure no one knows how shameful I actually am.

I'm That Girl from That Family. I didn't know Bernardo sees me that way

"And your mother?" Bernardo's dad says. He's so nice it doesn't sound like grilling me, but that's what he's doing. My mouth is dry and not working right. I don't want to admit any more things about how flawed and broken we are.

"Montana's mom's not around," Roxanne says, saving me from having to say the words myself. "But her sister is a sweetheart, and they're all very close. They're a really cool family. I spend, like, all my time there."

The moment of panic and shame shrinks.

"Montana's kind of the best," Bernardo says, neither agreeing nor disagreeing with Roxanne. Not saying anything more about my family. "We get each other."

"You're always saying that, honey," his mom says, not hearing until it's too late that she's said something mean. I keep reminding myself Bernardo and I have something different than Bernardo and Casey did. He said she made him feel like he was supposed to be more. And I know I make him feel like he's enough. I want his parents to see that. I change my posture and my smile, hoping to make it somehow more obvious.

His mom goes to get the dessert. Profiteroles with ice cream and homemade chocolate sauce.

"I'm in charge of dessert around here," she says. I like that their family isn't all one thing or another. That a Mexican feast is followed by French pastries and Ben & Jerry's. That sometimes his parents say the wrong things.

"I don't always say that," Bernardo says a few minutes later, when we should have already let it go.

He pouts and looks like the kid in the frame above him again. So strongly I think it's no wonder his parents treat him like he's a baby.

Luckily, the profiteroles are perfection, and the chocolate sauce is the buttery kind that hardens when it hits the ice cream, and the little kids zoom cars over the dining room table like it's a racetrack. Things here are flawed and brilliant, all at once.

Like love, I think, knowing I'll write it later on my List of Things to Be Grateful For.

We kiss outside his home and I worry about his family seeing, but he doesn't seem to be thinking of that. Roxanne sings "I Will Always Love You" when she gets sick of watching us and says it's time to get to the subway.

"They love you," Bernardo says.

"Um, hi, what about me?" Roxanne says, poking him in the back while he hugs me.

"Of course, you too," Bernardo says. "Thank you for helping our girl out."

I guess I'm their girl. I bury my head in his neck because I don't know how that's supposed to make me feel.

It feels a little like belonging.

June 21

The List of Things to Be Grateful For

1 The magic of guac wrapped in a soft tortilla rather than loaded onto a crispy chip.

2 Bernardo's littlest sister, Maria, who dresses exactly like her big brother—complete with winter scarf and a pink wig. So I guess she dresses like me too.

3 The subway ride back to Manhattan, after the nerves of meeting Bernardo's family had faded. Roxanne and I rode aboveground and looked out at the city like little kids who were seeing it for the first time. Before the homeless dude with a loaded grocery cart of recycled cans sat down next to us. One sweet moment.

twenty-one

Karissa is taking a bath in my bathroom in the afternoon.

When she finishes, the whole place smells like roses, but I'm miserable.

She comes to my room with her hair in a towel and another around her torso and the rest of her is bare and freckled and too much to take.

"We've been missing each other," she says, leaning against my door frame. Dad's at work, and Arizona is at her apartment eating peanut butter out of jars and talking with her roommate about who they've kissed so far this summer.

I'm here, but only part of me.

I can't tell if Karissa means we haven't been seeing each other or that we've been pining after each other, but I guess it's a little of both.

"You don't have a bathtub at your place?" I say. It comes out biting, and I can't stop thinking about the ring in my dad's pocket and the way it's bigger than all the other rings, and sharper-looking too. Meaner.

"Actually, I don't," she says. "It's something they don't tell you when you're looking for an apartment. They don't all come with baths or intercoms or working doorbells or reliable hot water. So appreciate this place while you can."

It occurs to me that maybe she's using my dad for things like fancy dinners and hot baths and endless supplies of toilet paper and the bar down in the basement. It wouldn't be okay, exactly, but I think it would be better than her actually loving him.

She looks like she's settling in against the door frame.

"How's Bernardo?" she asks.

"Awesome," I say. I can't stop thinking about his family and that they felt a little like they could be my family in some perfect world. We hung out with Arizona in her apartment this morning. Roxanne brought cigarettes and coffee and I brought cookies from the bakery that Arizona loves so that we could have cookies for breakfast, and Arizona's roommate told Bernardo and me how cute we are.

Arizona didn't say too much about that.

"He seems so into you," Karissa says. "And sort of deep, yeah? And spontaneous. Romantic. So few guys would be deserving of you, but he maybe almost is."

Karissa adjusts the towel, and I want to pretend we're in her apartment, not mine. She looks younger than Arizona right now, all naked and makeup-less.

If I'm going to say something about the proposal that's coming, now's the time. "What about you?" I say. She lights up.

"Are you asking me how things are with your dad?" she says. Her voice is high and eager and awful.

"Jesus, no," I say. "I'm asking what kind of guy is deserving of you."

"Your dad treats me really well," Karissa says. "I know you don't want to talk about it, but he does. He's really thoughtful. And gentle—"

"Oh my God, do not say he's gentle," I say. I have goose bumps and a cold feeling in my blood. An image creeps into my brain of my father stroking Karissa's arm and being gentle and I squirm, trying to get rid of it. I'm wondering if I can forget the word *gentle* even exists. Strike it from my vocabulary.

"Okay, all right, we'll keep taking our time with this," Karissa says, like there's this day in the future when I'll be able to withstand the image, the word, the amount of skin she's showing right now, her comfortable way of sinking into all our couches and armchairs, my father calling her *baby* once when they were in the other room.

"You want to move slowly, right?" I say. I guess I'm going for it. Having this conversation.

"With you and me and dealing with this new aspect of our friendship?" she says. They don't sound like her words. They sound like my father's.

"Well, like, with this whole thing." I can't bring myself to say anything close to *your relationship with my father.*

Karissa cocks her head and smiles. The towel on her head shifts and threatens to fall down. Tess had this detailed way of wrapping her hair in a towel that involved a special absorbent cloth and a butterfly clip. She used bottles of moisturizer, different kinds for every part of her body. She tried to teach me how to do it correctly. Karissa's still dripping a little. She has not moisturized, I'm sure of it. She's barely dried off. There are wet footprints from the bathroom to my bedroom. Her shoulders are bony.

"A casting director yesterday told me I need to wear more eye makeup," she says, looking in my mirror and apparently changing the subject. "I mean, what is that? That sucks. I'm not booking anything. Terrible, terrible actors who are really hot book everything, and I'm too weird-looking to get commercials and not fancy enough to get plays and not L.A. enough to get movies. You any good at eye makeup?"

It's impossible to imagine inhabiting Karissa's body and having any complaints about how you look, but there's always been that raw, insecure side to her. Our acting teacher told her to hang on to it.

"Confidence is beautiful," the teacher had said, "but insecurity is fascinating. Wouldn't you rather be fascinating?"

"Wouldn't you rather be fascinating?" I say now, knowing we both loved every word that came out of our teacher's mouth.

"I'd rather be able to act," Karissa says, shrugging. Six months ago I'm positive she would have answered differently. I can't stand that Karissa doesn't think fascinating is enough anymore. Almost as much as I wouldn't be able to stand it if Karissa became my new stepmom.

"Okay, I'm going to tell you something, but you can't tell anyone I told you," I say. "And you're going to think this is crazy and that my family is nuts, but I warned you, so don't lose your mind."

"I'm ready," Karissa says, grinning. Her towel finally falls all the way off her head, and she lets it go to the ground, her hair a mess of wet curls. She's dripping even more now, a puddle forming around her feet.

"My dad thinks he's, like, going to propose," I say. I start to laugh. Saying it out loud makes it kind of hilarious instead of totally panic-worthy. I can hear how ridiculous it is. How mismatched and nonsensical. How it will sound to Karissa. "On, like, Friday," I say. "Do not ask me where he gets this stuff. He's sort of nuts with women. So, like, I thought I should tell you so that you can tell him not to do it. Or make it clear that's not your thing. Or be prepared. Or whatever." I can't stop doing this low-level half breath, half giggle. I can't stop shaking my head at the absurdity of it all.

"Oh," Karissa says. "Wow. Oh wow."

"I know."

She starts smiling. But the smile never turns into a laugh. It stays caught on her face, stuck in confusion.

"Oh wow," she says again. "Oh my God! This is . . . this is . . ."

"So fucked up?"

"I can't believe someone like him can really see a future with someone like me," she says. She weaves her long hair into a sloppy braid, missing huge chunks.

"I mean, I know, right?" I say. I can't wait to tell Bernardo. I can't wait to tell Arizona! Arizona will lose her mind with relief. She'll throw herself on me, and we can celebrate with enormous ice cream sundaes from Serendipity. We can spend the rest of the summer in the park without this hanging over us, ruining everything.

Maybe we can even chill at Karissa's one night, near the end of the summer, when it's so over we barely remember it happened.

"Friday?" Karissa says. "Oh my God, Friday!"

She finally starts to laugh.

But the laugh is all wrong. It's happy. It's ecstatic. It's nervous.

It is the laugh of a woman who is going to say yes.

"Karissa," I say. I can't think of a sentence or question to follow her name.

"I, like, love him," she says. She is glowing. I'm choking on a feeling I don't have a name for that's close to disgust and panic and confusion.

"Karissa," I say, wild now, and frantic. I think if I slap her maybe she'll snap out of it. Pour cold water on her. Remind her he's my father.

"It's okay! It will be fun. I swear. You have to trust me. This is going to be so good," she says. I don't say anything, and in the pause she changes. Not much. Only a little. A little to the left, a little bit toward indignant and frustrated that I would interfere with her relationship. Her marriage. Her big moment. "I need this," she says. "I deserve a little happiness, after everything. And he makes me happy. And it's going to be fantastic. I'm promising you, okay?"

I don't answer. I wonder if it's possible to faint from feelings. I wonder if this is when I start loving her a little less.

She waits for me to say *okay* but I don't.

She leaves a puddle outside my door, and I feel like I'm drowning in it.

twenty-two

Two days later, Bernardo and I are naked on the couch in my basement, doing everything but. We are hanging out in the everything-but stage, and it feels good.

I haven't told Arizona and Roxanne what happened with Karissa. Instead I tell Bernardo's naked body about it.

It's Thursday afternoon and Friday feels like a death sentence, and when I tell him things, he looks in my eyes and says he understands.

"Would it make you feel better to see Natasha?" he says. I like the way his thighs feel against mine. I like that his shoulders and back and belly are paler than the rest of him. His knee is between my thighs and I like that too.

"How'd you know that?" I say. It's so obvious, that's absolutely what would make me feel better. Or if not better, more grounded.

"I know you," he says. He shifts me off of him and looks at me hard. I want to be kissing but he wants to be staring, so we settle for switching back and forth between both.

"You're getting to know me," I say.

"Don't get all scared," Bernardo says because he does, in fact, know me.

"Okay," I say. "You can know me."

Bernardo starts tickling me, and there's a manic two minutes of naked squirming and screeching and batting his hands away, even though what I want, what I really want, is for him to touch me so much more. Then he's kissing my neck and touching my thighs, not tickling anymore, and things start to happen, whirling-mind things, heart-expanding things, opposite-of-ticklish things, but he stops when I tense up. He has a knack for noticing the constant tensing and relaxing of my limbs. He said he's never known anyone who expresses so much in their biceps and toes.

There's a Sharpie on the coffee table down here from Karissa addressing big envelopes with her head shot inside, and Bernardo picks it up like he's made a decision. He draws a heart on my shoulder.

"Are Sharpies dangerous for skin?" I say, the chemical smell hitting me hard.

"Can't be too bad," Bernardo says. He draws another heart on my wrist and sneaks down my body to draw two on my upper thighs.

"I can pretty much feel the lead or whatever it is seeping into my bloodstream, just so you know," I say. The actual drawing feels good—the soft tip of the pen tickles my arm, and I like the intense focus Bernardo gets after we've hooked up, like I'm all he can see or will ever see in the world. He draws hearts on my knees and polka-dots my feet.

He twirls the marker like it's a baton. His fingers are sure. It's weird to feel like I know everything about him and nothing about him all at once.

He draws a ring around my ring finger. He draws a diamond and little dashes sprouting out from it so that I know it's a sparkly one.

I can't stop laughing.

"Oh come on," I say.

"Hey, someday," he says. I try to imagine any other guy I've been with saying or doing anything the way Bernardo does, but it's impossible. He's all raw and open and unafraid. He's an old soul and naive and strange and in love with me all at the same time.

"I wasn't kidding about the poison," I say. "I think it's, like, pretty possible that Sharpie on skin could kill me." I'm not all the things he is. I keep wanting to be, but it's like my brain is holding back my heart. Or maybe vice versa. I can't tell.

"Then we have to go together," Bernardo says. "*Romeo and Juliet* style. Poison me too."

"I love *Romeo and Juliet*," I say.

"I figured. You have three copies in your room," he says.

It's irresistible, the way he sees me and knows me and notices me and doesn't want me to change.

I draw hearts on all his joints and spirals on his arms. He takes the pen from me and writes his name on my back, flipping me over and running the marker along my spine. I can't stop shivering. He writes his name everywhere. Covering my whole body in him.

"We aren't going to be able to wash this off," I say.

"True."

"Natasha will think we are insane," I say.

"Love makes you do crazy things," he says. "She'll see that we love each other." He's so much smarter than me. So much more poetic. He knows something about love that I don't know, but I want to know it.

He hands the marker back to me. I write my name on him too. The pen gets stuck in the little hairs on his arms, and it's weird to see him, one big scribble.

"We'll match," I say. I mean it like it's sort of strange, which it is. We have the hair and the scarves and now the hearts and words all over our skin.

"We already do," he says. "Two parts of one heart." He will be a poet someday. Of that I'm sure.

He kisses all the hearts he drew, lips traveling over the marked parts of my skin.

"My dad's going to kill us. We're supposed to look good at the proposal thing tomorrow," I say.

"You're going to go?" he says. "You hate everything about it, I thought."

"If I don't go . . . I don't know. If I don't go, it's like I'm saying I'm not part of the family anymore, and I'm not ready to do that."

"Mmmm. You still want to belong to them," Bernardo says.

"I do."

"And you want to belong to me. With me," he says, correcting himself a little.

"I think I might," I say. He rolls his eyes like I'll come around soon, and I'm sure he's right.

"So there you go."

Bernardo has this kind of logic that turns me around. Like when you're little and playing Pin the Tail on the Donkey. Bernardo's the guy who straps on your blindfold and spins you around and around until you're so dizzy you don't know which direction to walk in.

He draws a line of hearts like a V-neck on the top of my chest. It feels good. I check us out in the mirror before we leave. We look good and carefree and in love. Natasha will like it. I almost convince myself of that. I look at myself in every window on the walk from my place to Natasha's with Bernardo. That's a lot of windows. I decide at some point, on window six or twelve or fifteen, that I love our reflection, the way we fit together. That I love the looks we get. That this is how to be in love.

twenty-three

Victoria and Veronica hug my legs when we get there, and Natasha gives us iced tea and cookies, and I'm proud to show them off to Bernardo.

"Are you treating Montana right?" Natasha says. I can't read what she thinks of him right off the bat. I've never introduced her to anyone, aside from back in the day when she was my stepmom and I didn't give a shit since I hated her.

"I think so!" Bernardo says. He isn't nervous. Or at least he's not showing it. In fact, he looks more comfortable here than he did when he hung out with Karissa. He lifts Victoria onto his lap and I lift Veronica onto mine, and I'm thinking this was the best idea I've ever had.

"It's probably my job to show you embarrassing pictures of her ballet class and the Halloween she dressed up as an old man, right?" Natasha beams.

"An old man, huh?" Bernardo says. "What ever happened to, like,

Cinderella or a cat or a ghost?"

"Not my style," I say, loving his teasing. "I made Arizona be an old lady, so we could match." I'm laughing, thinking of it, and Natasha is laughing too. She remembers.

"You bossed Arizona around, huh?" he says. I like how he's trying to paint a full picture of me and my life. Write a whole novel on it.

"Hard to say." Memories of growing up with Arizona are so vivid they hurt. "We bossed each other around, I guess."

Victoria traces all the hearts she can find on Bernardo's skin, and Veronica keeps laughing at the ones on me. Natasha doesn't mention any of it. Everyone else in my life would say something about it, but Natasha doesn't do judgment.

"Nothing like siblings," Natasha says, looking at her girls.

Victoria and Veronica run around tearing books off the wall for us to read to them, and Bernardo does all the guy voices and wolf voices and elephant voices and dopey voices while I read the fairies and princesses and narrators and monkeys.

"He's got a very gentle nature with the girls," Natasha says when I join her in the kitchen to grab more cookies. "I can see what you like about him." She rubs my shoulder where there's a cluster of hearts. "The girls love these."

"It's silly. We're sort of silly together. Obviously. We're weirdos together."

"Isn't that perfect?" she says. "My girl in love." It hurts like it always does when she uses the phrase my father uses. Itches, really. The off-ness. A woolly sweater two sizes too small.

When we head back to the couch, the girls have brought Natasha's List of Things to Be Grateful For diary to Bernardo to read, but he hasn't opened it.

"What's this?" he asks. I love that he didn't open it, and I think Natasha does too. I want her to see at least a dozen things that are amazing about him.

"Montana's never told you about our lists?" Natasha says, and he shakes his head. "Well then, I know exactly what you need." She goes to the bookshelf and pulls out a navy journal. It's masculine enough. "She'll tell you what to do with this."

She's bringing him into the fold. Letting him in on the thing that is ours.

We take the subway to his place and I tell him about the List of Things to Be Grateful For, and he sits on a stoop and writes out his three right away.

They're about me and Victoria and Veronica and what it means to love a city that smells like garbage all summer long.

He gets it.

twenty-four

Dad asks to have one more breakfast with Arizona and me, the morning of the proposal. I don't like the way he phrases it—one last meal—marking a before and after where everything is going to change. Again.

We're at the diner, of course. It's a sort of autopilot assumption for him that the crummy lighting and chipped plates will fix what's wrong between us.

He's waiting there for us instead of walking over with me. He's probably been there for hours. His paper has expanded, the way papers do when they've been unfolded and refolded, never again managing to take their original shape.

"No," he says when he sees my Sharpie-covered skin. "For the love of God, Montana, no."

"Can we please make this not about me?" I say. I'm bleary-eyed and weary-limbed and wondering when and why I've started drinking quite this much. It's not like we're from Wisconsin, where there's a sort of boredom that has to be drunk away. We're in New York City. But maybe the lights and sounds are more manageable when they're dulled, and maybe everything else is more manageable too.

Plus, I like getting tipsy with Bernardo. It enhances the falling-in-love thing and makes it even wilder and buzzier. We went to his place and poured gin into a bottle of juice and played a drinking game with old-timey TV shows where every time the guys were misogynists, we had to drink.

"I ordered you scrambled eggs," he says. He looks legitimately sad, not just irritated.

"I don't like them scrambled," I say, knowing a good daughter would say *that sounds fine*. "I like poached. Did you get bacon?"

"I didn't think about bacon," he says. I'm even angrier about this than I am about the proposal.

"How do you not think about bacon? It's the whole reason we come to this stupid place!"

"I like this place. And you can order some bacon. Change your order. Or maybe Arizona will eat your scrambled eggs and you can eat her fried ones."

"Fried's not the same as poached," I say. I sound seven. I sound ridiculous. I want to throw the napkin holder at him. I don't want to eat eggs and talk about the future.

He sighs but lights up when Arizona breezes in all coiffed and curved and blank-faced.

"You look beautiful!" Dad says, so loud half the diner hears him and turns to check her out. Dad forces a smile at me too. "My two beautiful girls," he says, and I can see him giving himself a mental pat on the back for complimenting us both even though it's clear who has won the day.

"Interesting look there," Arizona says. She mumbles under her breath, "This your solution? Drawing on yourself? Grow up."

"Don't worry, Montana's going to scrub that off by tonight," Dad says, as if we've discussed it already and some decision has been made.

"It won't wash off," I say. "Permanent marker. Gonna be a few days."

The waiter comes over at the exact right moment and drops scrambled eggs and fried eggs and no bacon onto the table.

Arizona picks her fork up.

"I'd like to order poached eggs and bacon, please," I say. "And coffee." The coffee here is thin and unlimited. I'm going to need a lot.

"I'll eat the scrambled," Dad says. He takes the salt and pepper shakers, one in each hand, and goes to town.

"Nothing is more important to me than you girls," he starts. "I want you to have everything you deserve. I hope you know that."

I almost want to ask him if he's talking about the eggs. I'm not in the mood for this conversation. Coffee gets poured, and the smell is a little burned but not terrible. Familiar.

"I haven't always done the best job at giving you what you need," he says.

It's weird to feel sadder about how sad he is for me than I am about my actual sadness. It sucks not having Mom around, but it's even more painful seeing how desperately Dad doesn't want us to have gotten robbed of something everyone else has.

"I'm vetoing," Arizona says. Her voice is higher and pointier than usual, but under control. Like she's practiced this in the mirror.

"I'm sorry?" Dad says.

"I'm vetoing Karissa," Arizona says again, like it's some rule we decided on when Dad started dating and marrying and falling in love with everyone. "I don't want her in my family, I think it's a mistake, I'm saying no."

It is beyond lame that my first thought is that Arizona left me out of this decision. That she planned some rebellion without me. That she probably talked to Roxanne about this plan but not me.

"Yeah, maybe you could wait, Dad?" I say. I'm trying to join in, even though I haven't been invited.

"Not wait," Arizona says. "Not do it. Ever. I think we deserve one unilateral no, and I'm using mine." She keeps digging into the eggs and makes her eggs-eating face that I've seen for years. Adds salt and pepper to each bite. Our diner trips are practically choreographed.

"Arizona Varren," Dad says. His voice is low and shaking. He pushes his eggs away like they're suddenly sickening. "Absolutely inappropriate. What's gotten into you?"

She doesn't even look down. Doesn't wince or stop eating.

"You're trying to marry a twenty-year-old who you met, like, five minutes ago. I don't think I'm the one with the problem," Arizona says.

"She's not twenty," I say, because I am literally the stupidest person on the planet. I wish I could time-travel back thirty seconds and unsay it, but I can't. Without thinking, without even considering the epic fallout from the choice, I've taken Karissa's side.

Arizona glares at me. I'm sure forks continue clattering and random conversations keep going, but I don't hear them.

"I mean, I also would rather you didn't marry her," I say, but it's so weak compared to whatever it is she's doing that it gets lost, maybe doesn't even travel across the table to my father's ears.

Dad takes a bite of eggs at last but makes a face like he's swallowing glass.

Maybe the images of his ex-wives are bouncing in front of his eyes. Maybe he's remembering that Tess's shitty Lean Cuisine meals are still in our freezer. If the former wife's food is still edible, you're not yet ready for a new wife. I'm pretty sure that's a rule somewhere.

"I expect you both to be there tonight," Dad says. "I expect you to support the thing that makes me happy, like I support both of you." His voice cracks, and I wonder if he's going to cry. If we're seeing him grieve something real and complicated and basic. His failed marriages. The things he's done that have made all our lives erratic and tense. Taking us for five-dollar eggs when he knows we'd prefer bagels and cream cheese and lattes and the park.

Arizona sees it too. She reaches for his hand. Holds it in hers. He stares at the ceiling and we wait in that moment, together.

"I'd like my girls there," he says. "It's that simple."

This is why hope is such a stupid thing to have. Especially when it comes to people you know well.

"You should have told me what we were doing," I say when he's gone and the rest of the diner has more or less stopped listening in and the eggs are cold and the coffee is refilled to the tippy top, where there's no more room for milk and sugar.

"*We* weren't doing anything," Arizona says. "I did something. You're in la-la land losing your mind over there. I'm trying to fix the situation." The hardness hasn't faded from her face, and I can't read her.

"That's not fair," I say. "I talked to Karissa about it. I told her what was happening. I thought I could stop it on her end."

"And?"

"She's not stopping it," I say. "But I tried."

"Well, see? You're doing a bunch of shit without me too. So." Arizona is bristly and flustered. I want out of the diner. Someone ordered tuna salad, and it's stinking up the place. "All that complaining about me being away for college, and you've spent all this time with freaking Karissa and that dude."

"Oh my God, you know his name!" I could slap her. I don't get frustrated with anyone the way I do with Arizona. I want to shake the table until she hears herself.

"I love you, but you're making a big mess, Sean Varren–style, and you need to know that," she says after rolling her eyes and picking a little at her cold eggs.

"I don't do anything Sean Varren style," I say.

"Whatever, dude," Arizona says. "You'll see. In like a year, when you leave and go to your own college, you'll see what really happened this summer."

I hate that she said the word *college*. I hate that she thinks I'm in need of some Maine-campus-induced epiphany. I don't respond.

She pays the bill and looks at me like I'm supposed to know we're leaving together. "Park?"

"I thought you hate me."

"I mean, I do, but it's our last day to be in the park before Dad ruins it with his proposal crap. Roxanne's already there. Told her I'd bring her a diner coffee to go."

"It's even worse when it's to go," I say, and somehow we're back to ourselves for a moment. We find each other, again and again. I'm happy that that, at least, hasn't changed.

twenty-five

That night, as planned, we hold candles in Washington Square Park and wait for Karissa to walk by, which she is supposed to do with her friend at exactly nine p.m., when the sun is mostly set but the summery sky is still sort of gray and blue and gold instead of black.

Arizona is there.

Somehow we're still unable to put a real foot down when it comes to this shit.

"Maybe she'll change her mind," I say. "Maybe getting proposed to is one of those things that seems like a great idea until it happens."

"I have a friend from school who thinks she's about to get engaged," Arizona says instead of postulating about Karissa. "I mean, this guy is sort of Christian-y or whatever, and I guess Christian-y people get married young."

"Midwest?" Roxanne says.

"Exactly," Arizona says, and I know I'm missing some joke about the rest of the country and the people you meet when you leave New

York City, and I try to lean harder on Bernardo. I hold his hand with one hand and a candle with the other.

"Karissa's not Christian," I say. "Or from the Midwest."

"I know," Arizona says. "I wasn't talking about Karissa." She has this edge in her voice that she used to use sometimes with Roxanne when Arizona and I would be using all this shorthand and Roxanne would struggle to keep up. Roxanne would keep asking who the guy from the beach two summers ago was, or which ice cream place it was that spilled the rainbow sprinkles down Dad's girlfriend's shirt one time, and Arizona would sigh and refuse to explain except in really short, irritated, fraught sentences.

I've never heard her speak that way to me.

The part of me that still thinks of Karissa as a friend has a strange instant of being happy for her, watching for her to come and for her face to light up. I can't stop hearing the words she said the other day, about deserving something good. I wonder if she'll be sad her mother's not here. I wonder if she'll wish she could call her sister.

I would want to call my sister.

I move to Arizona, to put my chin on her shoulder for a moment.

"Remember the girl with the bad breath?" I say. She's our favorite of Dad's girlfriends to make fun of. "I've decided I think it had something to do with Tabasco sauce and sex."

"You're disgusting," Arizona says. "And it was absolutely McDonald's french fries, poor flossing, and mouth breathing."

"Mouth breathing," I say, nodding my chin against her shoulder blade before moving back next to Bernardo.

She's not gone entirely.

Dad's a few feet away, and he keeps rubbing his hands against the top of his thighs, like he's nervous. But it seems like he shouldn't be nervous. He's had practice.

We're all new versions of ourselves tonight.

I haven't even tried to scrub off the Sharpie, and neither has Bernardo.

"It's pretty out here," Roxanne says, looking at thirty-five people with tea candles circled around the bench that was the site of Karissa's first date with my father. They are mostly doctor-friends and their wives because our limited extended family lives upstate and is uninterested in my father's engagements.

"I don't get when people want an audience for their freaking engagements," Arizona says. "And by people, I mean Dad. Also, fire hazard. Seriously. I'm tempted to preemptively call an ambulance."

"But *pretty*," Roxanne says again. Since my father is not her father, she has the luxury of finding him romantic on occasion.

"Yep. Pretty," I say. "Very hazardous. Extreme. Not his best, though. Maybe his second best. Definitely better than when he and Janie got engaged at Starbucks. And better than when he learned German to propose to Tess. Because that was truly awful."

"What was the best?" Bernardo says.

I tell him my favorite was and will always be the time he proposed to Natasha on the intercom as we passed over the Atlantic Ocean on our flight to Paris. He said he knew Paris was the most romantic city in the world, but he simply couldn't wait to get there.

It was bullshit, obviously. He'd planned the whole thing weeks ahead of time, but I liked the sentiment. And I don't know, sometimes even if something is bullshit it can still be beautiful. Like Natasha herself, for example, who was mostly plastic by the time they got divorced, but is still, aesthetically speaking, totally gorgeous.

Plus, I got to go to Paris and see Notre-Dame, which is so pretty when it's lit up at night that I dream of living next door to it. Preferably, at this point, with Bernardo. I told him my plans the other night when we were a little naked and a little out of breath and very twisted around each other. He said whenever I'm ready he'll take me there. He didn't seem to be joking.

Romance is weird. Things get said that seem too large. Even *I love you* feels oversize and ill-fitting. Like dress-up clothes.

He says it in my ear now, and I wish he knew it isn't what I need at this moment.

I do love him. And I don't want him floating in the things he said that went unreturned, so I say it back.

"Paris is all ham and cheese sandwiches," Arizona says with a nose wrinkle and a mini-glare in my direction. Her real problem with Paris is that Natasha was the wife who was there with us. No one could hate a Parisian ham and cheese sandwich. Melty cheese. Salty ham. All from some cheap place where you order at the window with your best impression of a French accent on the word *fromage*.

In the distance, I see Karissa. I see her long-legged gait and her wavy-messy hair and the distinct, almost symmetrical but not quite, unmistakable shape of her face. Her red linen sundress. Her knows-what's-coming smile.

I reach for Arizona instead of Bernardo. She reaches back.

"What is this?" Karissa says, her voice rising high above the crowd. It sounds a little like a song.

There's that wave of anger and nausea and compassion that I have for Karissa, and I wonder what exact combination of feelings is running through Arizona right now. Something very different, I'm sure. Another recipe. I settle into my own sick feeling. I can't breathe.

"I know you love the park," my father says to Karissa. "And I know you love candles. And dusk. And I know I love you." He gets down on one knee. It's always the right knee and it's always a blue box. And it's always a woman in a low-cut dress, and it's always his best suit and a warm night.

My father is a man who gets engaged in the summer to beautiful women who I feel bad for.

"Oh my God," Karissa says. They always say *oh my God*. I catch Arizona's eye, and she is squinty and pissed. She has her cardigan pulled over her boobs.

That Karissa is falling into the stepmom script makes me even sicker. Like she's passed over to the other side, and she's a Mrs. Varren already. I wanted her to respond differently. I wanted her to do everything differently.

It's funny to be able to pinpoint the exact moment you start losing someone.

"I want to give you everything you love," Dad says. "Your life will be filled with candles and dusk and the walk from the Washington Square arch to our apartment and my devotion." The light from the candle is hitting my face. It doesn't burn or anything, but there's a heat, a small, pointed intensity at my chin. "Will you share that life with me? Will you marry me, Karissa?"

Dude's romantic. Can't deny that.

I'm fighting the urge to scream. Violent feelings keep popping up, then simmering down. Little impulses that don't stick around but don't totally fade either. I wish I could be anywhere but here. I wish I could be at the top of the Eiffel Tower. At least up there nothing feels real or permanent. Down here, in my park, it's too real.

"Of course," Karissa says. She pulls my dad to his feet and people clap and Dad and Karissa kiss and then do more than kiss. Make out. Pet. Rub against each other in a completely non-park-appropriate way.

Arizona looks like she's going to knock the candles out of everyone's hands and start a fire. She failed at something vital. We both did, I guess, but it was the first time she took an actual stand. I think she thought she could stop this from happening.

Turns out it's always been far, far out of our control.

Roxanne's candle flickers out with a few others as a light breeze hits it. I lean into Bernardo. He is practically holding me up.

"She looks . . ." Roxanne doesn't finish her sentence. She puts an arm around my waist, which is awkward with Bernardo holding me close to him. She pulls me tighter, squeezes my hip bone, and he pulls me in harder, too. I'm crashing against each of their bodies.

"Yeah," I say. I blow out my candle. It was starting to hurt my hands, the wax bubbling a little.

"There's dinner at my place," my dad says, breaking apart from their embrace. She doesn't stop kissing his neck, his ear. "A celebratory dinner with everyone we love."

They're mostly colleagues, but a few of them helped when my mom first left, and I guess we love them, in a way.

I don't see anyone who looks like they belong to Karissa aside from the one friend who brought her here, and that girl's checking her phone and looking like she's going to make an exit. I don't see all her cool friends who we hung out with that day at her apartment, which was actually only a few weeks ago but might as well have happened in a different century to entirely different people.

Karissa hugs me before anyone else. She smells like raspberries still, at least. I have that flicker of happiness for her again, like my heart has a tiny space in it for truly selfless feelings. It's a very small space.

Her heart is beating so hard and loud in her chest that I get confused and think it's mine that I'm hearing and feeling.

twenty-six

Roxanne and Arizona sit knee to knee on the couch. I take over the floor, my legs long in front of me and my elbows behind me. Bernardo stands. He is not a floor sitter.

"They seem happy," he says. Arizona, Roxanne, and I scoff in unison.

"That's the most shrimp I've ever seen in one place," Roxanne says. As far as post-proposal parties go, this one is particularly lame. With Natasha we went to dinner on the top of the Eiffel Tower. With Janie we had steaks uptown with the biggest baked potatoes imaginable. With Tess, Dad rented out a German beer hall, and we chowed down for hours on sausages and pretzels and Tess taught us German songs and we danced. Even Arizona enjoyed that night.

Tonight's after-party is low music and shitty catering, and we are hiding out in the basement while the adults mill around upstairs. I feel like I can breathe, at least, with Arizona, Bernardo, and Roxanne. I can breathe as long as I'm not in the same room as the ring and all my feelings about it.

"What'd you get?" I ask Arizona, who has her tattered Trader Joe's tote bag, a sure sign that she poached a bunch of food from the party to bring down here. She smiles and starts unpacking. She's wrapped shrimp in napkins, and deviled eggs too, although they didn't survive the journey so well. She has boxes of crackers and an entire slab of brie, stolen from right under the caterers' noses. She has prosciutto slices and even attempted to pack bell peppers filled with goat cheese into a Tupperware container. The girl is a klepto rock star of epic proportions, especially when it comes to catered food.

She's so put together now in every other way, it's necessary that she has a few secret weirdo qualities. At a party like this, it's necessary that we all do. Otherwise the night would be unbearable.

Fuck I'm glad I wore zebra print.

I dig around in the bar, wondering if we should try to make our own crappy martinis while the adults rage upstairs.

"Looking for this?" Karissa has appeared at the bottom of the stairs. I didn't hear the door at the top open or her feet padding down the carpeted staircase, but Karissa has that whole lithe thing going for her. She flits. She's got a few bottles of white wine and a wicked smile and too much blush and not enough newly engaged sparkle in her eyes.

We all startle at her sudden presence among us. The exact way we've always done everything shifts, and it is as recognizable as a sudden drop in temperature. The wives are meant to be on my father's arm, showing his friends the new ring. The wives are meant to bury their faces into his shoulder with some combination of happiness and shyness when people congratulate them.

This is something else. Everything is something else with Karissa.

"Jesus. Don't be creepy," Roxanne says. "You can't show up places without announcing yourself. Unless you are a witch or a hologram or something. Are you a witch or a hologram?" She's like our id or ego or whichever one does all the shit you really want to do but stop yourself from doing.

"A witch," Arizona says, not quietly at all, and I think she maybe has already had a drink or two. Maybe she snuck one in while she was stealing food. I kick in her general direction.

"I'm a girl who likes escaping prissy parties," Karissa says. I think she thinks she'll win my sister over with coolness. It won't happen, but there's something nice about her trying. "My little sis and I used to sit outside whenever my parents had parties. But they had great parties, actually. You know the wine and pickle thing I do, Mon?" She uncorks the wine. She has the swift, expert movements of someone who has opened up a lot of wine bottles. She has a system.

I nod. She shouldn't call me Mon. I'm not ready and Arizona definitely isn't ready.

"Wine and pickles?" Bernardo asks.

Karissa gets choked up and starts swigging wine.

"Oh my God, so sorry, I'm such a freak. Sometimes talking about them gets me a little . . . like this." She wipes away a few perfect, beautiful, star-like tears.

"That's okay," I say, and try to make it sound robotic so that Arizona doesn't think I'm on Karissa's side, but also compassionate because Karissa must be hurting. There's no way right now to be a good person and a good sister, so I settle for good person—ish.

"I wish they could be here for this," she says.

"Of course you do," I say, and mean it, because even if I hate what's happening, I can't let that go unsympathized with.

Roxanne clears her throat. Karissa's not sobbing or anything, but she's shifting the feeling of the energy down in the basement, and Roxanne was deep in party mode. I start rubbing Karissa's back. She has a frailty to her that I would never have imagined.

I almost wish Arizona could feel it. There's some sort of truth in the way Karissa's bones protrude.

"I bet being up there and celebrating with Dad will help," Arizona says.

Roxanne smirks, and I blush at the half-hidden meanness. Bernardo doesn't react, which I love.

Arizona stands up so that she's face-to-face with Karissa. We've been in this situation dozens of times, with me and Arizona always surviving and the stepmoms always falling away.

Except.

Karissa is different.

I care that she's hurting and drowning herself in white wine in my basement. I care that her dress is askew and her eyes are wild. I care that none of her wine-and-pickles friends were at the engagement. I care that the ring is too loose on her finger, like my father confused her ring size with someone else's.

"I wish your dad could have met my family. He would have totally, like, gotten it. You know? Gotten me. He would have understood what kind of party to throw me." Karissa takes some of the stolen shrimp. Dips it in brie. Making something strange out of something normal, as always.

"Dad only does this type of party for these things," Arizona says. I think she's getting meaner, or else it's that I love Karissa more than I'm used to loving the stepmoms. That I'm not solidly enough on the side of anger and hate, even though part of me should be.

"Anyway, no one up there will notice I'm gone," Karissa says. She's not crying anymore, but she's spacey. Almost like she's already past drunk and into that hazy post-drunkenness that comes if you stay awake for too long after drinking. "Your dad will, obviously, but he likes my mysterious side, so he'll think it's charming that I disappeared." Karissa barely breathes when she gets on a riff. She talks right through. "I left my own birthday party, right after we started dating. He tell you that? I wanted pizza and met a cool drunk chick from Australia when I was grabbing a slice. I took her to Queens. She wanted to see the seediest club in the city. Thought Manhattan was too cleaned up. She wanted some, like, eighties experience." Karissa laughs along with her own story, but I'm still stuck on my father going to her twenty-third birthday party, surrounded by recent college grads and wannabe actresses. The same friends I hung out with a few weeks ago. What would he have worn? Did he buy jeans? Did they think he was her father at first? Did they see the similarities in our faces and demeanors when they met me? Did he play Never Have I Ever with them and drink wine and eat pickles and smoke outside in some weird parallel version of what I did?

She's changed him, at least a little. I noticed upstairs there were bottles of beer, which I know he hates, and chips and onion dip. He hates onions. And dip. And the greasy reality of chips. Maybe he loves Karissa.

Nope. Too gross. Too impossible. Letting someone eat chips at their own engagement party isn't the same as loving them.

"He didn't mind that you ditched him?" Bernardo says.

That's when I realize I'm still enthralled by her. I sit on my hands like a little kid while she speaks. I look at her eyes, which haven't changed at all and are grass-green and rimmed in purple eyeliner.

Except: she is going to be my stepmother.

And I feel, with an ill kind of certainty, that I don't want a stepmother who gets drunk on white wine and knows where the best strips clubs are. I don't want a stepmother who plays dirty charades and can't stop crying over her family.

That last part is true, even if it's cruel.

"Mind? No. Opposite. He called me an inspiration. Said I understand something . . . what was it . . . vital about life. Told me he loved me the next day. Do the honors, Bernardo?" she says, handing him the next bottle of wine. He pours it out in our little plastic cups better suited for rinsing with mouthwash than partying.

I have a feeling the wine is expensive. It tastes expensive. Like grass and lemon and it's light as air. I could drink bottles of it, I think, without stopping.

There's laughter and clinking glasses and elevator music drifting in from upstairs. I get a text from my dad asking if I've seen Karissa, but I don't respond. We can keep her with us. We can save her, maybe. If she's down here drinking and telling too-long stories, she's not lost yet.

They're not married yet.

I'm pathetic for even thinking that. For having some hope for normalcy even in the face of all this. For wanting things to go back even when they're so clearly moving forward.

"So. You're happy, then?" Roxanne asks when she has finished off her wine. Karissa is staring at the ceiling, which is tin and awesome and totally old-school New York. I wonder if she's picturing her new life in this pretty home with ancient details and old-fashioned moldings and sleek silver kitchen appliances and picture windows that look out at other brick buildings.

"Blissful," she says. I believe that she believes it, at least. "Like Montana. We're just two girls in love, you know?"

Bernardo's eyes light up.

"Slow down there," Arizona says, and elbows me like I'm going to be in on the joke of how ridiculous it would be to say *I love you* at this point in my relationship. My face goes up in flames.

"I mean, I'm in love," I say, the words sounding like they're underwater and I'm above water, and it's funny when your sentences are located somewhere different from your body, like I'm not the same as the things I say. It's deep thoughts like this that really take hold when I'm drunk.

"That's enough," Arizona says, like love is a thing she can Put a

Stop To. "That's enough." She says it again, because sometimes when you're drunk you have to say things twice.

Roxanne lights a cigarette and Karissa wiggles her fingers as a way of asking for her own. Arizona rolls her eyes, and I wonder why she's down here at all if she's going to stay pissed.

"One for me and Arizona too," I say. Everything is kind of the worst, but surviving this crap together is what we do.

"Me too," Bernardo says. He's been so quiet I almost forgot he was here. I'm not the best girlfriend tonight. I kiss him on the cheek and hold the back of his neck in my hand for a moment. It's not enough, but for him it seems it could be. "I get it," he whispers.

"It's Bernardo Day tomorrow," I whisper back. "We can go see a Mets game. Or buy more scarves. Or read comics."

"I don't read comics."

"Oh. You seem like someone who might read comics," I say. We forgot to keep whispering, so now everyone can hear. Arizona flinches.

"I'm good," she says. "I don't want to smoke. Or drink."

"Oh, come on, we need this," I say. I want us to be in it together, whatever it is. However messed up it is.

"I'm going to head back upstairs," she says. "Dad's gonna ask if I've seen his fiancée. I don't like lying."

"Since when?" Roxanne says, laughing.

"Montana, you should come upstairs too. For a slice of cake. And our ritual." She's saying this on purpose to leave Karissa out. I can tell from the lift of her eyebrows and the fact that her voice gets a little louder on the word *ritual*.

I thought we were making a new ritual down here, but Arizona wants our old ones. And I love her a little more for that. It's comforting, to know we both want the sister-bond we had. We both miss the things before this summer. Before this year.

I chug a little more wine. With enough of it in my system, Arizona and Karissa can both look the way I prefer them to, the way they do in my ideal world. I can force this situation into something manageable. Survivable.

"It's that time," Arizona says.

"Use more words?" Bernardo says. He tilts his head like that will help him understand what's happening.

Arizona and I have a ritual where we guess how long Dad will stay with his girlfriend or wife. We each write down our guesses— how many months—on a sheet of paper, fold the pages, and hide them under Arizona's bed in a jewelry box filled with old jewelry that Mom gave her before she left (ninety-five months, though we obviously didn't make guesses on that marriage). Whoever is closest gets a piece of jewelry from the box. I've had my eye on a string of turquoise beads.

Arizona always wins. She chooses the lowest number of months. I'm too optimistic, even when turquoise beads are at stake. I can't help myself. I've only ever won a single silver ring, a plain braided design from when he dated and immediately broke up with a girl named Fuchsia. For some reason, Arizona gave her three months. I gave it one. It lasted three weeks.

It is not our only ritual. There is also the Closet of Forgotten Things, filled with things the wives have left behind over the years. My father can never seem to bring himself to throw away the remnants of his failed marriages. We have a ceremony with that, too.

"Montana. Come on. Let's do this our way, okay? The Varren sisters way." Her voice is low and sweet and so comfortable and soft I could fall asleep in it. I almost do.

I want it to be me and Arizona against the world again.

But Bernardo is next to me, and his hand circles my wrist, and he holds up his cig for me to smoke from, a gesture so sweet and gentle and small and sexy that I lose my head in it. It's not comfortable, like the things Arizona is describing. It's something else. Irresistible. Bernardo puts his arm around me and I fit there. Arizona's phone dings with a text message, and I'm sure it's a friend of hers I've never even heard of.

"Stay down here," I say. "Have a drink. Have a smoke. Let's stay up all night and be crazy, okay? Let's do that. Let's get your hair pink too!" I leap out of Bernardo's arms and hug my sister. We're not historically huggers, but it feels good. We could do this a whole new way. I think she'll maybe even say yes. She sighs and squeezes me more tightly. She runs her hands through my hair and calls me a nut.

"I know this is fucked up, but it can still be a fun night," I whisper, something only for Arizona so she knows I'm not on board with it all, I'm not crazy. "We're in it together. You and me," I say, words that are sort of true and sort of false.

"I'll go pink too! Solidarity!" Karissa interrupts.

All Arizona's muscles tense, and she lets go of me.

"Or probably you two want to do that alone. Also great. I can help?" Karissa says, trying to shove the words back in her mouth, hearing her own mistake. It's too late. She's twenty-three and marrying our dad and overeager and freaking us out.

"I don't want to stay down here," Arizona says. She's whispering, and Bernardo is so on top of it that he turns the music up, so we can have a moment of privacy. Roxanne sings along to words she doesn't know and a melody she has only a vague grasp on.

"You can keep the turquoise beads," I say, because the look on her face says she wants to make a hope chest for failure. She wants to wish the worst on Karissa, and even though I don't want Karissa with Dad, I can't do a ritual that hopes for her heart to get broken.

"Keep them and the pearl necklace and the gold bangles and the heart locket Dad bought for Mom. You can have it all." I try to pull Arizona onto the couch with me. "Let's stay down here. Let's do it a new way, this time." I'm smiling and probably slurring, but I want her to agree to find some new way to be.

"You keep thinking I've done something to you," Arizona says. "I went to Maine. You're in a fucking fairy tale."

Her steps are loud enough to hear over the music all the way up the stairs, and when she opens the door for a second before closing it behind her, adult voices and classical music and the smell of baking feta and onion tarts waft downstairs.

I almost follow her. I am so close to following her.

* * *

"You know what's amazing?" Karissa says at the very end of the night, when everyone else is asleep and I'm somewhere past drunk. "You have, like, a whole life."

"You don't have a whole life?" I say. She opens the vodka and pours a tiny mini-shot into each of our cups. I don't want it, I'll definitely throw it up in, like, twenty minutes, but I take it anyway.

There's a grief-filled pause, for all the things she's lost.

"Well, I do now at least!" she says at last, and gestures, a circular motion with her hand that is not occupied with vodka. I don't know if she's gesturing to the basement or the whole brownstone or me and my friends, or my absent father, or the cloud of smoke that hasn't quite made its way out of the basement through the crack in the windows.

June 25

The List of Things to Be Grateful For

1 Stolen food.

2 The way Bernardo looks at me and not Karissa, even though everyone else is looking at Karissa. Maybe this is part of love too.

3 Someone beautiful thinking my life is beautiful.

twenty-seven

In the morning everything is terrible. Bernardo has escaped and left a note on my chest and a message on my phone that he had to make it home before his parents woke up. Arizona stands over me with a coffee and a grimace.

Roxanne and Karissa are gone too. In some ways the night never happened.

Except for my hangover.

"I stayed over," Arizona says. "I thought you might want me around today." I hear the bit of apology in her voice, and that she wants to be us again.

But she's in this shirt. Maybe it's from the Closet of Forgotten Things or maybe she bought it with her roommates or maybe she's had it forever, but it's never fit quite this way before.

It's white and V-necked with rhinestones along the cleavage and lace on the sides. I hate it. Arizona should hate it too.

"I do. But you can't wear that shirt anymore," I say, meaning it to come out as a joke. But it's not a joke, so it doesn't sound like one.

"I get it. You hate my body. I hear you loud and clear, Mon," she says.

"You look like a Varren wife. You hate Varren wives. You don't want to look like me anymore. I mean, how the fuck am I supposed to take it?"

"You wanted to become more you when you dyed your hair that awful color, right?" Arizona says. She doesn't wrap her arms around herself. She's decided not to be embarrassed about it anymore. "I wanted to become more me. This feels good for me. This feels better. You want some whole other standard for you than for me? You want me to stay the same but you get to change? I have no idea what you want!" Her voice keeps screeching and breaking and I've never heard her quite like this.

"I want one thing not to change. I want there to be one part of our lives that stays the same, that we can depend on. I thought that was you." I'm clear when I'm hungover. Or less able to twist up truths like they're straw wrappers or hair bands or hoodie strings.

I've finally said a thing that feels true to me, and maybe Arizona will hear the truth in it too. Maybe it will repair something.

"You're like Dad in so many ways," she says instead, and I know I've failed and that hungover Montana is every bit as irritating to her as sober Montana and drunk Montana. "The way you love and the face you make in the morning when you first wake up and the ridiculous way you hope for something that you know doesn't exist. But especially in the way you want us to be one very small and specific thing. That you have this idea of who I am, and you're mad if I don't meet the standard. You know? You see that, right?"

I slide down, far under a blanket to a place where Arizona can't see me, can't see my face, can only see the blanketed outline of my body.

"I don't want you to think that about me," I say. I know it's muffled from under the blanket, but she can hear me.

"You don't want to be Dad," she repeats back.

"I'm not Dad," I say. "I don't want *you* to think I'm Dad. And maybe Dad isn't even Dad! I don't know. I don't know." It has got to be the hangover that's making everything look different today. The hangover and telling Arizona I love Bernardo and watching Dad propose to the person I thought I wanted to be. They're all changing the world's shape and texture and feeling.

"Are you still drunk?" Arizona says.

"You know he never brings up the gift certificate? I think it was all Natasha's idea. And he forgets so many things and, like, when he was with Tess he was really into running and ran that marathon last year, and I haven't seen him even, like, speed walk since she left. And when he was with that girl Fuchsia, he went to some weird church thing where they stay in silence the whole time, but now he doesn't even know when Christmas is."

"You're completely still drunk," Arizona says. She stamps her foot a little, and underneath the new boobs and the way she's looking at me like I'm a huge disappointment, she's still the girl she was at eight, at least a little.

"No, I'm not. I wonder sometimes if Dad even knows the mistakes he makes. If maybe this whole thing, this thing that was the worst thing that ever happened to us . . . if it ever even really happened in the way we think it did. Or, like, what does it mean if it happened but he doesn't know it happened? What if he really does want a nice woman and a good life and for us to be happy? What if he loves us enough? What if he thinks we're great and he's actually in love? What if—"

"No." Arizona doesn't even leave room for me to breathe. She gets so close to my face I think she's stealing the air. She's more sure of this than I've ever been about anything.

And I guess this is what she meant, about hope and me having it. Because hope is space. It's having room for something even when things are cramped and hard to move around.

There is space for our father to be a little different than we thought. There's room for us to have a different ending, a different situation.

"I'll show you why you're wrong," Arizona says. "But you're not going to want to see." I follow her like a zombie to my dad's office. "They're out to brunch," she says, as if I've asked where Dad and Karissa are. "She looks excellent in the mornings, by the way. She was wearing one of his shirts and acting like nothing weird happened last night. You better not trust her. These people aren't real. This isn't real life."

I think for the thousandth time over the last three years that I should tell Arizona that I still see Natasha. That she is real, as far as I'm concerned. That she's my family too, and that Victoria and Veronica exist and are little mini-sisters and that things could have been different, that there was space for a different outcome there too.

Instead I shrug and watch her open up my father's desk drawers. She brings out a few folders. They are filled with pictures of women. Not the dirty kind, although some of them are naked-ish. They are women he is performing surgery on or women his partner wants advice on. The bodies and faces are covered in lines and marks and notes. Dashes under their eyes. Red marks drawn in under their breasts. Circles around their flaws.

I hate how their flaws are annotated. How he sees them as beings to be made better, instead of seeing them as they are. I hate the Post-it notes with surgical drawings that are really actually drawings of better versions of normal women. I hate the magazine covers and the Renoir painting with his dotted lines. But I hate his desk drawers filled with these poor makeup-less women most of all. They're too vulnerable.

"I mean, we've seen this before," I say. "This is his job. He does it at the counter."

It's shocking to see them all at once, bundles of women and his ideas about how they could be better. But this isn't a new thing.

Arizona scrounges around some more, opening and closing folders, flipping through photographs. "I found something else," she says. "I wasn't going to tell you, but you're being all crazy and reckless and fucking naive, and I guess the only way to stop that is to show you what's actually going on here."

Her voice is too loud for the small room and the headachy morning. She's edgy and off. She's breaking.

She pushes aside a brochure from a Pilates studio. Tess's Pilates studio, where she's started teaching. Her face is on the front with a few other pretty, skinny, rosy-cheeked instructors.

Dad has drawn on all of their faces too.

He's already done a lot to Tess's face and body in real life, but in picture form he still draws lines under her eyes and at her neck. Improving on his own work. His dissatisfaction so large and powerful I swear it's in the room with us.

I pocket the brochure. As evidence of how impossible it will be to ever be good enough for him. Maybe to show Karissa.

Maybe because I want to know where Tess is.

Finally Arizona finds what she's looking for. It's a photograph of the two of us.

We're in bikinis. We're fifteen and seventeen. We're squinting from smiling so hard. There are palm trees in the background and Tess's pedicured toes in the bottom of the frame. I have four tiny braids on one side of my head. Arizona has a sunburn on her nose.

It's hard to tell us apart.

Partly because there are lines on our faces. And our bodies. A few near my eyes and ears. A question mark near my nose. And a whole new shape drawn in around my chin. It's the shape my father wishes my chin were. Strong and solid and in proportion with my cheekbones and forehead. An ideal shape. Dotted lines make my hips smaller. The insides of my thighs touch in the photo, but he's circled the exact spot where they hit.

It's like a paper at school, all marked up with *needs improvement* and *has potential*.

Arizona is marked up too. Some lines on her face and vague

markings on both of our chests, like he forgot we were his daughters.

He probably did forget we were his daughters when he was doing it.

It doesn't matter if he doodled it while he was on the phone or spacing out. It doesn't matter that if I show him an issue of *Glamour* with a marked-up model, he doesn't even remember doing it. That he laughs at his own doctorliness. "You can't turn it off, I guess," he's said.

It hurts. My hangover turns into something else entirely. Something burning and drowning me. Something unsurvivable.

"I'm sorry," Arizona says.

I'm gutted and she knows it, because she was gutted too.

"This is what he sees?" I say, but I know the answer.

"They've only ever made it worse. His women. They make him less of a dad. And she's the worst one. You don't see it, but he's forgetting about us. He's not seeing us as daughters anymore. As family. As important. You think you understand Karissa and the other women. But you're missing the most important parts."

I want to be on her side and be upset about this together. But her boobs are pushed up too far, and they're all I can see.

"We're in it together," Arizona says. "You and me and no one else. Roxanne can hang out. She can help or make us laugh or give you cigarettes if you really need to do that. But stop trying to bring other people in. It's you and me."

"It's not," I say.

I'd go out right now if I could. See Bernardo. See myself through someone else's eyes. Never talk to my father again. But my head hurts too much and I'm dizzy. I wouldn't make it out of the building probably.

"You shouldn't have shown me that," I say.

I sleep away as much of the next twenty-four hours as I can. Because in sleep I don't remember that image of myself marked up beyond recognition, made into someone my father would love more.

twenty-eight

Bernardo brings me a bagel the next day.

I got up early and bought us huge blueberry muffins from a place that serves them with clotted cream to dip them in. He shows me the bagel and I show him the muffins and the cream and we marvel at ourselves.

I think that is part of love too. Basking in the wonder of how great you are for each other.

"You are the sweetest," I say.

"But you are also the sweetest," he says.

"So we're going to have to eat it all, right?" I say.

"I see no other option." He takes a bite of bagel right there on the stoop, followed by a bite of muffin.

"Clotted cream," he says. "Who knew?"

Being near Bernardo and eating clotted cream feels good, but nothing else does. I can't even look in the mirror. Errant marks fly up in front of my image, zaps like the kind that happen when you rub your eyes too hard or first try to adjust to the light after an evening of dark.

"You still hurting from the other night?" he asks.

I am still hurting, but not from a hangover.

"Are you ready for today?" I say. I haven't let go of the Pilates brochure or the idea that seeing Tess will do something, make me see something new. Arizona is so sure that I don't see anything clearly. Fine. I'll look more closely. At all of them. At my father and Natasha and Tess and Janie. At my mother. At Karissa. At myself.

"Use more words?" Bernardo says.

"Can we do something kind of crazy today? Are you up for it?"

"What are we doing?" Bernardo says. It's not yes or no, it's something better.

"I want to see Tess," I say. "The most recent stepmom."

He studies my face, and without thinking I bring my hand to my chin, to cover it up. It's funny, how aware of my weak chin I suddenly am. I've been walking around with it my whole life, barely even noticing, and now that I've seen my father's pictures I can think of nothing else. "You look sad. Are you sad? I haven't seen you sad before. All kinds of other things. Not sad, though. Is this what it looks like on you?"

I love that everything he says is a poem.

"I'm motivated," I say.

"And sad."

"Yeah. And sad."

He kisses me and I'm almost not sad anymore. I feel almost

beautiful again. The Sharpie markings on my arms and chest and thighs are blurry now. Not gone and not distinct. More like a fog over my skin and his. I miss them. Tess will hate it all. The hair and the scarf and the fog and the Sharpie and Bernardo and me being there.

I don't think I care.

The last time I saw Tess she was in the middle of moving out and Dad forgot to tell me. We have a rule that he's supposed to tell me and Arizona when someone is moving in or out so that we don't have to actually see or experience the change. It's a weird, chosen denial, like it's not happening if we don't see it happen. If a stepmom moves out and no one sees it, did she ever really exist?

At the time Tess was wearing pink leggings and too much makeup, and she was shaky and weepy on our stairs. I tried to sneak away unseen, but she heard my shuffling and looked up.

"Did you know this was coming?" she said. She looked young, then, underneath all the makeup and Botox and cascade of tears. She looked like a little girl. It was scary.

"I mean, I don't know," I said. "I've never seen it work, so I guess . . . sort of?"

"I'd never done any of this before," Tess said. "Movie night and making dinner and worrying about you getting home by curfew and cleaning the blades of the ceiling fan and saying I love you to someone every night before bed. That was all new to me."

"Yeah. See, it wasn't really new to us," I said.

"That's the worst fucking thing I've ever heard," Tess said. "This should make you feel something." She pointed to her pile of moving boxes, the truck outside, the burly men heaving the boxes from our apartment to their truck.

"I mean, we'll miss you for sure," I said, but I know it wasn't convincing enough. I couldn't muster up tears or even a crack in my voice or a big sigh or anything.

"Today I feel bad for me," she said. "But in, like, six months I'm only going to feel bad for you." She took one of the smallest boxes out to the sidewalk and stayed there, surveying the house and sipping a big green juice, and she never came back inside.

I don't have cute workout clothes, so I take Bernardo to the Closet of Forgotten Things, where I'm sure I'll find stretchy pants and tank tops with built-in bras and everything else I need to pull off Girl Going to Pilates Class.

The Closet of Forgotten Things is filled with handbags and failed pottery projects and expensive jewelry and jeans that are ripped in sexy places and books of poetry that are either sad or romantic but never both.

Arizona and I play a game sometimes, where we go through the closet and ask each other if the object is from the beginning or the end. If it is a symbol of manic falling in love or the spiral out of love and into despair. If it is a remnant from before they were a plastic wife or from the fizzy days where they're changing or the always depressing endings where they see how much they've lost and how little it mattered.

We played after Tess left, over the phone. I sent her pictures of objects and wished she were actually there.

Diet book: I say before, Arizona says after.

Gold bracelet with tiny diamonds: we both agree it's from the beginning.

iPod filled with sad songs: obviously it's from the end.

Never-worn sneakers: I say after, Arizona says before.

Arizona and I don't tell anyone about this or the betting box. They are things that make us terrible people. They are the things that make us sisters and help us survive.

And still, I tell Bernardo about it. Which must be love.

"I have never seen anything like this," Bernardo says, watching me dig through the contents and find a sweat headband that I decide was Natasha's.

The sweat headband is super eighties and neon and trying pretty hard to be retro-hip, so it could be from the end, but it's also unself-conscious and, like, exuberant and for someone who doesn't care what people think, so it could be from before or during. It's a tough call.

I point at the shiny black leggings I'm going to put on. "After," I say. Then at the headband. "Probably before."

"I want to play," he says, and picks up a stuffed giraffe. "What do you think? When's this thing from?"

"Oh, come on," I say. "Clearly from, like, week one. You don't buy stuffed animals after the first few weeks."

Bernardo nods his head like this is a research project and not a game. We head out.

It occurs to me on the subway, when I'm looking at my own Sharpied hands gripping the pole, that I have done to myself what my father did to me. "When do you think these markings will wash off completely?"

I ask Bernardo. I smile with the words so that he doesn't know how disturbed I now am by the thing we did.

"Another few days," Bernardo says. "Unless I do it to you again."

"No!" I say, too loudly. I want to wash my mind of the image of the photograph in my dad's office, but it's impossible with black markings crawling all over me.

"Are you sure you want to see her?" Bernardo says, knowing something's wrong but not knowing what and guessing incorrectly.

"I'm fine. I sort of miss the color of my skin. I miss how it looks, like, untouched."

"Well, I'm with you on that," Bernardo says. He kisses my shoulder, then my neck, then my cheeks, and then we're making out on the subway. Men in suits and women in empire-waist dresses and little kids on weird leashes avert their eyes. We stumble when the train comes to a halt, and our bodies fall against each other so that we both have to step back. I trip over a dude with a shopping cart full of blue garbage bags and cans. When I find Bernardo's lips again, we only have one stop left to kiss and we make the most of it.

The studio's near Lincoln Center, and everyone hanging out there looks the same. Looks like Tess.

Then there's Tess.

She looks good. Okay, at least. She hasn't changed except that her hair is even blonder and her body is contorted, with her legs above her head and her feet in straps and her hands gripping some medieval torture device situation.

I sit on a mat like I'm going to take a class, but there's no class going on, so I catch her eye immediately. And Bernardo catches everyone's eyes. He didn't take off his shoes or his scarf or anything. He is squarely himself.

"Montana," Tess says. Her voice goes hoarse mid-word, and I sort of know immediately this is a terrible idea. I'm not a regular girl to her anymore. I'm not me. I'm the symbol of the worst thing that ever happened to her. I'm the worst.

"I shouldn't have come," I say. It's a weird way to start a conversation, and we both know it.

"Are you taking Pilates?" Tess says. It hasn't even been six months, but I wonder if her prediction was right, if she feels bad for me instead of herself already. I blush from the idea of it. When I last saw her, she was the humiliated one. The one left behind. The pathetic pink-outfitted disaster.

I wonder if I'm now that pitiable and pink and unaware.

"Oh. No. I came to see you," I say. "And I have a boyfriend!" Bernardo seems like as good a distraction as anything else. He has a red T-shirt and a red baseball hat with the word *word* on it. I do a Vanna White gesture in his direction, like he's something to be admired and won, which he sort of is, in my opinion. Tess nods and waves, but there's no warmth coming off of her.

The studio smells like sweat and too-sweet candles.

"Can you grab some tea with me?" I say. I remember Tess liking tea.

"No," Tess says. "I'm working. And if there's something you need . . . I'm probably not the right person." She pauses and takes me in. All of me. The hair and the Sharpie shadows and probably the sadness, and she draws some kind of conclusion. "Are you okay?" she says.

"I'm great. I'm okay. I'm a little lost," I say. It's three different answers. I wish I knew the right one. Some of Tess's coworkers inch closer to us, like they know she might need backup. I'm almost happy for her, all these people looking out for her. A little family.

It is pathetic that my heart tugs at the thought of that word. And that I'm jealous she might have it already, without me, in this form.

"What am I to you now?" I say. "Do you miss me? What, like, are we? To each other?" I am ten. I am eight. I am five and thirteen and so small. It hurts, to be this little and exposed.

Tess closes her eyes. She tilts her head up to the ceiling and takes deep breaths.

"Let's pretend we don't know each other," she says. I am prepared for so many crappy things, but not that. "We don't, really. I don't know any of you. Not even your stupid fucking father."

Tess was not a swearer when she lived with us, so the word hits hard.

Arizona is right. I don't see everything. I am too hopeful. I am too into the stepmoms. I am silly and stupid and wrong about my own life. "I should go," I say.

"You and your brat of a sister," Tess says. It's not even a full sentence. "You're terrible people. Is that what you wanted to hear?"

It's mean. The last few days have been so full of mean things I feel like I'm learning something true and awful about, like, the world. Humanity. A few days ago I was simply Montana. Now I am terrible and ugly and ridiculous and a bad sister and a brat. My mind can't work fast enough to catch up with that idea of me.

"Don't talk to her like that," Bernardo breaks in, a new side of him emerging too. His voice is a little too big for the studio, and everyone's listening in now and all I want is to be on the street where you can say anything at all and no one notices. The other day some guy was talking on the phone about guns and knives and all his friends who have them. I want to be out there, with them, where I am pink-haired and fucked up but not in a way anyone notices.

Everyone here looks like someone my dad would like to marry or who he would have already married.

"I don't know what question I'm asking," I say. "But it's weird to have you live in my house and then never see you again. All of you."

I know even saying it like that, lining Tess up as part of a string of people instead of her own individual person, is sort of me being the worst. Even Bernardo cringes at the phrasing.

"I tried to make it seem like a family," Tess says at last. She's looking only at me, not at the people watching us. "But that's not the same as it actually being one, in the end, you know?"

"Maybe we didn't need you to make us a family," I say. I don't even believe it myself, but I can't stand her acting like we're not. I can't let someone else confirm my biggest fear in a sweaty, too-pretty studio full of boring people who don't eat pasta.

Besides, my father kisses my forehead some nights when he thinks I'm asleep, and that has to mean something.

Tess lets out a loud, singular, explosive laugh.

"I can feel bad for you. For all of you. Because you're so terrible you don't even know what you're missing. So yeah. I was right. You're the one who's meant to be pitied."

My heart's pounding and Bernardo is fuming. "Don't talk to her like that," he says again.

"You came here," she says, like the words came out of me, not him. I'm not sure if he's making things worse or better, being here. "To what? Make yourself feel better? Make fun of me? Feel all superior for knowing it wouldn't work out? You and your sister, both rooting for the worst possible thing to happen for me. Two teenagers actively rooting for my life to fall apart. Arizona said it under her breath a million times. Had a countdown of when he'd leave me. You're bad people. You don't care about anyone but yourselves. You don't care about anything."

Her face is twisted, and the other teachers come up to her, stroking her arm to calm her down like she's a rabid dog, which I guess she sort of is.

I want to cover Bernardo's ears. Because some of what Tess is saying is true, and some of who I am is a terrible person who roots for women's lives to fall apart. And I'm not ready for Bernardo to know all the bad things about me.

I know that that is probably love too. Knowing what makes someone awful. But after seeing what my dad hates about me, I'm not sure I can handle seeing what Bernardo hates about me too.

I'd sort of like to know what people love about me.

"You don't know Montana," Bernardo says. I stroke his arm too.

I'm scared of this version of Tess. I've never seen the ugly aftermath of my father, the stepmoms after they've been discarded. I've only seen the butterfly transformation of Natasha and nothing else. This is treacherous.

"I know her. I know all about her." At the end, Dad used to call Tess shrill, and I guess I know what that means now, even though I hate being on Dad's side. "You and your sister treated me like a joke."

"I liked movie nights," I say. I'm going to cry if I don't shut up. Maybe it's what I should have said to her on the stairs that day, maybe that would have meant something, meant that I'm a good person, meant that she was a real part of our family for a minute.

"I wanted to know something about forever and why it didn't happen for you," I say. I don't know why I came here.

"You need to leave," one of the managers says.

"I'm only trying to understand," I say.

"I'm not some project," Tess is yelling. Then she's pushing the other teachers out of the way and coming at me. Her hands reach my shoulders and she gives one giant push before they can pull her back again. Bernardo pulls me into a protective hug.

"We're going, we're going," I say. The tears are coming, but I don't want them here. We make it into the elevator before they splash out.

"We can press charges," Bernardo says. He's hot, his whole body feverish from indignation.

"It's my fault," I say.

"She touched you! She hurt you! She's insane!" He punches his own thigh. I can't stop crying. I don't have any anger in me. She's right. And Bernardo doesn't see it. Which means he either really loves me, because he only sees the good. Or he doesn't love me at all, because he doesn't really see me at all.

"We were rooting against them. Arizona and me. Like it's a game. We root against all of them. We're the worst," I say.

Bernardo rubs my back and tells me I'm the best over and over again, but he says it too many times and it loses all meaning.

June 30

The List of Things to Be Grateful For

1 My new pet turtle, Floyd, a present from Bernardo, who says he will live longer than my chameleon did back in the day. Turtles are sturdy and don't change. Bernardo gets me.

2 Emoji-only texts from Arizona that are half apology and half octopuses and cats with hearts for eyes.

3 Outdoor movies with Roxanne in the park and the tiny relief of summer nights after summer days.

twenty-nine

I wake up a few mornings later to the sound of Karissa rummaging around in my room.

I'm asleep in the clothes I wore out with my Bernardo the night before. I took him to Reggio to explain to him why I continue to love my dad. I still smell like the café: espresso and butter and toast and candle wax. I am not ready for Karissa. Not this early. She has on blue-striped pajama bottoms and a cropped white lace top and this oversize sweater cardigan that is all wrong for a summer morning, except that the AC is on so high that it's almost warranted.

"Morning!" she says at the first sign of me shifting into wakefulness.

"You're in my room," I say. I want to be cool with it, but it's too early to be cool. I can't feel anything but confused and exposed and deeply awkward. The thing that shifted last week when she said yes and put a sparkly ring on her finger didn't unshift because we got drunk right after. The shift happened, and I'm not sure it can unhappen. When the earth quakes, does the land go back to its original state, or do things stay slightly askew? Do the fault lines become faultier?

They must.

"I need a strapless bra," she says. There is zero hesitation on the word *bra*. I make a grumpy morning coughing sound.

"It's early," I say, like that's the real issue here. I want to be having a fuzzy dream about what sex with Bernardo will be like. I do not want to be watching her tornado through my room.

I don't want her anywhere near my room. I don't want the life where she has access to my room.

"It's actually late. I waited. But then I figured, what the hell, you've had a sister your whole life, no big deal, right?" Karissa is rummaging through my sock drawer. I have no idea if she's made it to my underwear drawer at this point or not.

"No. Not right. Not okay!" I shake my head back and forth to wake it up and adjust last night's tank top and jeans. I feel chalky and dry. The AC makes my eyes burn first thing every morning, a blast of cold air after a night of warm dreams.

Karissa stops unpacking my socks from the top drawer. There's a pile of white athletic ones at her feet. T-shirts are strewn all over the floor. My closet is open, the contents rustled and misplaced.

The Karissa I loved and still maybe love is there, but so is someone else. Like a third person in the room with us. Old Karissa and Stepmom Karissa. I do not seem to like Stepmom Karissa.

There's a look crossing her face that I've never seen outside of acting class. A hurt look, pained and confused. I'm not following her script. If it were afternoon and not morning, I would defer to the look.

But my head hurts and my mouth is salty and dry from eating Goldfish in bed after Reggio, and not seeing Arizona at the café made me miss my sister even more. "My sister and I shared a closet," Karissa says.

I think I'm simply tired. But maybe I am also, horribly, a little tired of this story.

"Sometimes I couldn't even remember what was whose," she continues. "Like, if I'd bought a certain shirt or if she had. That closeness . . . it's beautiful, right?" She's getting choked up, like she always does when she remembers her family, but it's so early for grief that I don't know what to do.

The grief has turned a little sour. Or possibly I'm exactly like my dad—thinking something's beautiful until I look too closely, then seeing everything I want to change about it.

"That's so cute," I say, careful and not convincing enough. "But we don't really do that." I want to also say *and you're not my sister*. But I don't. Arizona would.

It's weird to start getting sick of someone's grief, but it happens. Or maybe it doesn't happen to everyone, but it happens to me. Maybe this is proof positive that I actually am the terrible person Tess accused me of being. I can't even work up early-morning sympathy for someone whose entire family died in one fell swoop.

"Look what I found, though!" Karissa says. She's made her way back over to my closet and pulls out a dress I bought secondhand with Arizona last summer, when she dragged me to some boutique with too-girly clothes. The dress is butter yellow with doily-looking white sleeves and a blue ribbon that wraps around the waist. It's pretty and extremely not me. I have been planning on wearing it out with Bernardo, since he promised we'd spend the summer eating at sidewalk tables, and it is the exact kind of dress a girl wears to eat in the sunshine. I have a whole plan where I wear my hair in loose curls and barrettes and act sweet for an afternoon. Order éclairs. Drink tea with my pinkie up.

"That's mine," I say. I get out of bed fully, since she is clearly not going to stop. I try to feel that compassion for her again, like I did a few weeks ago. "I mean, I guess you could borrow it sometime if you want," I try, but it comes out pissed, and Karissa's not paying attention to me anyway. I'm like an object in this conversation. A lamp or maybe something truly useless, like an ottoman.

"Well, I mean, you have to wear this. Let's picnic. That's a picnic dress if I ever saw one." Even Karissa's voice is grating at this time in the morning. I get the feeling this is an apology, and it's not enough. We can't picnic away her marrying my father.

I want to see her with a cigarette on the stoop or a beer in the basement or sitting cross-legged on her kitchen counter, pickle in hand, or perched on a bar stool at Dirty Versailles with strangers watching her.

I do not like this new part of her.

Her eyes say *nothing has to change*, but that's not true, and I can see that, at least.

"I'm saving it," I say.

"For the boyfriend? We can all go. Call him up. I'll buy baguettes and cheese and salami or something. It will be very French. It will be romantic. I have a dress I made a few summers ago when I was into making clothes. It's perfect. We'll be perfect." Karissa holds the dress up to my body and gets her face too close to mine. "Have you picnicked before? Mom used to take me and, like, my dolls on picnics when I was little. We'd just go behind the house, but it was my favorite thing to do. Let's do that."

"Are you okay?" I say, trying to root her behavior in something specific. "Is it, like, another anniversary or birthday or something?" I want to put a name to her grief. Maybe it will feel more controlled then, less wild. I want to make it not about us and our relationship and how to fix it.

Karissa shakes her head.

"I want to spend time with you. I want to have a Karissa-Montana day. This is about us." It is the exact thing I didn't want her to say. I never would have guessed, in Dirty Versailles that night a few weeks ago, that we could have gotten here so fast. Her saying the wrong things and making my head hurt. Me wondering how long I have to smile around her for. When it's appropriate to scream.

"Don't you have an audition or anything?" I check my phone. Bernardo has texted a few times already, and Roxanne sent me some link to something, and I want my room to myself so badly my skin itches.

"No auditions today," Karissa says. "But I should have some soon! I have a plan. What if we did a little dress shopping?" I wonder for a moment if she's on something. She's that hyped up. It seems like she may throw her arms wide and start spinning around and around until she falls down from dizziness, the way little kids sometimes do.

"Like . . . summer dresses?" I ask.

"I was thinking maybe wedding dresses. I sort of want to look around. See what's out there. It's, like, what you're supposed to do when you get engaged, right?"

I am the expert, clearly.

"I guess. But maybe you want to go with someone else?" It isn't until I see the look on her face that I know I've said the wrong thing. I forgot, for long enough to ask one question, that her family is gone. And that we pledged best friend status when we were drunk. And that somehow I am the person she has to do this with.

"I'm engaged," Karissa says, her eyes big and her mouth drawing down. "I want to do things other people get to do."

I think of how many times I have said and thought this exact sentence.

She hasn't made a move to get out of my room, so I wonder if she's expecting me to change in front of her. I cross my arms over my chest and wish they were wide enough to cover all of me. I have sweat marks on my shirt and the image of my bikinied body with lines on all the ugly parts in my head. I don't want to be seen.

"Can we go get croissants? I'll meet you at Pain Quotidien in, like, fifteen?" I say, desperate to change the subject. Chocolate croissants should be a strong enough force to put a stop to almost anything. But they are not strong enough to stop her.

"I was thinking you could be my maid of honor. I know that might be weird, with Arizona and stuff, and of course she'll be a bridesmaid.

But what do you think?" Karissa smiles. She's flushed and wild-eyed. She still hasn't let go of my yellow dress. She uses her free hand to grab my hand. "You remind me so much of my sister. And I really meant what I said, at Dirty Versailles, you know? I want you to know I wasn't just drunk. I feel that bond with you. That was real."

I don't like the desperate edge to her voice or the way she keeps half pacing around my room. Taking little steps in every direction.

"Oh wow," I say. I'm queasy and hot. My heart's pounding out a particular rhythm that means this is wrong and weird and scary. I decide to put a T-shirt over my tank top and actually change clothes later. I run a brush through my hair and tie it into a side ponytail, and I flip through my texts some more. If I knew how to unlock this moment and move into a different one I would, but my phone doesn't seem to have an app for that.

"That's a yes, right?" Karissa says. "I'm thinking red for you. A red dress. Because, like, screw pastels, right? I am not a pastel bride. Your sister will be a pastel bride. You will definitely be wearing pastel pink or whatever when you are her maid of honor. So let's get you in red for mine."

HELP, I text Bernardo. *Attack of the crazy stepmom.*

Tess????? he says in some kind of text panic. It's too many question marks for so early in the morning.

Karissa, I text back. I should text Roxanne to come over and join us for the day. She could at least create some distance. Poke a little hole for me to breathe out of.

I'm suffocating, I text her. I sort of know I won't hear back. She has friends visiting from Bard, and they're going on some weed-smoking bender that Arizona and I weren't invited on, since we don't smoke weed.

She seemed okay at the thing last week, Bernardo texts. I think what he means is that we were all too drunk to care that she's unstable. Or maybe Karissa's too pretty for a guy to worry about in that way.

I guess I'm going to spend the day with her.

Good luck, he writes back.

I try to think about Dirty Versailles and acting class and Karissa's cool apartment and the way she smokes her cigarettes and the way she uncorks wine bottles and how talented and funny and exciting she can be. I try to hold on to that part of her, the part that I wanted to have.

"You're the reason I found your dad, right? You deserve to be up there during the wedding." Karissa climbs onto my bed now that I've left it. I would never climb onto someone else's unmade bed, and I sort of wince on her behalf. I'm sure it smells like sleep and Goldfish and cigarettes.

Feelings are clawing, feral cat–like, all over me, along with the realization that in any other version of this, I'd be thrilled. If Karissa were marrying Will from acting class or the bartender from Dirty Versailles or the ex-boyfriend she told me about who started texting her old roommate, I'd be on board. I'd be silly with the thrill of being her maid of honor. I'd be advertising it.

It's hell, wanting a slightly different version of a situation you're in. Or getting what you want, but it being wrong anyway.

"I'm okay being a guest," I say. It is the most polite I can be.

Karissa gives me a long stare. She looks the way she did when she played Laura in a scene from *The Glass Menagerie*. A disturbing kind of naive.

"You don't want to do it," she says. That's when she drops my dress to the floor. She gets up on her knees, pushing aside more of my blankets, and tries to get a look at my phone. "Who are you texting? Are you texting everyone? Your friends? Your mom? Arizona? You think she doesn't hate me enough?"

"No, oh my God, no," I say. "Nothing about you, I swear. I'm saying good morning to Roxanne. I'm making plans with Bernardo. We talked about maybe getting grilled cheese somewhere with really good grilled cheese? Because there are all these places that specialize in random classic foods, and we vowed to try them all?" I sound too panicked, I'm sure, and I turn my phone off so she can't catch sight of the series of distress signals I sent out to basically everyone.

"Sounds fun," she says. She's still side-eyeing me. She's still furrowing her brow. "I know we have work to do. On our relationship. But I want to do it. I don't want things to change."

Then you shouldn't have gone and changed everything, I think.

I don't want to talk about us or the relationship or what we are to each other, because the more we talk about her marrying my father, the more real it will become. So I find a smile and imitate a person whose life isn't getting blown up by a beautiful disaster.

"I'm sorry. I'm not a morning person. But sure. We can hang out for a little," I say in slow, measured sentences. Karissa makes me a little breathless.

Maybe she does that to everyone.

"So then we'll dress shop? Today?"

"Aren't you planning on a wedding next summer?" I say.

"Well, sure, but that doesn't mean we can't shop now!" She is brimming with energy. I'll never catch up.

"How about instead I help you with your monologue?" I say. "Aren't you learning a new monologue for auditions?" I want to see her do her acting warm-ups—windmills with her arms and swooping sounds with her mouth, followed by an intensive session of rolling around on the floor. There's nothing quite like watching Karissa roll around on the floor. She's as comfortable as a puppy and emerges vertical and dust-covered and victorious. Her hair turns into a tangled mess, which makes her even prettier, and by the time she is upright, her back is straight in a mathematically perfect way.

I could stand an afternoon with the Karissa that she used to be.

"I'm going to hold off auditioning for a few weeks," she says. "I'm not quite ready to be auditioning right now. But soon."

"Oh."

"Your dad's helping me," she says. I nod but don't know what help Dad could be. "He thinks I could make it in L.A. Or maybe London. There's a lot of theater in London. We're thinking of getting a place."

I want to go back to bed for the rest of my life. But a tiny part of me wonders at Dad changing alongside Karissa. Changing for Karissa. I don't think he's ever thought about moving or supporting or adventuring with his wives and girlfriends. It's a little bit beautiful even if it's mostly awful.

"Dad loves New York" is all I can think to say.

"Well, sure. But what if we could love other things too?" Karissa shrugs like she hasn't asked the world's biggest question, or at least my biggest question. What are the things we are supposed to love the most? And what happens when we want to love other things too?

thirty

Karissa and I go to a street in the East Village that is crowded with bridal shops.

"It's like a fairy tale, right?" she says.

She knows I don't want to answer, but she keeps asking anyway. Like if she says it enough times, I'll give in. It makes me think she doesn't need my actual approval, only the surface of approval.

"I have a secret," she says. "I already booked us an appointment at this one place." She smirks and elbows me like it's all a big joke.

I think it's not cute and it's not okay, but I'm sort of held hostage by her energy and her dead family and the promise that every hour or so I get a moment of the person she was. Plus the tattoo of her own eye on her back and her crazy beaded sandals and the fact that she knows awesome places to get egg sandwiches and coffees, which we did before heading to Wedding Dress Row.

Karissa tries on eight gowns in an hour.

"You must be so happy for your sister," the clerks say, one after the other. I don't tell them she's not my sister.

"You try one on!" Karissa says, twirling around in something full-skirted and skimpy-topped.

"I'm just here for moral support," I say. I try to imitate a person in a movie. I play with the train of the dress Karissa has on, holding it up and dropping it down. Smoothing it out with the palm of my hand.

"No. That's not how it's done. Get her something crazy expensive and crazy beautiful," Karissa says. She slips back into the dressing room, and I try to signal to the clerks that I am seventeen and not in the market for a wedding dress, but they don't listen, and the gown they put in my arms is spectacular. Something a bohemian princess would wear.

"Holy crap," I say. "Are you sure I can put this on?" The clerks nod and smile, but I'm pretty sure it's forced. They do not actually want me trying on gowns. My armpits smell like men's deodorant because I bought the wrong kind, and the rest of me smells like smoke because we split a cig on the walk here.

"Oh my God, did you find the one? Let me see!" Karissa says. She comes out in her underwear. I think the clerks want to shove her back in the room, but they're enchanted by something in her too. Something I used to call magnetism but now I am searching for a new word for.

Danger.

"Clothing!" I say. I don't want to see her in her underwear. But I especially don't want the East Village to see her in her underwear.

Before I have a chance to object, Karissa grabs my hand and drags me into her dressing room with her. It's cramped and absolutely brimming with fancy white fabrics. Karissa is so close she's almost touching, and there's nowhere to look but at her body or the dress.

"Okay, okay, step out and I'll try it on," I say. I take a mini-step backward to get some space, but there's no room, so I collide with all the hanging dresses, tulle and silk and satin and lace coming at me from all sides. It's like we are in the center of a cloud. The puffy kind. Cumulous or whatever.

She squeezes into a stretchy, short dress, the kind of thing a Playboy model would wear to her wedding. I don't make a move to take off my own clothes and try on my own gown. Karissa nods, getting it. Doesn't check herself out in the mirror before stepping out of the dressing room, which I sort of love.

She pulls the curtain closed behind her so that I can change alone. It doesn't feel any less cramped. If anything, the dresses seem to have expanded, ballooned. I am trapped in tulle. It's not easy getting into the dress. There are so many folds in the fabric I can't be sure where my arms or legs go, and it droops on top where my boobs aren't and hugs my hips too tightly. I'm worried little beads are going to fall off from the pressure of my not-rightness, but I step out so that Karissa can see and have her perfect, gown-shopping, best friend moment.

She has her phone out and trained on me, snapping pictures the instant I pull aside the curtain.

"Look at you!" she says, turning the screen to me so that I am face-to-face with myself. I look shocked and pale. The hints of scribbles make my arms looks unwashed. My dirty-blond roots are even more obvious in the ugly overhead lighting. The pink in my hair even sadder, more depleted against the white of the dress. But there's something pretty in the contrast between me and the flounce of the dress.

Maybe not pretty, but interesting.

Karissa wraps her arm around my waist and holds the phone up so she can get us both in the picture. The clerks rush to help, and we have an impromptu photo shoot. It's awkward at first. The dress itches and keeps sliding around on top, the straps falling down every time Karissa moves my body this way or that. But with the clerks egging us on and telling us how beautiful we look, and Karissa's frenetic energy pulsing against my body, it's hard not to get caught up in the fun.

We try on a few more dresses, until each of us ends up in princess-y things. Skirts like bells. Bodices that cling and sparkle, ribbons criss-crossing up the back. Karissa gets behind me and twists my hair on top of my head, so I can see what I would look like if I were a whole different person.

"Gorgeous," she says.

"You too," I say, and it's the truth. We both look kind of incredible as princess brides.

"This is exactly how I always thought this moment would be," Karissa whispers, and it sounds like truth. "We'll take them!"

"You're getting the dress?" I say. I pitch the question up, so it sounds excited, and I wonder how well I'm pulling off this whole maid-of-honor situation.

"We're getting both dresses."

"That doesn't make any sense. I'm not getting married."

"But for someday! Or for pretend! Or prom or a tea party or dancing in a fountain or going to a football game, because why not!" she says, and she giggles that loose, bubbly giggle followed by her patented unexpected snort, and I don't want to be a girl who says no, so I don't say anything.

Karissa has my dad's credit card and a mythical mania and this strong, strong, planetary kind of pull.

Besides, I looked good and strange and dreamy, and that's what my dad gets for marrying a twenty-three-year-old.

thirty-one

The next day, I go to the park at our regular time, not expecting Arizona and Roxanne to be there. It's surprisingly comfortable, the idea of being alone in the park again like I was all year. I'm used to the loneliness, and them being back in town for a couple of months doesn't change that.

In some ways, they're barely here anyway. Or barely here with me, at least. I know for certain that they've hung out a few times without me this summer. I noticed matching tans one day. And a conversation about this Thai place, Republic, that we all used to go to together but they clearly went to alone. The leftovers were in Arizona's fridge.

But here they are with big iced coffees and smiles.

"Let's have a normal day," Roxanne says. "Like, a good day. We can pull that off, right?" She looks from Arizona to me, and I wonder what it's like to be her, always caught in the things that happen between us and around us.

"I could use a normal day," I say. Arizona hands me a to-go cup of hot coffee. She knows that even in the most extreme heat I stick with steamy drinks.

The coffee's good. And being in the park with Arizona and Roxanne is good too. Calm. The eye of a hurricane. Hurricane Karissa. Hurricane Falling in Love.

Roxanne has taken to wearing summer hats. Arizona has taken to wearing enormous sunglasses. I am in flip-flops and jean shorts, like I was last summer and the summer before, because I am the only one of the three of us who knows that whatever you wear this summer will look stupid by next summer, so you might as well wear what's most comfortable.

"I'm sorry. We need to talk about these jean shorts. They are truly, truly disgusting," Roxanne says in her too-loud voice. I hike them up a little, like that will somehow help. "Like, there are strings. Hanging off of them. Long strings. I'm gonna say it. Tampon-esque strings. Your cutoffs are tampon-esque."

"Don't say tampon in public," Arizona says.

"*You* just said it," I say. Roxanne laughs, and Arizona huffs and takes a long sip of iced coffee that results in her bitching about her teeth hurting from the cold. I am so happy not to be Arizona.

"How about sex? Can we talk about sex?" Roxanne says. She's got a smirk on her face, and I finally notice a hickey on her collarbone and specks of last night's mascara gathering in the corners of her eyes.

"No," Arizona says. "Stop trying to rile me up. I get it. You guys are edgy and I'm a prude."

She turns away from us, toward a pack of ladies crossing their legs and checking out one another's manicures.

"I slept with someone last night. Met at a party. Goes to Cornell," Roxanne says. I wasn't invited to the party. I look at Arizona to see if she was there, but she looks shocked, so she must not have been.

"Whose party?" she says.

"Friend of a friend in Chelsea," Roxanne says.

"I would have gone," Arizona says.

"Me too!" I say.

"You were with your roommate, and she gets all weird and possessive," she says to Arizona. "And Mon, I bet you anything you were with your guy. So."

"Bernardo," I say, because they never say his name. "Sorry I'm all in love and doing that whole thing." I'm not sorry, but I feel like there's an empty space where my apology is supposed to be, so I fill it.

"Don't apologize for being in love," Roxanne says.

"Do we have to keep saying they're in love?" Arizona asks.

"I love him."

"You met him, like, yesterday. You know better. Come on," Arizona says.

"Please stop hating the only thing I actually like," I say.

And just like that, I miss Bernardo with as much ferociousness as I missed Arizona and Roxanne all year. I miss him even though I saw him last night, like they assumed. I miss him even though Arizona thinks I barely know him.

Arizona pushes her glasses and watches a violinist gather up coins and lock up his case. It's like a whole performance series out here. As soon as the violinist vacates, a human statue takes over. She's dressed as the Statue of Liberty and is so unmoving it's scary.

Little kids throw things at the statue lady, trying to get her to wince. She doesn't. She stays solid and still. She's sort of incredible. Her eyes don't even blink as almonds and drops of water come flying at her painted face.

"The park doesn't feel the same today," Arizona says. "Maybe I'm over New York."

It's meant to be the meanest thing she can possibly say.

"You need a day on my roof and Mexican and sushi delivery at midnight," Roxanne says. "Then you'll love it again."

When our coffees are gone and the statue lady has been replaced with a little boy break-dancing, we leave. And I call Bernardo. His family's having chicken and rice and beans tonight, and I want to be in that warm house with people who are positive they are doing it right.

thirty-two

"Absolutely not," Bernardo says the next day as we're walking around the Upper East Side, Bernardo in a suit and me in one of Janie's old dresses, like we belong there. We're near my dad's office, heading to this French place I've been going to since I was little and wanted to show Bernardo.

"I don't mean I'd be getting surgery, like, tomorrow," I say. "I'm just wondering if I should consider the possibility." It's getting harder and harder to stop thinking about that photograph. I've been avoiding my father in the house, playing a weird kind of hide-and-seek that he doesn't know is going on. I don't want to see his gaze slip from my eyes to my chin. I don't want to see what I know he's thinking.

"When I was with Casey and after she dumped me, I felt like I had to change everything," Bernardo says. "But you made me feel like I can be who I am. Or we can become new people, but together."

"Casey wanted you to change?" I say.

"I mean, not my chin. But be older. Be different. Have more

direction or something. Be a different kind of better person that she'd like more. It's a losing battle, though."

"I made you dye your hair," I say, covering my face in embarrassment for being every bit as bad as Casey.

"You did not make me dye my hair. You inspired me to be a weirdo," Bernardo says.

I want to cover him in kisses but I can't, because we reach the restaurant and I catch sight of Karissa in the window.

Bernardo hadn't understood why I wanted to come all the way uptown to go to a bistro when there are so many identical French bistros all over the city. I couldn't fully answer except to say I like the predictability of the menus and the always-red chairs and the waiters' accents. So I like Café Moche. Especially for their french fries.

I've known my dad comes here for lunch when he has to work on weekends, so maybe Karissa in the picture window shouldn't be so much of a surprise, but it is. A breathtaking one. I stop Bernardo before he barrels in to say hello and steal some of her fries.

"Jesus," he says, his exclamation for everything from terrible weather to great kissing. "Tiny city we live in, right?" I nod but keep holding him back.

"What's she doing?" I say.

"Probably waiting for your dad?"

As soon as he says it, my dad comes back from the bathroom, and they make out right there in the window. It's disgusting and I turn away. I can almost see Central Park from here. It's a green haze in the distance, and I wish I could leap straight into it. I keep wanting to be somewhere other than the place I am.

Maybe I simply want the summer to be over, even though it's what I waited for all year.

"I'm sorry," Bernardo says, like he's responsible for me witnessing this reality. "It's over. I think they stopped."

I turn back to look at them, hoping they have taken up residence on their own separate sides of the table. I don't even want to see them holding hands after that display. But I catch something else, a last gesture that looks affectionate except for how well I know it.

My father uses two fingers on her jaw and turns her face to the light. Even in the daytime, French bistros manage to stay pretty dim, so he has to move his face closer to hers to see properly, and he does. He inspects her face. Not for loveliness. For flaws.

I know because he's done it to me.

Karissa doesn't wince away from him. She smiles. She nods her head when he's done telling her what I'm sure is a laundry list of things that would make her better. She grips his arm while he's inspecting her.

He is going to change her.

He keeps chipping away at this person I thought I had, and soon she won't even exist.

"You wanna say hi, or no?" Bernardo says. I picture, for a moment, eating burgers and fries and drinking big mugs of latte with Karissa and my dad and my handsome, perfect, crazy, solemn boyfriend. It could almost be nice, but I can't shake the nausea of Karissa giving in to Sean Varren, like the rest of them do.

The sad-happy look on her face isn't something I can look at while eating.

"I hate my father," I say to Bernardo. Karissa's settled back in her chair, but her grip on my dad's forearm hasn't loosened, and she keeps touching her hair and her face like she wants it to stay in place.

"Nah," he says, and I know he's right. He's all I have, parent-wise, and he's good, sometimes. He's even great on occasion. For small spurts of time. For moments.

Across the way there's a whole bunch of scaffolding—buildings getting torn down or built up. I try to remember what used to be under the bars. Maybe a bakery or a frozen yogurt place. Somewhere I used to go when Natasha and I would meet my father after work. Now who knows. It will probably be a bank.

"You know what I love?" I say. "That your dad makes rice every night and guac on Sundays and that you get pizza every Thursday and watch TV with everyone and that your mom grew up with in the place you now live."

I must look like I'm going to throw my shoe through the window or something, because Bernardo holds me unprompted. Pulls me to him. Lifts my face up.

"It looks like something perfect," he says, "but it's not. There's no room there to be your own whole person. They want me to be the oldest kid and not much else. And I don't want pizza every Thursday. Some Thursdays I want sushi. Or steak. Or pancakes for dinner. And guess what? I don't like rice. I don't like rice and beans or knowing what's going to happen next."

"I want to know what's going to happen next," I say.

"I don't," he says. He runs his hand through my hair and smiles at the way it curls and splits and knots.

"I'm tired of everything changing," I say.

"We'll change together, then," he says. And maybe he understands me more than I think. Maybe he has some instinctual blueprint of me. He touches my face but doesn't hold it to the light to examine it. His fingers find their way to my mouth and he traces my lips. Pulls on the bottom one a little. He's about to kiss that same spot, maybe pull on it with his teeth, something I didn't know I'd like so much, but I get an idea and stop him before his lips have landed on mine.

"I should pierce it," I say. I didn't even know the words were in there. I've never wanted a pierced lip.

"Your lip?" Bernardo looks fully surprised. He finishes his journey to my mouth and kisses me so hard I think I might faint. His hands tug at my hair, and I'm glad I've kept it long and messy. There's so much of it for him to pull and play with and weave through his fingers. When we're done, I have the chaos of my hair as proof of passion, and I like it. I won't brush it out when we've broken apart.

"Maybe not my lip," I say, and I can tell from his rare smile that that was the whole point. He likes my lips the way they are. A lot.

He looks at my face for a long time. Pedestrians have to change their paths on the sidewalk. They sigh and their dogs bark and little kids barrel into our legs because we are taking up too much room. It's one of those gorgeous summer weekends and the Upper East Side is packed, absolutely drenched, with men in bright-colored shorts for their weekend-wear and women in expensive sundresses that are meant to look inexpensive. We get whiffs of cologne after terrible cologne, a parade of smells and frustrated noises and elbows and shoulders banging against our bodies, but we don't move until he's done looking.

"I got it," he says. "Nose."

I almost say yes. It feels natural, to let him look at my face and tell me how to change it.

Until it feels awful. I start walking toward the subway and let him follow behind me, asking if I'm going to do it. I get Karissa and my dad out of my head.

"Eyebrow," I say.

"Cool. Me too."

"Really?" I reach behind me for his hand and pull him so we are walking side by side. It's annoying for everyone else on the cramped sidewalk, but I don't care anymore.

Shit, I'm in love.

"You definitely don't have to do it," I say. He'd look good with an eyebrow ring. It would fancy up those serious eyebrows.

"We're in it together," he says.

"I love you," I say. Nothing has ever felt so true or big. Everything is melting away. Or I'm melting into him. Or maybe it's so hot and humid on the streets of New York today that it feels that way, and that's close enough. Maybe we're simply melting, period.

"Let's go say fuck you to the world and pierce our faces," he says, which is basically the same as *I love you too*.

We take the subway down to the East Village and find a place that's the right mixture of dirty and clean.

"Here?" I say. There's graffiti outside, but the pretty kind. The artsy kind. Inside there are chairs that look like they could be in Dirty Versailles—gold arms and red velvet seats—and a neon sign.

"Here," Bernardo says, completely sure of himself. "I've heard of this place. They don't check IDs." I wish I could have a little of what he has, so I launch myself at him and press against him, sucking on his neck a little, like sureness and stability might be something I can extract from that one place.

I've never thought of myself as a girl who would get a facial piercing, but that's sort of the point.

"Do you think Victoria and Veronica will be mad at me?" I say. I'm not sure why I'm even thinking of them now, standing in the doorway of this place. But they're so small, I don't want to freak them out. "Like, will they think I'm a monster or something?"

"Who?" Bernardo says. It hurts, his forgetting. He's the only person in my life who knows them, who's met them, who knows what they mean to me. I need him to know without explanation.

"The girls. Natasha's girls. My, you know, my not-sisters," I say. I should have said sisters. Or stepsisters. Or almost-sisters.

"Oh, of course," Bernardo says. He kisses the place that I'm about to pierce and squeezes me again. "They'll get used to it," he says, a thing I'm not sure is ever true. "This is a you and me thing, anyway. Not a them thing."

I feel a pull of missing them. A gasp of it. Then it's over and I want to be with Bernardo.

I tap my eyebrow when the guy asks me what I want. Bernardo

mimics the gesture. The guy rolls his eyes, but I don't care. He doesn't get it. He doesn't know.

He does me first, then Bernardo. It hurts, and I hadn't realized it would be a real needle. It's not like with ears, where there's a gun punching a hole in your skin. This seems more hard-core.

I feel hard-core. He slips in a silver ring with a shiny red bead. And like that, I'm new. I'm more. He lets me stare at myself in the mirror, and I move my head this way and that, seeing myself from every angle.

Bernardo needs me to hold his hand while his is done, but he doesn't yelp or anything at the pinch. His ring is gold and thicker than mine. I want to play with it. I want to ruffle his hair and touch his face. I want to feel the way he belongs to me.

We walk down the street after and probably aren't getting any more looks than usual, but it feels like they can all see the way we fit together.

thirty-three

When I get home, Karissa is on the couch, blitzed out of her mind and holding her phone in one hand and a lit cigarette that she's not even smoking in the other. I don't tell her I saw her uptown with my father. I don't tell her I saw the way he looked at her face for flaws.

She doesn't notice my eyebrow, but she cuddles into me on the couch.

"My agent dumped me," she says. She shows me an email from the agent who signed her in the fall. Someone fancy and skeezy.

"No way," I say. Karissa isn't a little bit good. She is a lot good. She is arresting.

"He says my look isn't selling," she says. "He says after auditions the feedback is that I'm really good but I don't look the way they need me to look." She's crying not only from her eyes but from her chest.

"But you're gorgeous. He's insane. That's literally insane."

"I'm all wrong," Karissa says. She doesn't move from the couch, doesn't let me move. "Thank God I have you guys," she says after a while. I think she means my dad and me, and the sentence makes me tense up. She doesn't have me. She probably doesn't even really have him.

My shirt's wet, soon, from her crying. She is getting messier and stranger and more and more a part of my life.

I touch my eyebrow ring, like it's a portal to a better place. To Bernardo. To the place I actually now belong.

Dad gets home an hour later. My arm is falling asleep from holding Karissa, and I want to be anywhere but here.

"She needs you!" I say.

"Sean!" Karissa says, and Dad comes right to the couch before putting down his briefcase or pouring himself some water like he usually does.

"What happened here?" he says, and takes her from my shoulder to his own.

"Agent stuff," I say. I get up to go to my room and let them do this alone, because I don't want to see love and kindness and warmth between them. Even if that's what I've always wanted for my father and what I want for Karissa, I hate seeing it between them.

Then they're kissing, and it's even worse seeing it up close and not through a window. I take another few steps away.

"I can't do this all," Karissa says. She is soft and scared. Her voice shakes.

"Sure you can. We're here for you," Dad says. "Right, Montana?"

I don't respond. I can't. I notice a new lamp on the table next to the couch. It gives off an orange-pink light through a thick glass shell. It's odd and shadeless and totally from Karissa's apartment. It is the first new addition to our home.

Soon there will be vintage floral armchairs and gold sheer curtains and beaded pillows and ironic coffee mugs and framed posters instead of original prints.

"I want to be married to you already, you wonderful man," Karissa says.

"Do you now?" he says. I'm going to be sick. I need to leave the room, but I'm compelled to stay. It's an awful thing I can't stop looking at.

"I do," Karissa says, then laughs. "Like *I do*, I do, you know?" She's giggling and my dad's giggling and the sound has the approximate effect of nails on a chalkboard.

"I do," Dad says, all mock serious like he's in his own wedding and yep, that's what he sounds like when he's getting married. I know it well.

"That sounds good," Karissa says. I should leave. I need to leave. I've watched sickly sweet moments like this before, but always with Arizona and always when I didn't know everything about the woman, and always when it was funny instead of terrible.

It's bizarre to think my dad carries this baby-talk-using, skin-crawlingly cutesy side of himself all the time. That it lies dormant in him except when it pops out, surprising me every time.

"Well then, let's do it," Dad says.

Every part of me stops—my brain, my heart, my churning stomach, the world around me.

"What do you mean?" Karissa says, but her voice is so glee-filled I'm sure she knows exactly what he means.

"Let's get married soon. Now. We don't need to wait. We don't need to plan a whole thing. You want to be married already, let's be married already."

"Really?" Karissa says. Her tears are gone, but the mess they made on her face is not. I'm sure she still smells like cigs and maybe wine and me too, from staying against me for so long.

"Really," Dad says. He sounds proud, which is how he always sounds when he feels like he's fixed something. Every time he gets married. Whenever he buys us something expensive and useless when we're sad. When he has news from our mother, like it's an accomplishment for us to get to hear she exists.

This is one of those moments where he thinks he's solving a problem, but he's making it worse.

"You got engaged five minutes ago," I squeak from my place at the bottom of the stairs. "I think that would be a little . . . hard . . . for us . . . to adjust to." It's impossible to piece together a statement explaining something that should be obvious.

I was wrong, the lamp's not the only addition to the apartment. I notice for the first time paint samples on the wall. Coral and violet and mustard yellow.

I don't like any of them. I like the almost-green-but-mostly-gray walls Dad's had forever. He's never let anyone paint.

"You don't get engaged unless you're ready to get married," Dad says.

"Karissa," I say. I think I don't need to say more than her name for her to understand me.

"Montana," she says back. I guess I was wrong.

"This is a lot. At once."

It is the gentlest way I can think of to say it is not okay, it is unacceptable, it is ridiculous. I even say it with a little smile, something warm and easy, a smile I would have given her after a hard scene in class or when we were standing on the corner and she lit my cigarette. It is a smile she knows.

She bursts into tears.

Dad shakes his head at me. At my insensitivity.

Karissa cries even harder, moaning a little. "Even my best friend doesn't understand me," she says, and I try to calculate how very wrong I might have been about her and how truly scary that is.

"I know," Dad says, and I wish I couldn't hear. "I know, I know." He shoos me away with his free hand. Doesn't even look at me.

I take the paint samples off the wall and go upstairs. The tape was too sticky, and some color tore off when I pulled too hard, leaving behind tiny squares of white.

It's a little bit ruined, our home.

July 4

The List of Things to Be Grateful For

1 The little scab near my eyebrow ring. A sign that I did
something real and dangerous and unlikely.

2 The little scab near Bernardo's eyebrow ring. A sign that
we're in it together.

3 Fireworks in the far, far distance, seen from Roxanne's
roof. All four of us watching them together, something we
can agree on. The wonder of colored lights flickering and
thundering in the sky while we sweat and sink into the
summer.

thirty-four

Bernardo goes home to Brooklyn after the Fourth of July finale is over—dozens and dozens of fireworks toppling over each other in the sky until the whole thing is so lit up and crowded that we can mostly see flashes of light, smoke, and nothing else.

Arizona, Roxanne, and I head to our place and have a sleepover after, all of us bundled in the basement like the old days. Karissa's upstairs with my father and doesn't wander down all night, and Arizona, Roxanne, and I stay up forever with a six-pack and cigarettes, so it's a mellow end of the night and Arizona doesn't even make me defend my eyebrow ring.

"How soon is soon?" Roxanne says when I tell them about the conversation Dad and Karissa had on Saturday in front of me. It feels so effing good to share it with them that I don't even wonder what kind of fallout it might have. I couldn't hold on to it all by myself.

"Like a few weeks, I think," I say. "She has a dress already." I don't tell them how I know that.

Roxanne shivers and rubs her goose-bumped arms. She used to do the same thing when we'd tell each other scary stories with flashlights under our chins. She scares easily. We scare her.

"I'm talking to her tomorrow," Arizona says before we fall asleep.

"About what?" I say. I didn't drink enough beer to make me drunk, but I'm close to sleep with one toe in a dream about a forest and a bear and a chandelier.

"If she would leave, everything would be okay," Arizona says. "With Dad. With us. With me. We'd all be okay. I'm sure." Or it could be the bear that says it. It's hard to tell.

"Be careful," I say, because I've seen something unhinged in Karissa that is too hard to explain when I'm half-asleep.

Arizona scoffs, misunderstanding. "Everything with Dad would be fine without these women," she says. I think. Maybe the bear in my dream said it, not Arizona at all, because it sounds like something that would be said in a dream. Something we want to be true but probably isn't.

When we wake up in the morning, I don't have time to try to discern dream from reality. There's a lot of noise and smells and Top 40 pop music coming from the kitchen, so we wander up without the proper transition from sleeping to waking. We emerge from the basement in our clothes from the night before and reeking a little of the things we did. Karissa practically attacks us with friendliness.

"You're finally up! Been waiting for you so we can have a girls' afternoon!" she says. Arizona recoils from the sound, and I back off from the smell on Karissa's breath—sour margarita mix. It's past noon but not by much, and she has that shiny-eyed look she did the morning she came into my room and kidnapped me. "My mom and dad always used to do margaritas the day after the Fourth of July! It was a total family tradition," she says.

Of course. There's always a corresponding family memory whenever things are awkward for her. I wonder if it's the same for Arizona when she's at college. If everything reminds her of me. I hope that's the case.

I rub my eyes and try to adjust for the hundredth time to Karissa in our kitchen. I wonder if it will ever feel normal. Seeing her now I want to shove her back into her own kitchen, her own space.

"You are getting so punked out!" she says, touching my eyebrow ring. "I've always wanted to do that. Stupid acting."

"Stupid acting," I repeat like a robot.

"I love you," she says, and it's light, with a giggle, the kind of *love you!* I've written at the ends of text messages or said when hugging someone good-bye even if I haven't meant it.

But still. I don't want to hear it.

Arizona looks like she is getting strangled, and I guess she sort of is.

"I should go home," Roxanne says. They see the strangeness in Karissa's eyes too—something in between elation and depression—a sparkle that could be tears or joy. It's uncomfortable, not knowing where someone is on that spectrum.

"I'm not really in the mood for drinking," Arizona says.

"I can make a virgin!" Karissa says. She's plastered. The wedding gowns we bought are hanging from the curtain rod by the fridge. She's unzipped them so they are on full display, and I wonder if she wants Arizona to be pissed, or if she's actually that naive.

I'm a little bit terrified about the possibility that Karissa is going to tell them all about our shopping trip and that the extra wedding gown is mine.

"Look," Arizona says. "If we talk, will you remember what we talked about when you sober up?" She's looking at the dresses but talking to Karissa. "Or are you too blasted? Are you, like, blackout right now? Or can we do a conversation?"

I'm vibrating inside, like my stomach and heart and spine are leaning against a washing machine on a heavy cycle.

"You don't want to start the day with serious talk, do you?" Karissa says, making her eyes wide and licking salt from her fingers. "I am not in serious talk mode right now, ladyfriend." She pours herself another margarita and slides one across the counter to me too. With Arizona and Karissa both looking at me, it's impossible to decide if sipping is a good idea. I roll the glass between the palms of my hands instead. Seems like a compromise. "My dad had a saying—margaritas and bad moods don't mix," Karissa says. I cringe.

"Please don't call me ladyfriend," Arizona says. When she and I shared a room years ago, she drew a line in thick black marker across our light-green rug. One side was mine, one side was hers, and we weren't allowed to cross the line. I feel like Arizona has her marker out again today, and she's drawing another thick, uncrossable line.

"It can be a really good idea to talk things through," Roxanne says. I think she and Arizona have rehearsed versions of this scenario. They seem to be unsurprised by the twists and turns.

Roxanne takes another step toward the door, and I wonder when her cue to leave is.

And why I don't know the script.

"Well, okay then," Karissa says. She makes a big show out of emptying her margarita into the sink. "We can talk, but I won't go against my late father, as I'm sure you understand." She pouts. I don't like it. I can't stop cringing. I'm getting hiccups in my stomach, a new sensation that feels a lot like nervous anticipation for something awful.

"We need to zip the garment bags up first. And you really need two?" Arizona says, gesturing to the gowns. "You already planning the second wedding? With husband number two?" She puts a hand on her chest to stop herself from saying more. "Shit. Sorry. I want to talk nicely. I'm sorry. Okay. Let me start over, but can we zip those up first, because they're distracting me."

Karissa blinks and gets this funny Zen look on her face.

"Sure. Let's start over. Arizona, can I get you a drink?" she says. She has the beginning of a smile on her lips, but she doesn't let it come through fully. It's a power move, like she'll forgive Arizona if Arizona will take one.

Arizona is desperate to say no, but yes is easier.

"Thank you. That's nice," Arizona says, and Karissa pours her a margarita. Pours herself one too, even after the whole show of pouring it out. She crosses her arms and watches Arizona take a sip. Roxanne clears her throat, and I look at my phone and try to think of a succinct way to alert Bernardo to the massive power struggle quietly going down in my kitchen. Arizona sort of sputters on the alcohol or the salt or the lemon-lime sourness of the drink. Karissa zips up the dresses, and Arizona relaxes a little in spite of herself. Something bad is happening.

"You wanted to chat about something?" Karissa says, like all is right with the world. There's a glimmer of the person she was before. Cool. At ease. Open and wounded and pretty and wild. She pulls up a bar stool, offers one to Arizona. Leans in too far, aggressively far, to hear her speak. Their faces are inches away from each other. She puts a hand on Arizona's skinny arm. "Let's have a conversation. You liking your drink?"

Arizona takes another strained sip. Nods and musters a weak smile. Probably silently hates herself.

"Don't marry my dad," Arizona says.

Roxanne lets out a huge exhale and I drink, a long painful suck on the rim. Karissa nods and leans forward one more precarious inch like she's super, super interested. She knew this was coming.

"I see, tell me more," she says. I've seen Karissa plenty drunk before. But I've never seen her like this.

"Don't do it," Arizona says again. "It will destroy my relationship with him, and the marriage is gonna last, like, two years tops anyways, and you're going to hate yourself and he's a terrible husband, and I will make your life hell if you do. So I'm asking you. Girl to girl.

Like, honestly. For your own good. Because he has only had terrible marriages. Don't do it."

I keep going on my margarita and pour myself another as soon as the first one is done. Karissa doesn't say anything but stares at Arizona until she drinks more. The silence is excruciating.

"Maybe we should go out?" Roxanne interrupts the quiet. "We could just, like, walk? Around?"

"Keep drinking, Arizona," Karissa says. I don't know why my sister's still listening to the command, except that maybe she thinks if she obeys everything else Karissa says, Karissa will give in and leave my father. It's terrible logic, but Arizona has a desperate, delusional look on her face, almost as desperate and delusional as Karissa's, which begs the question: Is this how my father makes women feel?

I feel a little desperate and delusional this summer too.

"You don't need him," Arizona says. "You're . . . look at you. You're some goddess. Who should be with, like, a puppeteer. Or a poet. Or a merman. You don't need to be with my father. He'll ruin you. You've lost so much in your life. And you will lose him too. I don't want to see that happen to you."

"Don't pretend to give a shit about me," Karissa says. "Don't say awful things and pretend it's because you're such a nice person."

Arizona picks at her knuckle, even though there's nothing there to pick.

"Don't pretend you know what my relationship with Sean is simply because you don't like it. I don't know about these other women. But with me he's kind. And accepting. And my life has been a mess.

I lost my family. And I can't book a fucking acting role to save my life. And I've hated who I am when I look in the mirror, even when other people are looking at me or wanting me or whatever. I sat in an old apartment with no working heat, drinking two-dollar wine with coked-up friends who have no direction. Then I found Sean. And we met halfway. And look at him! Do you even look at your father? He's happy. You can't tell me he's not happy!"

"He's happy now," Arizona says. She's getting a little sloshed. Drinking too fast on an empty stomach is a bad idea. "Being happy now isn't the same thing as being happy forever."

"News flash. No one's happy forever," Karissa says. It's something true and terrible. It takes my breath away. It makes me take a long sip of margarita. In the cross fire between Arizona and Karissa there's no right and wrong, only horribly depressing. "We're all trying not to be lonely. And you, Arizona. You are fucking lonely." She pours herself more margarita and smiles the smile of someone who is winning.

"Hey now," Roxanne says, which is nothing really.

"Arizona has me," I say, because it finally clicks that I have to pick a side this morning. And it's no contest. I pick her.

Karissa looks back and forth from me to Arizona like she's trying to see what's between us. I hate myself for ever telling her about missing my sister, about not feeling close to my sister, about wondering if my sister and I will ever feel the same way again. I hate so many things I said when I didn't know Karissa was dating my father. It was such an unfair place we were in. She was in one relationship, and

I was in a whole other relationship, a different reality. And I guess that's what betrayal looks like.

"I'm not like you," Arizona says. She puts down her margarita and gets back in Karissa's face. "I can't compete with someone like you. I get that now. I thought I could maybe, but obviously that's not in the cards for me. I don't have my dad, I guess, and I don't have some Bernardo loving every tiny thing about me." She's getting choked up, and it's so strange she'd even bring him up, because even though it feels like he's existed for me forever, he's barely been around. "We can't all be strange and lovable and quirky and free, okay?" She stops herself, realizing she's said too much. She's given Karissa power in the very moment that she was supposed to be taking control of the situation.

The words Karissa said—*you are fucking lonely*—echo in the kitchen. They did something to my sister.

"You're great, Arizona," I say. It's so quiet and small and pointless. It's so much tinier than the things I should say to her. I wonder if she has a friend at Colby who could say something more powerful. Someone who knows her better these days. Someone who isn't a little bit angry at her still.

"You're sad," Karissa says. It's cruel and cutting. It gets worse. "Your father loves me in a way that makes you jealous, and I get that. I so, so get that. You wish he loved you more. Loved you enough to do whatever you say. He doesn't."

Me, Arizona, and Roxanne inhale together. A sharp sting of a breath. Karissa has a wicked look on her face, like she's won something none of us understood was up for grabs.

"My father would have done anything for me," Karissa goes on. She sees the looks on our faces, and instead of them holding her back, they propel her forward. "He told me to stay home the day they died. Said it was too dangerous to drive. He protected me. That's love.

"My father said I was the most beautiful girl in the world," Karissa continues. I can't believe she's not stopping. The air in the room is thick with heat and shock.

Karissa's going for the kill, and it's an awful thing to have to watch.

"I don't trust you," Arizona says when she's regained the balance she lost from how deep the words cut. She downs the rest of her drink without being instructed to. She slams it on the counter when she's finished. "I don't trust you and I don't like you and you're not going to like how this all goes down."

"Neither are you, honeybun," Karissa says. She pours yet another drink. She's drowning in margaritas, and I wonder if she'll even remember all of this tomorrow.

I will. I won't forget.

thirty-five

I spend the rest of the day and that night at Arizona's apartment, but by the following evening Karissa is blowing up my phone with desperate texts, and I can't stop myself from meeting up with her.

She brings an orchid.

"It's special," she says. "It's sensitive."

"I'm not sure I have a green thumb," I say.

"I'll help you with it," she says. It's a beautiful and weighty peace offering. Janie was the wife with the green thumb, and it's funny to be thinking of her now, but I can't stop the rush of thoughts. I miss her little boys and Saturday mornings we spent at a community garden planting vegetables.

I wonder what she would think of Karissa. What she would think of me now.

I wouldn't mind seeing her. Even after the Tess fiasco. I wouldn't mind her knowing who I am now. Maybe it would complete something—me seeing all the stepmoms.

Karissa orders a martini. A French one.

I don't get a drink.

Dirty Versailles is slow and grimy tonight. It was so fun a few weeks ago, but tonight my bra's too tight and Karissa has that freaking rock on her finger. Someone vacuumed all the fun out.

"I'm over your sister," Karissa says. "Do we have to keep her?"

"Hey," I say. It's not exactly a strong response, but it's something. I try again. "You crossed a line. And my sister and I are a team. Okay?"

"I know, I know. She's wonderful. We love her. But aren't you glad you have me and Bernardo? That's how I feel about your dad."

"I'd like to have everyone," I say, but it tastes bad. It is Arizona and me against the stepmothers. That's what it is supposed to be.

Although I guess if I'm honest with myself, it never has been. Not since I made an imprint of my sleeping body on Natasha's couch. Not since I hugged her kids and babysat them and pretended to be somewhere else. I've been betraying Arizona all along.

I have absolutely zero idea what I'm doing, and seeing Karissa face-to-face right now feels all wrong. Like I'm not Montana anymore at all. I eye the door. It'd be easy to sneak out and make my way back to Arizona's. Bring her a carton of ice cream or a pizza.

"Another!" Karissa calls to her bartender.

I watch her get drunk, and I sip on a glass of water and then an orange juice to keep things interesting.

"Are you looking for a new agent?" I ask, wanting to talk about things that aren't about Us.

"Soon, soon," she says. She grins. "I'm going to be the girl they want me to be." I think that's what she says, but the words are sloshed and jumbled. Her eyes are unfocused.

"I bet you'll be famous someday," I say, and this at least I mean. All the things I've started to find wrong with her don't mean she's not crazy talented and impossible to stop watching.

"Maybe I'll be the girl Arizona wants me to be, too," she says, nonsensically. There is no version of Karissa that Arizona would be okay with. I take the smallest sip of Karissa's French martini, and I'm surprised by this fizz and the sweetness. It's nothing like what she made me and Bernardo that night in the basement. It's better, lovelier, fancier, more compelling. I could get used to it.

"Look," I say at last, part of me still watching the exit, willing my limbs to take me there. "Maybe you could at least wait? On the wedding? I know we keep saying it and it's a total broken record situation, but it would help so much if you and Dad would slow down and breathe and let us adjust and make sure you actually love each other."

"Don't pretend you don't understand love," Karissa says. "I know you do. I've seen it. We're the same. We'd do anything for it." She reaches out and touches my eyebrow ring. It's still sore, and her finger on it hurts, sends a wave of pain behind my eye.

I miss Bernardo like he's a limb, and I'm also certain that our love is nothing like whatever she and my father have.

I should have gotten drunk.

I also should know better. I should know better, but when Karissa and I leave, I walk us up the path Natasha and I walk with the girls when we're trying to get them to fall asleep in their stroller.

And maybe it's what I wanted or maybe it's the exact last thing I ever hoped would happen, but we run into them. I don't see them until they're close. Natasha's in pajamas and I'm maybe vicariously drunk through Karissa or potentially so mad and confused that I feel drunk.

She sees me, though. And sees Karissa's drunken stumble.

"Montana?" Natasha says.

"Monana!" Victoria calls out. Veronica screeches and reaches for me. I can't breathe. I don't reach back.

"Hi," I say. Not *Hi, Natasha*. I guess some desperate part of me believes I can get out of this situation unscarred.

"Hi!" Veronica says. She has a tiny vocabulary, but what words she has she loves.

"Hi," Karissa says. She wipes her mouth with her hand, like a little spit maybe came out on her greeting. "Who are you people?"

Natasha squints. "Who are you?" she says. "Friend of Montana's?" I almost can't believe that Karissa and I still look a little like we belong to each other, like we fit. I feel so far away from that time.

"I'm Karissa!" she says. She trips over her own feet to grab Natasha's hand, and I'm collapsing inside. I am red and wish I'd drunk my weight in vanilla vodka at Dirty Versailles. I grab my phone in my pocket like it's Bernardo's hand and think I can't manage the world without him sometimes. Not when it's like this—tense and ready to fall to pieces.

"So this is Karissa," Natasha says. I shake my head at her, begging her silently not to tell Karissa who she is. I'm clenching my jaw so hard I can't open it to speak. If I grind my teeth hard enough, maybe I'll magically leave this place, like Dorothy clicking her heels. I have to believe there's a miraculous escape.

"This is Karissa!" Karissa says. Her drunkenness hits every sense. You can see it, smell it, hear it, touch it. I'm sure my dad will taste it later if he has his mouth near hers.

"Okay, well, good to see you guys!" I say.

"Monana!!!!" Victoria says, loud and insistent and undeniable.

"I'm Natasha," Natasha says. "I'm sure you've heard of me."

Karissa is the worst amount of drunk. Too drunk to be presentable, but not drunk enough to miss what's happening. She looks at the girls and at me and back to the girls.

"They know your name," she says.

"Monana!" Victoria says again.

Karissa looks Natasha over like she has all the time in the world. Like she could take notes on her if she felt like it. Open up a notebook and go for it, right here and now.

"And how's Sean?" Natasha says, not wincing or shying away from Karissa's gaze. If anything, she sticks her chest out more. Even messy and late night and mother-y, she's hot in the Sean Varren wife way.

"Happiest he's ever been," Drunk Karissa says. Drunk Karissa wants to be strong and powerful and messing with Natasha. Drunk Karissa is shooting eye-daggers my way every few moments, too. Drunk Karissa can't stay steady. She swings like a pendulum, back and forth and all around.

"Montana? I'll see you soon, I hope? The girls would love to spend another day in the park with you," Natasha says.

"Montana and I love going to the park!" Karissa says.

I am territory. I am a thing to put flags in. They want to claim me as their own. It's a whole new thing. I am used to being the thing abandoned. A left-behind spare sock or a toy you outgrow but sort of vaguely remember as symbolic of some time in your life. I am Montana who watches Tess move out or Montana who gets one card a year from her mother or Montana whose dad wishes she had a different shape or Montana whose sister has a better time without her.

"One of the last times Montana saw her mother was at the park," Natasha says, because even if Karissa knows me in the wildest ways, Natasha knows me deepest. She's read the lists, she knows everything that's ever made me happy or grateful or nostalgic. She knows I sat and watched cupcakes float in the fountain and that I'm grateful that I remember the moment so clearly.

I have never seen Natasha petty like this until I realize of course I have. When Natasha was with my father, she'd make sure we knew that she knew him best. "That's not his favorite tie," she said to me once when I brought him what I thought was his favorite tie—a purple one I'd given him for Christmas. "Your father prefers red."

It's not like I've forgotten the things I used to hate about Natasha or the way she made me feel when she lived in our apartment and tried to change us. But I let those memories fade a little, and now there's the outline of the person she used to be, and she never did get her implants taken out, and she's grasping onto me and some life we had together, and I guess maybe people change but they also don't.

"Montana and I don't live in the past," Karissa says. She puts an arm around my shoulder. She smells sweet and alcohol-y. "We have adventures in the here and now."

I shrink away from her. I don't want to be a thing they both own. I don't even want to be a thing Bernardo owns, a piece of a whole. Even though I miss it so desperately, I'm not even sure I want to be part of a set of sisters, at the end of the day. I want to be whole, all on my own.

Natasha narrows her gaze. She sniffs the air, maybe seeing if I'm drunk too. Sussing out what these adventures might be. She stands in front of the stroller instead of behind it, blocking the girls from Karissa or, maybe, from me.

Another flash of memory: Natasha sniffing at my father's collar, wondering if he'd been with another woman. The kind of sick that made me feel.

"You're a drop in the bucket," she whispers to Karissa. "Don't you forget it," she says to me. I am the rope in a game of tug-of-war. They both want me, but neither of them really wants me. They just want to win.

"So were you," Karissa says.

We're close to home, and Karissa's smoking what I assume must be the world's last cigarette by the way she's hoarding it.

"Hey, me too," I say, and reach for it.

"I thought you were all good now," she says. She doesn't give me a drag. She scarfs the rest down, quick, unpleasant inhales and exhales, and pounds it with her heel into the pavement. "What the hell have you been up to? What was that?"

"You're drunk," I say. We're a block away from the apartment, and we can't get there soon enough.

"They know you," Karissa says. "They know you well. You said you hated all your dad's exes. He told me that too. You're not in touch. We're starting fresh. I'm not like any of the rest of them. I mean, I'm not making this crap up. Those are things that came out of your mouth. And out of your dad's mouth. Those are things that were said."

"I'm allowed," I say, but my voice is small and meaningless next to her.

"Do you even want me in your family?" Karissa says. It's not safe to answer. I never said I wanted her to be my stepmom. I only ever wanted her to be my friend or my fearless leader, the girl with the cool hair and the cool clothes and the perfectly imperfect smile who I could have adventures with. "You're so fucking greedy. Some of us would settle for one moment with their mother, one instant looking at their sister or father again. And you run around needing more, more, more, *lying* to me. You're a huge LIAR!"

Her arms are making wild swinging gestures, and I dart a little to avoid them.

No one notices.

"I see her sometimes," I say. I reach out to bring one of Karissa's arms down to her waist, but it's too out of control and I leap back. "And her kids and whatever, it's nothing, it's a thing I do when I need mom stuff. It has literally zero to do with you. Zero."

"It has everything to do with me! Are you crazy? ARE YOU

CRAZY?" The question should be asked of her, honestly, but I don't say that. A bike delivery dude rushes by us and Karissa yells after him too, angry at the world. "You and your fucking sister! So selfish! So unfair!" The words are fast and furious and so much louder than I've ever heard her, and it's disorienting to be called this many names in such a short period of time. To have a kind of consensus between her and Tess, that Arizona and I are awful.

"Arizona doesn't know," I mumble. "It's my thing. It's mine."

Karissa softens a little at that.

"Arizona doesn't know?" she says.

"Please don't tell her."

"It's between us?" Karissa says. Her face is nearly familiar again, almost becoming a recognizable set of features in an arrangement I have seen before.

I feel used. Like one of the old cashmere coats at the thrift store I went to with Bernardo. Something to be tried on and left behind. Something that's been worn by a million variations of the same type of person, who think it's all sort of a joke.

My mind rushes with metaphors when I'm overwhelmed. And I am so, so overwhelmed.

"Yep," I say.

Karissa nods and thinks. A little rain starts to fall. Summer-in-the-city rain, which is light and misty and makes my hair feel thick and frizzy on contact. It's getting ugly out here, summer turning the way it always does away from sun and freshness into something fuzzy and uncomfortable and smelling like the big bags of garbage they haven't picked up yet.

"Okay. Well. It's me or her," Karissa says. I need to know exactly how drunk she is.

"You're leaving my dad if I don't stop seeing Natasha? What does that even mean?" I say.

I try walking up the stoop to our apartment so that at least we can fight under the miniature awning, but Karissa stops me.

"No. We're doing this here," she says. She takes out a cig and tries lighting it, but either the lighter is running low on fluid or it's too wet to get it going. The thing is probably soggy in her mouth already. "Your dad barely remembers being with her," Karissa says. "He's shut it all out. It was all a big mistake. You should be moving on too." It is impossible that Karissa would know more about this than I would, but she's certainly proclaiming to.

The first part rings true. Dad doesn't do memories.

"Did he ever tell you about the gift certificate she gave us? They gave us?" I say. I can barely get the words *gift certificate* out. They catch in my throat and burn like a summer cold caught in there.

"I don't know what you're talking about. But you need to be staying away from her. Do you have any idea what this would do to your father? You can't decide to invite her back in. It's unfair."

There are one million things to say about my dad doing that exact thing to me, not the other way around, but I can't put words to it all. That he's allowed to change everything but I'm not allowed to change anything. That it's my job to roll with whatever new family construction he comes up with, no matter how much it hurts. And that I'm expected to let it all go whenever he says it's over.

"Look. I know things have been hard lately," Karissa says. She takes a deep breath and her cig finally gets lit and she blows a whole bunch of smoke into the sky. It only makes the sidewalk hotter and more insufferable. "I know we don't know how to fit together quite yet. And that I'm a little off. But you know me. Remember?"

I do remember.

"Remember that scene we did together in class? Those long nights we spent at the studio rehearsing the shit out of it? How fun that was?"

Yes, I do.

"Remember convincing Donna to let us all order Ethiopian food when everyone was really cranky that one day? Teaching them all to eat with the spongy bread?"

Yes, I do.

"Remember when I took you swing dancing?"

I do.

"Remember when we hung out on Valentine's Day and made each other Valentines and I told you about every guy I ever loved?"

I do.

"Those were real things," Karissa says.

I shake my head. They were real, but they're not anymore. They're real, but they don't mean what they used to.

We finally make our way up the steps, under the awning.

"I can't go inside until we're okay," Karissa says. "Until you remember that you love me."

My head hurts.

"We can't go inside until you choose me."

We stand on the stoop for a long, long time. Karissa's face gets lit every few seconds by passing cars, and she's chain-smoking and I'm chain secondhand smoking and about a thousand conversations pass in front of us but we don't speak.

"Okay," I say at last, because I can't stand the gross weather anymore and Karissa reminded me about one more day—the one I came in crying that Tess was leaving, and she bought me hot chocolate and listened to me explain the way it feels to have something taken away that you weren't totally sure you wanted but that you were trying to want.

"Let me in," she says.

"Okay," I say, and we go inside where it's air-conditioned and my dad's white noise machine is humming the perfect non-sound and he's left out apple and cheddar sandwiches for us both.

July 9

The List of Things to Be Grateful For

1 Pasta for breakfast.

2 French toast for dinner.

3 The sunset, as seen from Battery Park with Bernardo.

thirty-six

Days later, when the heat wave has passed, Bernardo and I are sitting in my basement, drinking white wine and smoking ridiculous clove cigarettes, and he asks what my dad did with all the old rings.

"Do the women keep them?" Bernardo asks. "Do they keep everything he gives them?"

"I mean, the boobs for sure. And the new catlike faces."

When Bernardo thinks something I say is funny, he kisses me instead of laughing. It's one of the million things I love about him. I find something new every day, practically. The texture of his hair on a particularly humid afternoon. The way his lips move a little when he reads the back of a book. I love lying on a blanket in the park in his arms while he runs his fingers up and down my spine. I even love the noise my phone makes when he's texting me. It sounds different, somehow, that *ding ding!* when I know it's him.

It's all stuff I can't tell Arizona and Roxanne, exactly. Things that are too small or cheesy or random to say when they ask me how it's going with him.

"What's gonna happen with Karissa?" he says.

"Maybe she'll surprise me," I say. "Maybe it will be okay."

"Natasha turned out okay," he says. He rubs my back, and any other day it would be the perfect thing to say, but I'm trying to let go of Natasha, in my head first, and then I'll do it in reality. I'm trying to give Karissa what she wants.

Because yesterday we had coffee on the roof and got tans, and the day before we drank white wine at my favorite movie theater, the Angelika, from thermoses, and laughed at a documentary about supermodels, and those are things that make it seem like it could be okay, even if there's a snaky feeling in the pit of my stomach that tells me it's all wrong and even if every few hours something is dark and strange on her face. And because the real truth is that I'm afraid of what she'll do with the secret I've been keeping. I'm afraid of Karissa.

Bernardo's eyebrow ring scrapes my forehead a little when we kiss. "You are the best kisser," I say.

"You too," he says before kissing me again.

"Better than Casey?" I say. I say it because I'm drunk and lost in the kissing and because he teared up a little when we were in Battery Park the other evening. I asked him why, and he said he and Casey used to go there together.

"You miss her?" I asked.

"Sometimes," he said, and I thought it would hurt except it was so real and true that I didn't mind. It was better than pretending she'd never existed or never mattered.

"I decided something," Bernardo says now, and I'm worried he's decided he's not really ready to love someone again. "I'm over her. In the real way. In the over-over way. In the I-don't-miss-her-anymore way."

"But in Battery Park—," I say. I don't want to hear a lie that is simply easier than the truth.

"That was the last little bit of feelings for her," he says. "That was it. I'm not sad about her anymore."

I trust him so deeply that when he says it's over, I know she's gone and there's only us.

"Bye, Casey," I say, waving at some ghost of a memory of her.

"Bye, Casey," he says, waving at the things he loved about her that have stopped mattering.

"I love you," I say to him in the simplest, clearest voice I have.

"But seriously, Mon, does the dude have a ring collection, like, in his sock drawer?" Bernardo says. The words are thick, but I like the way his hand moves from my knee to my hip bone. It makes me feel a little like a cat, which isn't the worst way to feel when the rest of the time you feel like a mouse.

I adjust his glasses and shiver at how close it makes me feel to him.

"I'm sure he returns them. Or sells them to some diamond expert. Or, like, puts them in a safe at the bank," I say. I'm actually not sure about this at all, so I add it to the list of things I don't know or don't understand about my father.

"Your dad is not selling those rings. He's classy and shit," Bernardo says. I've noticed he never swears, so him saying *shit* is a mini-revelation, one more thing to fall in love with. It's amazing how many things you can love about one person.

I almost understand my father in this moment. Almost. I get how sudden and drastic the feelings come on when you meet someone you like, and the pull to tie it all down and guarantee that it won't ever go away. I have never felt more feelings than right this second. I'd like to tie Bernardo here. Both of us. I'd like to tie us to this moment, anchor us to each other and how it feels to be in love in the summer in New York City when you're seventeen and pink-haired and braver than you were before.

We are fixing each other's broken parts but not in the manic temporary way my dad and his wives and girlfriends do. I can finally un-hear Arizona's voice in my head about *too fast* and *too much like Dad* and *delusional* and *don't know what love is.*

"Is Karissa's ring the craziest? Because that thing is crazy," Bernardo says. "That's what you should have. Something crazy." He keeps drinking, even though we're past the point of no return. So I keep drinking too. I don't mind being dizzy when I'm with him. I'm already dizzy around him, even sober, so it almost evens out. Like a double negative or whatever.

I have the best thoughts when I'm drunk.

I smile and drink more wine and take the cigarette from between his fingers and put it between mine because I want our mouths to taste the same. I want to be in that cloud of smoke with him.

Plus, I am cool when I smoke. I'm a girl in a movie.

"Maybe he lets the ladies keep them." I never know what to call my dad's exes, so I'm always trying different phrases. The exes. The ladies. The Sean Varren Club. Fakes. "That would be classy, right?"

"Let's look," Bernardo says.

"Look in my father's sock drawer?" I say. I cock my head and take another drag and put the cig back into Bernardo's mouth, like a distraction.

"Worth a shot, right?"

I can't stop laughing. Love and wine make me laugh. Bernardo, of course, doesn't laugh, but he looks content watching me.

"You better not be plotting a heist of my father's diamonds and socks," I say. I lean back on the couch, which is too stiff and too leathery to be comfortable. It squeaks under my bare legs, and I can't stop laughing.

Bernardo moves closer to me. He stubs out the cigarette in the crystal ashtray on the coffee table and looks at me like I'm beautiful, like even the parts of me that are not so great are actually amazing. He looks at each part of my face, feature by feature, and does these mini-sighs each time his gaze shifts.

He moves his hand from my thigh to my face, and the other behind my neck. "I want you to have one," he says. "I think we should do it."

"Do it?" I say, trying not to squint in confusion or drunkenness.

"We should get you a ring."

"Like a *ring* ring?" I say. I laugh because seventeen-year-olds don't get rings. I look very closely at his face to determine exactly how drunk he actually is. I can't stop laughing. Bernardo is serious and I'm a mess of feelings, plus my head is heavy, heavy, heavy.

"You're drunk," I say. It's a fact, and it's the only explanation for what we are talking about.

"We're drunk," he says.

It's nice, being a we.

"When your dad was proposing, it hit me. He's done it, like, a million times, but he still believes. That's cool. And, like, getting married doesn't make sense for anyone, which means it makes sense for everyone," Bernardo says. He's smart; it's one of the things I love about him. Smart and deep and romantic, and I am four-leaf-clover, rabbit-foot, double-rainbow lucky. I drink some more wine, dizzy from the strangeness of what I guess is a proposal.

I'm seventeen, I say in my head over and over, but I don't say it out loud. Maybe because I'm sort of over being seventeen. I don't feel seventeen. The way I love him isn't the way seventeen-year-olds love.

I think about my father on one knee, proposing to Natasha. Or the photograph of him and my mom on their wedding day, holding hands on the beach like the world made sense.

I wonder if showing Bernardo that picture would make him feel the same weird tangle of feelings—hope and hopelessness, fear and excitement. Belief and faithlessness. Wonder and terror.

"You're insane. And adorable. And you know, someday, obviously," I say. "Oh! What about a promise ring? Roxanne had one of those once with the guy she dated who had a mohawk and a coke problem. But they got a promise ring. It was the Irish kind—a claddagh ring. It was cool."

"And they broke up," Bernardo finishes. "And it was like a joke, right? Like, their parents thought it was totally adorable?"

"Sure," I say. Roxanne's mom gave one of those soft, sweet laughs and said she'd had a boyfriend who got her one when she was young too. She said it like we'd all understand how silly we were when we'd grown up. Roxanne hated her for it, but she was right. A promise ring doesn't mean anything. It doesn't have an impact. It isn't a real thing. "Yeah. You're right. It's like a kind of joke to the rest of the world."

"We're not a joke," Bernardo says. "We're not high school sweethearts. We're not Roxanne and her coked-out boyfriend." He puts his hands on my face. My cheeks are cupped in his palms. He is breathing hard, and soon I am too. "I think I love you more than most people love other people. I want us to be married. You're going to be eighteen in a few months. And why be jealous of people who do romantic and crazy things when we could do those things ourselves? Why not be the people in the books and movies and in our heads?"

I don't know if I understand or agree or even hear Bernardo over the buzzing in my head and heart.

I wonder what he's been reading, which characters he's jealous of. Which love story he thinks we could rival.

"I saw your list of things, the gratitude diary thing," Bernardo goes on. "I know I shouldn't have looked, but I will show you all of mine. I've been doing it, like Natasha told me to."

I'm speechless. I try to remember everything I've written in those pages, so I know how much he's seen of me.

"Those aren't for you," I say. I wonder if more wine is going to make it better or worse. I take a few sips to find out. "I read you the ones I wanted you to read, but the rest weren't for you."

I'm not sure I like being seen. Not so fully.

"You show them to Natasha, you said." He sounds genuinely confused, like he must be missing something. Bernardo doesn't let go of my face, even though I'm sure it's getting hot under his hands. I'm blushing with confusion. "You showed them to me. We know everything about each other. That's why I was so honest about Casey."

"That's different," I say, trying to find a voice under the love and the wine and the lost feeling of my world changing. It's hard.

"You can't be closer to Natasha than you are to me," he says. It's weird, because it's the second time in three days that someone has said essentially that to me. I get cold inside; I don't want Bernardo and Karissa to have anything in common right now.

"I'm not. Of course I'm not," I say. I pretend this doesn't feel so bad. I try to understand that this comes from love and him wanting to know me. "The lists are a thing between us, though. Like, a Natasha-Montana thing. And I sort of wish you'd asked to see it. I would have shown you."

"She gave me my own notebook so it could be a Bernardo thing too," he says. He's still speaking gently; nothing's a fight with him. And maybe he's right. Maybe Natasha gave him the notebook so that he could join our club, so that I wouldn't have anything without him.

Bernardo's not Karissa, I say to myself. Then I say it a few more times, to make it true.

But I feel a little like territory again.

"Right," I say, and my messy mind tries to make order of all this.

It's confusing, learning what love is. It's some of the things I thought it would be, plus some other things, and I keep getting off track. I can't seem to stop myself from feeling the wrong things in the right moments.

"I want to know all of you," Bernardo says. He touches my cheek, my hair, my eyebrow. "I wanted to see the secret parts, and I did, and I love them too, and I think we should do this." Bernardo grabs my ring finger, the one on my right hand, and I love that he doesn't know that's the wrong one. It's a mistake my dad could never make, and I love the idea of being the First, the Only, the One.

Yes, yes, yes, my brain says, even though it's confused about absolutely everything else in the whole wide world. Bernardo sounds so sure, and I get lost and happy in the sureness.

We are not Roxanne and her coked-out boyfriend. We are not couples from school who have sex in someone's parents' bed and call it love. We are not some adult's idea of a cute couple. We are not my dad and the way he falls in love without really knowing someone or caring to know them. Bernardo knows me, wants to know more. We are something new.

We're more. We have to be. I've only ever wanted more.

"Yes," I say. "Let's do it."

thirty-seven

It turns out my father keeps all the rings in his office, in one of his desk drawers, like they're business contracts, which I guess they sort of are. I almost don't go in, even though we've searched everywhere else. I don't want to be anywhere near that photo of me and Arizona ever again, but I can't stop myself from looking for it.

I look in the folder again and it's gone.

Arizona must have taken it and destroyed it. I have a surge of love for her, and sadness that what I'm about to do with Bernardo will take me further away from her still.

"A drawer of diamonds," Bernardo says, all poetic in his disbelief.

"A drawer of empty promises," I say. The wine says it, not me.

There are eight rings in the drawer, but only four ex-wives, so I have to assume he intended to propose to some of the girlfriends and never got around to it, or he's planning ahead for three more wives after Karissa. It's a small fortune sitting in my dad's office. I fantasize that he's saving them for my college education or something, but the sad reality is that he probably got half of them back after the divorces and promptly forgot they existed.

I swear if I said the name Natasha to him, he wouldn't even know who I was talking about.

They are perfectly lined up in the drawer, a row of boxes where pencils and spare staples and unpaid bills should be. My stomach turns.

"Let's try this again," Bernardo says. He holds one of the rings to his face, then another, and settles on a simple one I've never seen before. "He won't miss this for a few weeks until I can buy you one myself, right?" I laugh and kiss his shoulder, but he has a serious look on his face and he's lowering himself down to one knee and we are doing this in the real way now.

"I can't . . . we can't . . . those things are probably bad luck . . . and I hate diamonds . . . and there's no way you're actually . . ." I'm finding it impossible to finish a sentence. Bernardo is on the floor of my father's office, on one knee, holding a blue Tiffany's box up to me.

"Will you marry me?" he says.

I grin. It's hard to say yes in a normal way, because the moment is so ridiculous and the ring is so shiny and my body is still rocking back and forth a little from the wine. I cover my face and laugh into my hands.

"Let's not be like everyone else. Will you not be like everyone else with me?" I like this question better, and that Bernardo's shoulders stay squarely back and his knees aren't buckling or anything. The ring in the box in Bernardo's hands gives my heart this unexpected leap, a feeling I wasn't prepared for, and my knees are the ones that buckle.

I don't want to be like everyone else.

I don't want to be like my father or my sad mother or the creature that Karissa is becoming or any of the other women who used to be my family but are now scattered all over the city in new lives. I want to be like Karissa was in acting class, and like Natasha told me to be in my journals. I want to write this down tomorrow. I want to be grateful for a stolen diamond ring and an hour-long kissing session on the floor.

"Yes," I say, and go for the kiss, which is long and overpowering and adult.

The ring goes on my finger. Only for the afternoon. "I'm not actually keeping this," I say.

"But we're actually engaged? I can get you a ring of your own?"

"We're engaged," I say. I can't stop laughing. Or kissing. Then we are tangled on the floor, the drawer of rings still open and the contents probably watching us.

We're naked and then we're more than naked. We're doing it, or trying to. It's quick and fun and the whole thing is not as big a deal as I thought it would be, but maybe nothing is too big anymore when you have a massive diamond on your ring finger.

"That's what engaged people do?" I say when we've held each other and made eye contact and done all the things it feels right to do afterward. I mean it as a sexy joke, but Bernardo stiffens at the implication.

"That's not why I proposed," he says. It's not that I forget about his seriousness, but I sometimes think it's a transitory state, not an actual long-term condition. I assume if he loves me, he has to have a deep laugh and a lighter spirit somewhere in there.

"Of course! Oh my God, of course. I'm kidding, babe," I say. *Babe*, as a word, doesn't come naturally to me. But he likes it. It softens him.

"I'm so bad at your jokes," he says. He plays with the ring on my finger, and I think he wants me to keep it on, wants me to show my family, wants to make this even more real somehow. But I like it as dress-up.

"You really are," I say. I smile big so he knows it's teasing, but he's too busy kissing the very top of my forehead, along the hairline, to notice.

"Who are we telling first?" he says.

"Oh God, no one for a while," I say. I start getting dressed. I'm still getting used to all the nakedness.

"What do you mean no one?" he says.

"Well, it's not like we're getting married tomorrow or anything, and we can wait until people don't think we're insane." With my clothes on and my hair up and no longer sweaty on my back, I feel more in control.

"Since when is this about other people?" Bernardo says. He puts some clothes on too but doesn't look happy about it.

"Exactly," I say.

It's quiet between us for a while.

"I want it to be real," Bernardo says.

"I do too. It is real."

His face is cracking open with a sort of sorrow, and I know that even if he's over Casey, the echoes of heartbreak are still there. Ready to light up and take over at any moment. I've said something that reminds him of that hurt.

He doesn't have to tell me. It's an energy shift so distinct he might as well be changing colors, like a mood ring.

Bernardo is a person who is scared he's not real enough.

Bernardo is a person who wants me to help make him real.

"I want to tell my family. And your family. We don't hold back. That's not us," he says. It's strange, that there's such a strong sense of *us* already. But there is. And we do things big and strange and together. We don't hold back. We don't try to fit someone else's idea of what's right.

And I love that about us.

Muscles I didn't know I had are aching a little. A beautiful kind of soreness in mysterious parts of my body. It's possible I like after-sex even more than actual sex.

"I don't want to be engaged the way my dad is engaged. I don't want it to remind me of that." I think Bernardo understands me the same way I do him. The sensitive bits, the little zones that grip up with feeling, are different but equally strong.

He nods.

"I forget sometimes," he says. "I don't know anyone else who's been married more than once. I've never even been to a wedding."

"I was so little at Janie's wedding. She was so . . . into it. I was a flower girl. She was a princess. Her little boys had seersucker suits. They did this whole ritual. With sand. And, like, pouring sand into a bowl together? I thought that meant it would work."

I spin the ring around a few more times. I can't keep it on. But I do like how it looks on me. That we can both look at it as a symbol of Something Big.

"I don't know whose ring this was," I whisper.

"Maybe it's one of the spares?"

I take it off and hand it over. I can't go downstairs with that thing on.

"It's cool," Bernardo says. "We can do unexpected, big things." He's flushed and dimpled and his glasses are hooked around one ear still, but not the other.

I'm sure I look the same: disheveled and happy and off-kilter. I think of when Dad proposed to Tess in broken German in our flower-filled living room. Tess had on a navy suit and had gotten a blow-out earlier that day, and her makeup was understated and pretty.

She'd kept touching her new nose.

That's how I know this is good and real. We are the opposite of put-together and perfect and planned. We are spontaneous and romantic and falling apart at the seams. I'm certain that's how it should be.

I take the ring off and look for clues of who it might have belonged to.

And there, on the inside, engraved and a little rubbed off: *My Always Janie.*

July 13

The List of Things to Be Grateful For

1 Talking to Roxanne about sex, now that I know what it actually is. The speed at which the words come.

2 Natasha listing *terrible things that make you realize how much you love someone* on her latest List of Things to Be Grateful For.

3 The picture Bernardo's littlest sister drew for me. Me and Bernardo. I'm in a wedding gown, like she knows even though she doesn't. She simply happens to think we'd look good getting married.

thirty-eight

"I figured out where to get you a ring," Bernardo says a few days later. We're at Reggio, which I've taught him to love so that I can come here with him when everyone else in my family isn't talking. I need to teach him everything Arizona and my dad do, so that as it keeps falling apart, I'll still have the best parts.

"I found Janie," I say to Bernardo while I'm shaking way too much sugar into my latte. "I want to see her. I know it went badly with Tess. I need to do it anyway." I put her ring back in the drawer as soon as I saw it was hers. It made my finger numb. It was a little too small. And a little too beautiful. And a little too reminiscent of the things I used to think I'd have.

She now works at a rooftop restaurant in Williamsburg.

Finding people is so easy it's a little scary. They're close, even though I haven't seen them in years.

"Perfect," Bernardo says. "Williamsburg works for the ring too."

"Janie first," I say. I need to get her out of my system before anything else. My very first stepmom, whose changes were the most extreme. Her mother visited us once, a little over a year into their marriage, and she didn't recognize her own daughter waiting for her at Penn Station.

It was awful. Janie waving maniacally while her mother looked everywhere for her skinny, big-nosed, brunette daughter. A pretty mole near her right eye was gone. Her squinting, happy eyes were opened wide and intense. She looked like an alien.

It's been years since I've seen her, so I'm half expecting her to be entirely plastic now. More mannequin than person.

"I think I need to do it alone," I say. I lost sleep practicing that sentence last night. It's hard to tell Bernardo I need something other than the thing he wants to give.

"I messed up last time," he says.

"No, no. You were great. I needed you. And I need your support with this too. But I want Janie to see me. Only me. I want it to be about her and me and things we were and who we are now and . . . I don't know. Maybe there's something about the first woman you see in a wedding gown. Maybe it's that simple."

"I want to see you in a wedding gown," Bernardo says, which means it's okay and I can stop apologizing.

We go to Brooklyn together, and Bernardo finds a bookstore to wander around in while I see Janie. He heads right for the mysteries section, and I think there are so many things I don't know about him at all. As I'm leaving, he sings along with the Beatles playing over the loudspeaker. He doesn't hum. It is not quiet.

I add it to the List of Things to Be Grateful For.

* * *

I ask the hostess to seat me in Janie's section.

The menus are huge, and I could still choose to hide behind mine and never actually talk to her.

I decide on a lobster roll with bacon on it, because it's impossible to think of any greater combination. And for the most difficult moments, it's always a good idea to have bacon.

Arizona would agree. And I know—with as much certainty as I know that lobster and bacon is a perfect combination—that I should have told Arizona to come with me.

I recognize Janie when she comes over, but only barely. Everything about her is bigger except for her nose and her waist, which are both terrifyingly smaller. Her forehead is a flat, motionless desert. Her hair has grown to three times its size. Her nose looks strange and smushed. Her lips are rosebud red and so inflated I'm sure they could be popped with a needle, like balloons.

She doesn't recognize me. I order the lobster roll and watch the expression on her face, which doesn't change except for the light in her eyes, which goes dimmer and dimmer with every passing moment.

"Janie," I say, when she's turning away to put my order in.

"Uh-huh."

"I'm Montana," I say.

"I'm Janie," she says. But before she's even done saying her name, she startles herself into remembering who I am. "Montana! Montana? Like, little Montana?"

"Stepdaughter Montana," I say, like giving myself that title will somehow make her be something special to me. I'm increasingly ashamed by myself and how pathetic I'm turning out to be.

"Are you here on purpose?" Janie says. She looks around like maybe my father is here or maybe a hidden camera is trained on her surprised expression.

"I should totally not be here, right?" I have some kind of PTSD from what happened with Tess. I'm filled with the most humiliating type of regret, and I'm getting out of my seat.

"What do you want?" Janie says. "Did your dad send you? Are you in AA or something? Are you, like, getting closure?" She's deeply nervous, but not pissed like Tess was. I am trying to remember everything about her and her kids. Little boys, Frank and Andy. They fought over toy trucks and grew from little to not-so-little in the time our parents were married. I feel a deep need to know how they ended up.

"How's Frank?" I ask. I'm gripping the bottom of my chair and trying to calculate how old he'd be now. Two years younger than me, I guess, so fifteen. He's a teenager.

"You came to catch up?" Janie says. She looks confused, but still not mean, so I soldier on.

"And Andy? Is Andy okay?" Andy would be thirteen or fourteen now. Maybe his voice is changing. Maybe he's smoked a cigarette. Maybe he's kissed a girl. My heart is fluttering, not pounding, a sweeter kind of excitement.

"They're both . . . good. Andy is at boarding school in New Hampshire. Frank plays baseball." She clears her throat, and I guess that's all I'm going to get about the boys who used to be my brothers. I almost never think about them, but even these two tiny details give me a rush of feeling for them. An ache. Maybe I'll go to New Hampshire or start attending middle school baseball games.

"I miss them," I say, a thing that isn't really true until I say it, and then it makes me weepy.

"I wonder if they remember you," Janie says. It's mean and I don't know if it's on purpose. "So how can I help you? I'm not giving you their emails or anything. I'm not comfortable—"

"I wanted to say hi?" I say. Arizona would have had something better to say. She'd smooth over the situation and make it something good, worthwhile. I can't imagine what I was thinking, doing this again. Janie's in the middle of a busy lunch shift. Hipsters in plaid shirts and bushy beards are signaling at her to get them more beer, and she smells like seafood and garlic. There are out-of-season Christmas lights all over the place, not only the white kind, but colored bulbs and reindeer heads. It is not a place for a serious conversation.

Janie blinks. It looks painful, the movement of her perfectly smooth eyelids and the unwrinkled corners of her eyes. She's had so much work done on her face it doesn't even look like a face anymore.

"I got engaged. I'm engaged. It made me think of you. That was the best wedding. Everyone was so happy."

Janie does math on her fingers. She shakes her head like it can't be right.

"So you're, like, twentysomething now? How old were you when we broke up? I'm all off. Jesus. I haven't thought about you in years. Like, literally. Years and years."

"Oh," I say. I need that lobster and bacon situation immediately. I need something else to swallow down with the humiliating starkness of that particular reality. I'd rather be shoved around by Tess at this point than reminded by Janie in a dozen little ways that I meant nothing to her or to her boys.

Maybe the saddest feeling ever comes with the knowledge that you think about someone every day who never thinks of you. It's a type of loneliness. All the time it's been me and my memories and nothing else, even though I assumed there was an equal and opposite force coming at me from the stepmoms.

"I mean, no offense," Janie says, seeing something in my face, surely, that turns her momentarily kind.

"I'm seventeen," I say. "You left when I was eight."

She laughs.

She may not remember me, but I remember so many little things about her, like her breathy laugh. I wonder if Frank and Andy blush like that, laugh like that. They can't possibly look like her, because she doesn't look like her. But maybe there are other things they've gotten from her. Maybe they even got something from me. I wonder if they still speak the pig Latin we taught them or if they've ever retold the scary stories we shared late at night.

"Oh, Montana. Wow. Wow. Your family, huh? A mini Sean right here." Janie fluffs her hair. Her whole demeanor shifts from confused to cocky, like she's been proven right about something very important and scientific. "Your family really falls in love fast and loves getting married, huh?"

"This is totally different," I say, which is what people say when it's not so different at all. "I'm not my dad. I'm his exact opposite."

"Honey," Janie says. I try to remember if it's something she called Arizona and me when we were little. I think she's going to say more—give me advice or a warning or a punishment or a congratulations, but she doesn't have any of that for me, I guess. I wonder what she'd tell Andy or Frank if they came to her, wanting to get married so young. I imagine myself as a real child of hers, but I don't know what that looks like either.

I'm lonelier than I've ever, ever been.

"What do you mean you haven't thought of me in years?" I say. Something that hurts this much needs to be worth it, so I'm not leaving without lobster and bacon and answers. "We were family."

"No, honey," Janie says. "That's not family. We didn't even know each other."

Déjà vu is supposed to be something kind of mysterious, but this is a pretty literal mirror of the last conversation I had with Tess. More like one of those paintings. The infinite ones—a painting of a person holding a painting of a person holding a painting, and on and on forever. Inescapable and repetitive and strange.

"I know a ton about you," I say, and I believe it too. "I know how long it takes for you to do your hair and what you sound like when you're yelling at your kids and what you like for breakfast and what time you go to bed, and I've seen you cry. If you see someone cry, you know them."

"That's not knowing someone," Janie says. "You have no idea what you're doing. And it's not your fault. But if you think those things matter, if you think anything you know about me makes me family to you, you are deeply confused. And you're seventeen. And your father is a weenie who won't stand up to anyone aside from some huffing and puffing. So he'll probably tell you this is fine, that you're getting engaged or whatever, or he'll give you the silent treatment or some other terrible parenting decision. But he won't tell you what you really need to hear. So I'm going to say it. You cannot be engaged. You cannot get married. And that? Me saying that? That's family. That's what that looks like." She waits, like maybe I'll have a response to that, but I can't even get in a full breath.

I look for the Janie I used to feel I knew under all the plastic surgery she's gotten. Her eyebrows hike up to her hairline. I can't read what emotion she's feeling—they're all convoluted and wrong on the tight expanse of her skin.

"Maybe you shouldn't be telling me all this, honey," Janie says. "Maybe you should be telling your mom. But if I'm the best you've got right now, that's the biggest favor I can do you."

"I'd like that lobster bacon roll," I say at last, since she's waiting for me to respond and I don't know anything except that that will be delicious.

Everything else is too complicated to tackle.

Janie brings the lobster roll with bacon piled on high and says it's on the house.

"You should tell your real family," she says before leaving me with the food perfection.

"I have no idea who that is," I say.

The lobster roll with bacon is fucking delicious. It's the best thing I've ever eaten. Dripping with mayonnaise and loaded with fresh lobster.

thirty-nine

"We don't have to get our rings today," Bernardo says when he sees my face. He's bought me a graphic novel about love and religion called *Blankets*, and we look at it from the floor of the store for a while until I start to cry. "I thought you wanted me to be into comics."

Love is really sad, when you get right down to it.

"I need to walk," I say.

"You want to tell me about it?" he asks.

"I want to tell Arizona about it," I say. But I know I won't.

Bernardo nods and I can see the thing on his face again—the heartbreak and pinch—but he lets me have it.

"You are one great fiancé," I say.

We wander Williamsburg, and it's never as pretty as I think it's going to be. It's gray and half-run-down and half-industrial and doesn't quite live up to the promise of coolness that it makes when you're riding the L train toward it.

"We should get the rings," I say.

* * *

Bernardo walks me to a tattoo shop.

"I can't do that," I say. It's the cool, clean kind of tattoo parlor. But still.

"My cousin works here. It's cool, you're eighteen-ish. He won't tell," Bernardo says. It is the most beside the point he's ever been.

"I don't have tattoos," I say.

"Well, yeah. Me neither," Bernardo says. "But it seems like something we'd do, doesn't it?"

"No!" I say, because my reflexes tell me to. But I think back on the weeks we've been together. Weeks that could be years for how enormous and life-changing and real they've been. This does seem like something we'd do. This is sort of who I am now. Who we are together.

"We don't have to. I thought it'd be cool. Maybe put each other's initials on our ring fingers? Or something? I don't know. You came up with the hair and the piercing, so I guess I thought you'd like this." Bernardo is rubbing my ring finger with his thumb.

"Yeah," I say.

The Arizona in my head tells me this is a terrible idea. But I like the idea of permanence. It's something Sean Varren would never do. For all the women he's changed and done surgery on and married, he's never once done something permanent to himself. Only Botox, which doesn't stick. He makes little changes, becomes variations of a different person, but doesn't make a real leap. He marries them, knowing he can get out. He can slip the ring off. He can leave them behind.

I won't be able to leave Bernardo behind if I do this. It will be a real kind of forever. That's the kind of forever I'm looking for.

"So I guess we'll be telling people tonight," I say. "We won't be able to hide anything."

"I'm ready," Bernardo says.

We say *I love you* when I'm in the chair. We kiss. It's like a ceremony but not. It's a lot like the piercing—doing something we aren't old enough to do, but pretending we are.

The guy with the needle leans over my ring finger and starts drawing a cursive letter *B* in the place where a diamond might go.

There's a buzzing pain, something that I feel in my finger and my brain. I'm panicking and wishing myself somewhere else entirely, so I keep looking at Bernardo.

It sort of works. I try to breathe through the jolts of pain and pre-regret.

DO NOT FEEL THAT, I tell myself.

Once upon a time, Roxanne and Arizona and I planned on getting tattoos together.

It wasn't that long ago. Maybe a year and a half. Before they went to college and before Arizona's surgery and before the first time Roxanne had sex and before Karissa. Back when Dad was still with Tess. We were going to get matching best friend tattoos. Roxanne suggested a sketch of our bench. Arizona said we should get three hearts tattooed underneath our belly buttons. I said we should get our initials in a line on our arms. *ARM*.

We laughed and looked places up online and bragged to people at school about our plans.

Then Arizona said it would look ugly, and Roxanne and I didn't want to do it without her, and Dad got divorced again and the idea fell away, the way great ideas sometimes do.

It hurts but not that badly, getting Bernardo's initial on my finger.

It hurts more thinking of the things that have vanished this year and past years and that maybe everything I've ever thought was real wasn't.

This is real.

Nothing that stings like this and stays like this could be fake.

I don't look at it until Bernardo's is done too. I'm hyperaware of that finger and nothing else, and I hope that feeling lasts for a while, because it's exactly as it should be. Bernardo breathes heavily while they draw the *M* on his finger, and it's fast but before it's done, I can't help being a scaredy-cat.

"Is this really happening? Are we insane?" I say.

"We're the good kind of insane," Bernardo says. The tattoo artist forges ahead, and I do my impression of a girl laughing it off. Everything's throbbing. My finger, my ears, my heart, my tongue. My eyebrow. I don't know that I want to be insane, even the good kind.

"Look. Beautiful," he says, and shows me his finger. It's red but the *M* is fancy and sweet and fits the space perfectly.

I finally look at my own finger.

The *B* is an alien force, a foreign being on my skin.

"It's big," I say.

"You two are all set," the tattoo artist says.

"We are?" I'm having trouble thinking. Everything around me is spinning, and I have tired, heavy eyes and Bernardo's initial forever on my ring finger and a whole mess of a life that I can't even get a handle on anymore.

The world shuts off for one stunning minute. And I faint. I've never fainted before, but it's like a mini-break from the world. Brief and long at the same time. When I come to, Bernardo's face is over mine and the tattoo artist is standing by with water and fanning me with a tattoo pamphlet.

"It happens," he says.

Bernardo kisses my eyes when they're open, and he says I scared him and I say I scared myself, but I mean something different from what he means.

"My family first or yours?" he says.

We do his first.

They hate the tattoos and the engagement. They smile anyway.

The kids actually love it all. His sisters and brothers swirl around me like I'm a maypole. They ask questions about dresses, and I decide not to let it slip that I have a gown already too.

"You think this is what you want?" Bernardo's dad asks us both. "You don't know what this is."

"We're in love," Bernardo says, and it would be sweet if he didn't sound like every movie about stupid kids. Everything he said about the pointlessness of promise rings and how adults don't take them seriously is coming back to me. We are every bit as not-serious when he talks about our Deep and Unwavering Love like it's a thing no one else has experienced.

His mother rubs her husband's hand in hers while he fumes, and I know they know what love is. We sound small and stupid in comparison. There's chicken sizzling on the stove top and a supply of beer in the fridge and coffee brewing in the machine at all times. They exchange looks that tell whole stories between the two of them.

Bernardo can't even tell what I'm trying to say when I speak in half sentences.

"This is a huge mistake," Bernardo's dad says. "You're always in love. You have to get ahold of yourself, *mi hijo*. Not everything is one and only and forever and the biggest and best. You're a kid. You're not able to make these sorts of decisions. Look at you! Look what you do!" He says words in Spanish that I can't understand, and his mother tries to make everything quiet and calm again.

"Not that we don't love Montana!" his mother says. "You are a sweetheart, honey. You seem really wonderful, and I know Bernardo is so happy to have met you." She pours me a cup of coffee without asking if I want it or how I take it. She loads it with sugar and milk like that may make this whole conversation go down easier.

"Yes. You're a good girl," his dad says. "It's not about that. It's about being real adults. And responsibility. And college. And growing up. And knowing the difference between love and *love*. And what were you thinking, doing this to yourselves? What if you change your mind next month?"

"That's the whole point," Bernardo says. He is indignant. "This is about us not changing our minds. I mean, you can see, now, how permanent this is. How serious we are. I'm not a kid. I'm not being ridiculous. I'm being very, very serious."

I cringe.

When it's me and Bernardo alone, the things he says sound true and wise. But with my throbbing finger and post-fainting brain, I hear him through his parents' ears, sounding impetuous and impulsive and intense.

"No," his mother says, "this is about you rebelling or trying to prove something. I don't even wear a ring. I don't need to. You see?"

I see.

His brothers and sisters write *B*s and *M*s on their fingers, to match our tattoos.

"Look what you're doing," Bernardo's dad says. "Look at the example you're setting. We should never have let you sit in that room and read poetry all day long. Did something kooky to your head."

"Raul!" Bernardo's mom says, smacking her husband on his shoulder. "Poetry is fine. Loving Montana is fine. But the rest of it. We can't support. We can't let you do this. Okay? We can get this all undone. It's not too late. Okay?" I have never heard anyone sound so desperate. Whereas Bernardo's dad is filled with a controlled anger, his mother is eager and trying so hard to stay sweet.

"You didn't know what you were getting yourself into," she says to me, like she has a world of knowledge about her son and I do not. "I'm sorry."

"This can't be undone," Bernardo says. He puts a hand on his mother's shoulder and looks her right in the eyes so she can't pretend it's not happening or that it's something else.

I bury my nose and mouth in the coffee mug and wish everything were as simple and perfect as the smell of coffee.

forty

We don't talk much on the way to my place.

I don't want to storm into the house and announce our engagement to the angry masses. I don't want to have another terrible conversation today. I'm exhausted from Janie and fainting and Bernardo's parents. And my father already disapproves of the most basic things about me—my fucking face, for instance—so he won't like this newest complication.

"They don't get us," Bernardo says.

I'm desperate for him to stop staying stuff like this. I don't want him sounding like some broken record of misunderstood youth. It makes me feel stupid. I try to think of a way to tell him so.

Instead I shrug. I'm losing my words.

"They're always like this," Bernardo says.

"Always?"

"They didn't want me even dating Casey, so I guess this is an improvement."

He says *Casey* with a little whistle on the *s*, like he's used to saying it in a whisper, in her ear. We are still so, so new.

"I thought they'd be happy," he says. He wraps his scarf tighter around his neck, like he's hanging himself in protest.

"Really?" I say. We weave through the park and I buy myself another coffee at a cart near the exit. It's the crappy kind, but it still smells exactly like coffee always smells. What I actually want is to get drunk, but getting hopped up on coffee is going to have to do for now.

"Let's tell Karissa first," he says.

"That's random," I say. I'm sweaty and pink and wishing I hadn't worn my cutoffs to announce our engagement. I should have gotten dressed up for his family again. I should have worn something with a trim or a ribbon or a patch of lace or a polka-dot pattern.

"I think she'll approve," Bernardo says. "I think I need to hear someone approving. I need to hear a congratulations. We haven't heard congratulations, you know?"

I beam at him. My fiancé. He sounds like the person I love again. It's so true, what he's said. So right. So exactly what we need. I trample on all those doubts and focus on how often he says the perfect thing.

Karissa's on the stoop. She's drinking green juice and smoking a cigarette.

She has a new face.

Not a new face, but a new chin.

"Holy fuck," I say, because that is what you say when someone looks like themselves but like someone new. It's what you say when the thing you hoped would stay is gone.

The new chin is still swollen and bruised, but I know what it will look like later. It will look the way my dad wants my chin to look. Defined and strong.

"I know it's a little shocking," she says. "It's still healing, so it looks scary now. But it is going to look out-of-control gorgeous. It's going to change everything."

"Jesus," Bernardo says.

I think she got Botox too. Her forehead has an eerie stillness, a plastic, inhuman look that makes me sad. She had this one line in the middle of her forehead that I bet had been there since she was younger than me. Not a wrinkle, but a piece of her. Now it's gone.

"I know, I know, I look like someone punched me," Karissa says. I have all these fighting words to say, but I can't get the energy to say them.

I try to let go one more inch of who I thought Karissa would be. I try to sink in one more inch to what Bernardo could be for me.

He looks confused and overwhelmed, and I must look the same. We are two people who have been unprepared for the things happening around us.

"We want to go out," Bernardo says. "We want to do a celebratory night out. Are you allowed?"

"Awesome!" Karissa says, as willing and filled with unquestioning as usual.

I'm missing her face.

"Where are we going?" she says. "Dirty Versailles?"

"Fancier," Bernardo says.

"So what are we celebrating?" Karissa asks. She grabs my elbow. "You didn't celebrate whatever it is with Natasha already, did you?"

"No. You're the first," I say. I'm shaking from the pressure. She's holding this thing over me like it's a boulder she could drop on my head at any moment. She could crush me.

"Well, let's make sure you don't feel the need for any other celebrations. Let's make sure this one is truly epic." Karissa takes a drag of her cigarette and hands it to me, and I don't give it back. I hide the hand with the tattoo on it. We have to reveal it at the right moment. With champagne and house music and sparkly clothes that I'd never in a million years wear otherwise.

Karissa delivers on the celebration. She gets us a table at some fancy club she used to go to a lot before meeting my father. She has friends there, the way she did at Dirty Versailles, but they're different kinds of friends. Sadder. Dressier. Older. Drunker.

"You. Are. Perfection," one woman says when Karissa kisses her cheek on the way to our table. The swelling of Karissa's chin has gone down a little more after icing it, and she's covered the yellow with makeup. The lights, or lack thereof, hide the things we don't like about ourselves from others.

The drinks hide the things we don't like about ourselves from ourselves.

So we get drunk. Blasted. First me, then Bernardo, then Karissa.

Karissa has something else too. Pain pills from her surgery. She takes one, then two.

We go through two bottles, then three. We talk to guys in suits and girls in crop tops and thousand-dollar shoes. I can't stop shimmying in the fringed dress Karissa lent me. I love how the fringes hit my arms and the backs of my legs when I twist.

I've never gone out dancing before, and adults dance differently than we all do at high school dances. I can't put my finger on what it is, but it's something about the way they throw their hands in the air and the movement of their fingers and who they are looking at and dancing for.

"I feel awkward," Bernardo says. He's barely dancing, mostly moving his head and his arms, and I tell him to have another drink.

"It's our engagement party!" I say, because it's all become both lovely and a big joke.

"This doesn't feel how I thought it would," he says. "I hate this music. People keep bumping into me. This place is gross. Depressing. Like, this is what we have to look forward to?"

He'd hate Dirty Versailles if he thinks this place is gross. Which is sad, because I'd pictured us there together when we're Karissa's age, kissing the bartender's cheek and taking shots of whatever bright-blue or green or pink thing he felt like making us. I thought we'd entwine our legs under the bar stools and make out under precarious chandeliers.

"Don't you want to be in love and reckless and wild and us?" I say, which isn't exactly the point I wanted to get across, but it's close enough.

"We are," he says. He points to his finger. My initial marking him.

"Remember when it was only Sharpie?" I say. That day in the basement when we wrote all over each other felt permanent and scary, but this is even more. Bernardo shakes his head and points to his ear. He didn't hear me.

It's for the best. He'd take it the wrong way.

"Let's hear that congratulations," I say. "She's wasted, we can tell her. She'll be happy. She'll scream and jump and tell the whole club. That will be fun, right?" I want his mood to match mine.

"Okay. Let's do it. And I have another idea too," he says.

"Telling Arizona and Roxanne?" I say, unsure if I'm kidding.

"Better than that," he says.

Karissa dances over to us, her bracelets jangling, presumably, but we can't hear it in the booming room. She hasn't asked what we're celebrating. I guess once she found out we'd chosen her, it didn't matter what for.

"I have to tell you why we're celebrating," I say. I yell directly into Karissa's ear for her to hear me.

"Oh right!" she says, like it's a side note to the rest of her night. "I figured you and the big guy finally did it?"

"We did," I say.

"You had sex? It was your first time, right? Was it good? Was he good? That is so freaking adorable," she says. She hugs me and I'm astounded, even though I shouldn't be, that she thought I'd run to her to celebrate losing my virginity. At a *club*. I guess in some alternate universe where we are the old Karissa and Montana, I maybe would have told her, at least. And she would have bought me a glass of wine or talked me through it or laughed with me about the awkward bits. But that alternate universe is so far away.

I hold my hand out to Karissa, palm down, like it has a ring on it. Like I am waiting for her to kiss it, all royal-like.

"What. Is. This," she says. She pulls my ring finger close to her face so she can get a good look at what I've done to myself.

"Bernardo proposed!" I say.

"And you're telling me first?" she says. The thrill is all over her face, but it's for the wrong reasons. I nod. It's almost true. "MONTANA! OH MY GOD!" she says. She pulls me into a huge hug, and the clubbers in our vicinity look over to see what the commotion is about. Karissa keeps me pinned to her with one arm and grabs Bernardo with the other. "I'm so happy for you guys!" she says, exactly like we wanted.

Bernardo finally smiles.

I'm too drunk to remember what a smile feels like.

We drink and dance more, and Karissa starts to fall apart a little. Her limbs get swingy and cumbersome. Her face gets droopy. She moves her jaw strangely, like she isn't yet used to her new chin.

"Are you okay?" I say, and bring her to the bathroom. Bernardo goes to the bar to get us all water.

"You told me something important," Karissa says. She isn't looking at me directly. She looks to the lights above my head and the sign on the bathroom door and at her own shoes and my tattoo. "You really, really did," she says.

"Yeah, I did," I say.

"I should tell you something too," Karissa says. "Now that we're family."

"It's okay," I say.

"No but, like, we need to be close. In the real way," she says. "I want that. Don't you want that?"

I shrug. I don't want anything right now, except for her to be more sober.

"I miss my mom," Karissa says. "We had the same face. Now we don't. Now I have a new face. And I don't have anything else of hers. Maybe I should have kept the face."

"I know, I know," I say. It would be impossible for me to compete with the way she misses her family, so I don't tell her I miss mine too, or that I'm sort of tired of hearing about her family. Instead I nod and rub her back and fight against throwing up.

"But, like, I miss her," Karissa says.

"I know, you must miss them all," I say. My knees are giving out a little, so I lean against the wall.

"No. Only her. They're all around. I hate the rest of them. But my mom I loved."

It's one of those sentences that's hard to hear or put meaning to. I almost ignore it, it seems too drunk and impossible and indecipherable.

"I don't know what that means," I say, shifting even more of my weight to the wall. My head to my shoulder. "I think I'm really drunk."

"They didn't die," Karissa says.

I try to lift my head from my shoulder and my body from the wall.

"I don't understand. What? I mean . . . what?" I say. I'm yelling, but only because the music is loud. She has a look on her face that's a little too cute and not enough ashamed.

"My family's all . . . nice," she says. "Nice in a way that's awful. And I left them. It's hard to explain to people. Especially people like you." All her vowels are long and singsongy. Her eyes are foggy, and I have a feeling this will be another night that is erased in her mind, but not in mine.

I will never forget this exact moment.

It's the worst moment. Of all the things I've been told that I didn't want to be told, this is the one I hate the most, because I didn't anticipate it. Not even a little.

I leave the bathroom and lean against a wall on the side of the dance floor. Everywhere is too cramped and close. I want to be on the street. Karissa follows me out and stands next to me. I can't get away from her.

"I wanted us to be close," Karissa says. "And I *feel* like they're dead, you know? Like they died when I left? Like it could have happened, and it was something you would understand better than me leaving them. I know you don't like people leaving." She's sort of falling asleep by the end of the sentence. A thing that is sliding away from her. She looks like her mouth is trying to catch up with her words.

"But you told us so many stories about them and all the crying and stuff and, like, what the actual fuck are you talking about?" The music shifts from one dance beat to another, and there's a whooping from the crowd. I look over at Bernardo. He's got three glasses of water lined up in front of him at the bar. He waves and I wave back, but I think even from across the bar he can see what's happening to my face. It's falling. It's cracking. It's breaking down, and I wish this news was sobering me up, but instead it's making me drunker.

"I mean, I really, like, lived through them dying," Karissa says. She takes another one of her painkillers, and I can see future-her, all doped up and tight-faced. "Like, in my heart, it happened. Like with acting. When you're really living through it?"

Bernardo finally comes over with two of the glasses of water. He hands one to Karissa and one to me and holds my face in his hands.

"Hey. Hey, Montana. You okay?" He's a little drunk too, or at least he smells like whiskey and beer and sweat. "What's going on? Should we leave? What are you guys doing?"

I smile a lazy smile in his direction. "Nothing was true," I say.

"It's not like that," Karissa says. She grabs hold of my arm, and I let her stay there but only because I don't have the energy in my limbs to shake her off.

I have a thousand things to say to her.

I have nothing to say to her.

forty-one

"We can say good-bye to everyone," Bernardo says. The cab ride home smells like french fries and Axe body spray. Whoever was in here before us was the worst. I'm motion sick and trying to will away the drunk.

Karissa is slumped against one of the doors. We'll have to carry her upstairs.

I've told Bernardo what happened, and we can't think of anything to say about it, because the lie is so large and strange and impossible.

"Say good-bye?" I say. I keep checking Karissa's breathing and heart to make sure she's still alive. I don't know all the rules about drinking.

"We could leave here. Leave all these people. Maybe meet your mom? Out west? And then get jobs. At bookstores or flower shops or whatever," Bernardo says. "We're engaged. You're almost eighteen. We can do whatever we want." When I'm drunk, I'm messy and confused. When he's drunk, he's clear and insane.

"What are you talking about?" I say. I nuzzle into him so the words come out sweet and affectionate instead of bewildered, which is what I actually am, by literally every conversation that's happened tonight.

"What is going on here is nuts, Mon. Absolutely absurd. We need to get away from it. From her. And from everyone. But her especially. She's fucking toxic. She's a toxic crazy person who is manipulating everyone, and we have each other so we don't need this shit."

He's swearing so much it makes me sad. I don't like him all worked up and growling.

"Don't leave me," Karissa says, waking up long enough to hear about us running away. Long enough to try to keep me close. She grips my thigh.

The cab is extremely rickety and speeding like crazy.

Karissa passes back out, but her hand stays on my thigh. Her nails dig in.

She is always attaching herself to me. Bernardo puts an arm around me. It's too warm to feel good in this stuffy car. I need out.

"I'd love to take a weekend trip to find my mom," I say. "You're the best boyfriend. Fiancé. You're the best fiancé of all the fiancés I've ever fiancéd." I sort of know the words are twisty and wrong as they come out, but I don't care.

"I don't mean a weekend trip," he says. "We need to get away from this. This is bad. What's happening with your family is really, really bad. And you saw my family. They're not okay with us. I don't want to sit around while they judge us. You want to live in disapproval land for the next year or whatever?"

"I've always lived in disapproval land," I say. They're sad words but sound funny right now. I cackle. The cabdriver looks in his rearview mirror.

"I don't usually drive around drunk kids," he says. "And your sister there looks sick. You gonna tip well?"

"We're not kids," Bernardo says like a mantra.

"She's not my sister," I say, because that's *my* mantra.

"I'm asking if you're gonna tip well," the cabbie says. He's angrier than I'd noticed, and I wonder if maybe the Axe cologne and french fries were his, and not the people before us. It's weird, when you think about it, that we let strangers drive us around when we're wasted. It's not safe. I want to tell Bernardo my epiphany, but he's handing over a twenty and sighing.

Karissa groans and Bernardo covers her mouth with his hand, like she's going to get us kicked out despite the ridiculous tip.

It's nice, though, having someone take care of me.

The cabbie slams the brakes at a red light, and all three of us pitch forward. Karissa and I hit our heads on the glass. It hurts.

"Do you really need to stay here for this?" Bernardo says, like the inside of the cab is all that my life and my city really have to offer.

"We'd go to California?" I say. All I know about California is palm trees and a warmer ocean than the one we have here.

"Or Portland. Or Seattle. Or Hawaii. Anywhere you want," Bernardo says. "I just thought you might want to see your mom first."

"Maybe I do?" I say, but it seems like a big, huge question. I've seen the rest of them. The almost-moms. Do I want to see the actual mom? These are questions I don't want to answer in a stopping-and-starting cab next to the biggest liar I've ever met.

"We don't need any of this," Bernardo says. The cab's pulling up to my brownstone. It's gorgeous in the streetlights. Tess's potted plants are still on the stoop, and they're drooping in a kind of tragic beauty.

I can't stop thinking about Bernardo's mother's empanadas and the way his littlest sister hangs on to his legs even when he's walking. The tiny coziness of their apartment and the way they sit around reading books on the two couches every Sunday night.

"We don't?" I say. I'm trying to fit the things he's saying in with my feelings. I thought love had something to do with feeling the same things in the same moments, and I want that back.

"Okay, here we are," the cabbie says. "Get her out. Bring her right inside. Lay her on her side so she doesn't choke. Put water by the bed." He's listing it off like he's said it a million times to a million drunk people. Bernardo piles Karissa into his arms. We bring her upstairs and tuck her into bed. We keep her on her side. My father's nowhere to be found.

We go back to the stoop when we're done with Karissa and after we've downed a frozen French bread pizza to soak up the alcohol and the feelings.

It's humid and smells a little like garbage, but everyone in the world walks by and I make up stories about them in my head and listen to their private conversations and think about the sidewalk as being a quilt of moments, and man I'm deep when I've been drinking.

I take out a cig and offer one to Bernardo. We sit like chimneys on the stoop, blowing trails of smoke into the sky.

"I really meant it. We should go," Bernardo says. "Aren't you tired of being the one who stays here and takes it?"

I am.

I really am.

"I'd have to check with Arizona first," I say. It doesn't make sense, since she doesn't live here anyway, but I don't want to not have anyone to check with. I don't want to be quite that free.

"Fair," he says. "We can tell her tomorrow. But she's not deciding for us, okay? It's our decision. As a couple."

I nod, and the cabs blur together on the street in front of us. I'm still too drunk to move my head painlessly.

"I don't want to tell my dad about Karissa," I say. "I don't want to be part of it."

"Okay," Bernardo says.

"She's not mine," I say, and it's finally and totally true.

"Agree," he says.

"None of it's really mine," I say, meaning my family and my life here and all the things I thought were real. But I don't say any of that. "I guess we could go away after the wedding."

I light another cigarette. I can't pause, can't let my hands still. Bernardo puts a hand under my butt, so I'm sitting on it.

I'm thinking maybe Bernardo is the only thing that is right about my life.

I get an intense urge to tell the people I love about my engagement. I have no idea what I was thinking telling Janie and Karissa first. It's the first time I've been scared of my own actions. Like my impulses are all off, and some sort of terrible neuron is firing in my brain that's making me do the opposite of the things I should be doing.

I want to tell Roxanne and Arizona and Natasha. I don't want to let go of those things. When Bernardo keeps saying we should be over NYC, I'm not sure I can be over them.

"Maybe it's not that New York sucks. Maybe everything feels impossible after a while, and we get tired of everything. And everyone," I say. I try to figure out what percentage of me is drunk, what percentage is sober, what percentage is reeling from Karissa's lies, and what percentage is in love.

"Well, I'll never get tired of you," Bernardo says.

"Me too," I say.

I light another cigarette. I don't usually chain-smoke, and it goes down rough. Everything's spinning, and I feel like crap. I feel like I'm in someone else's body. I'm saying words that one part of me means but another part of me is scared of.

"Okay," I say, because I want to make out, not fight. "We'll go far away."

"We'll get married on a mountain," he says. "Romantic and just us."

"Right," I say. "Sounds great."

We make out. It should be gross, the sweat and the queasiness and our smoky mouths and boozy lips, but it's not. I feel less vomit-y, less like death, more like myself.

That must be love too.

After we head up to my room, Bernardo falls asleep, but I can't. Everything's spinning and Karissa is scaring me. I don't like her sleeping down the hall, a stranger.

I call Roxanne, missing her voice and the way we planned to spend the whole summer together but didn't. Won't. I need to tell her everything, immediately.

I'm choking on all my new decisions and the things I miss.

She answers the phone all sleepy and strange.

"I'm going to get married," I say, and she wakes right up. "I'm going away," I say.

Roxanne doesn't say too much, but she's there and that feels right, at least.

Nothing else feels right.

forty-two

I fall asleep eventually and wake up a few hours later. Bernardo's passed out cold. He's beautiful and fretful in sleep. I could wake up with him every day. I could do that. I will.

I shake him a little, wanting to talk or hook up or something since I'm awake and the rest of the world is asleep. But he doesn't even grunt in response. I get out of bed, and as soon as I'm upright I realize how seriously fucked up I still am. The room's at a solid forty-five-degree angle, and my mouth is dry even though the rest of me is damp and sweaty. I can't totally keep my head up. Or I could, but I don't really want to.

I take out my gratitude journal and try to choose three things from the day that make me feel lucky. Champagne. Bernardo. Potted plants on the stoop. The idea of palm trees being a part of my everyday life. Being engaged. My new tattoo. Roxanne. There's sort of a lot to be grateful for, even when I'm drunk without wanting to be and overwhelmed.

But writing it down doesn't give me any kind of certainty.

I'm looking for certainty.

I still can't stomach telling Arizona all the epic ways I've changed and ruined our family by letting Karissa in and the ways I'm ditching her to be in love. But there's Natasha, and the fact that she exists makes the day feel more manageable. I text and ask if I can come over.

Natasha is the kind of person who responds to late-night and early-morning texts. She's the kind of person who gives a shit, all the time, even when she's not mine anymore. Even when I've disappointed her.

Come on over! her text back reads. *I'll put on the coffee.*

I leave a note on Bernardo's chest that I'm heading over to Natasha's. It feels illicit, traveling the city at five in the morning with boozy breath and unchanged partying clothes, and I love it until I realize how much Natasha is going to hate it.

I'm right. She does.

"Oh, come on, honey," she says. "Is this because of the new girl-friend? Is she lending you stripper clothes? What happened to your T-shirts and your pretty fresh face?"

"Don't start with me," I say. "I didn't come over for a lecture."

Natasha recoils a little, and I do too, from myself and my obnox-iousness, but actually I sound the way Roxanne talks to her mother. Normal teenage girl. I sound like a girl with a mother.

"The girls have been asking about you," she says. I'm sobering up fast.

"I'm going to get away from the girlfriend. Dad's fiancée. The whole situation," I say.

I tell her everything.

We have an entire pot of coffee.

She doesn't say anything any other mother wouldn't, and that's nice. Almost nicer than the congratulations we'd been looking for. She tells me I'm too young. I have only known him for five minutes. Love and lust are different things. I don't know what I want. I have to tell everyone about Karissa. This is all dangerous. I can't leave town.

"We're in love," I say.

"Been there," she says, and it's like a sunrise, something coming to life in front of my eyes. She tucks some hair behind my ear. Part of me wants to stay here with Natasha, be some other kind of seventeen, the kind that comes with a mother who tells you what to do.

"What do you think my mom would say?" I ask. I never bring my mother up with Natasha. Somewhere along the way I learned that all the mothers had to exist in different, separate spheres. That I, too, had to be chopped up—different bits of me reserved for different people.

I thought having a person would stitch me up. Make me whole. Fix me. The way Arizona used to make me feel—like I belonged to something solid even if I was in pieces. It hasn't been working.

I catch sight of myself in Natasha's mirror and leap at the unfamiliar image. Smudged makeup under my eyes and a scab on my eyebrow and the metal ring pinching the skin and my hair the tiredest, saddest, least pink shade of pink.

"I wish I could tell you what your mother would say," Natasha says. "Or I wish you didn't need to know."

Victoria and Veronica call out for her from their cribs, and she holds up a finger to tell me she'll be back in a minute.

I sneak out while she's in the other room. Some dark and hidden part of me doesn't want to be face-to-face with the things other girls get but I don't. I can't see her be a mother. I don't want to know what that looks like and continue having to live without it.

I don't want to live without it.

The walk home is long, that truth finally unlocked and unrelenting.

forty-three

We don't get to tell my family.

When I get home, Karissa has made a feast of fried baked goods and my father, Arizona, and Roxanne are at the counter with coffees and grimaces.

Bernardo is miserable against the stove. He doesn't have coffee but looks like he needs it.

"She came into the room," he says.

"Bernardo slept over," I say. We were going to tell them that anyway, so it doesn't matter, and I don't know what the tortured look on his face means.

"I saw the note you left for him," Karissa says. "So I told them everything."

She does not mean she told them *everything*. She means she told them everything about me.

"I was at Natasha's," I say, even though it is now a thing everyone knows.

"I told them that. And I told them about you and Bernardo," Karissa says. "We're family. We shouldn't have secrets."

Her words pummel me. She doesn't even blink with shame over how insane that statement is coming from her mouth. Instead her voice is cool and strong. She should be hungover, like us, but she's not. Or else her coffee is magical.

"This isn't true, right?" Arizona says.

"I'm hungover," I say. "Sorry, Dad. Can I eat like seven of those things? And I'm sorry about the sleepover. I know. I get it. I'm rebelling or whatever, I guess."

"I mean, Natasha? Natasha's the fucking worst," Arizona says.

"I should go home," Roxanne says. She can't stop fidgeting on the stool.

"Stay. I thought you should be here to hear about Montana's engagement," Karissa says. It's hard to decipher exactly what the look on her face is. She seems proud of herself, kind of sarcastic. Then I realize what it is: smug. She's smug.

"Montana is not engaged," Dad says. Arizona nods. She is red-eyed, and her face has that post-crying droop to it. Like it's worn itself out with too much emotion.

I keep eye contact with Bernardo and hope that he somehow saves me from having to do this here and now and in this way. The things that were beautiful about our love are breaking, and it hurts. I want to take the perfect parts that are still left and bury them in the backyard so no one else can get them.

"Let me see your hand," Dad says.

"No," I say. I'm remembering we live in New York and don't have a backyard. I have nowhere to bury all the good things. They're going to be taken from me.

"Who *are* you?" Arizona says. She looks like she might punch me. Her shoulders are back and her hands are up.

"Who is *Karissa*?" I say. "Did she tell you about herself? About her lies?"

"Come on now, Montana," Dad says, and of course I'm the one who sounds crazy. Karissa threw me under the bus first, so that anything I say is now suspect. Desperate.

Karissa serves me a whole bunch of French toast pastries. They are too eggy, and she puts too much syrup on them, and she's wearing one of my father's crisp white work shirts, and I hate her more than I've ever hated any of them because she lied the most. She glares at me.

"Everything Karissa's told you about herself is a total lie," I say.

"We're talking about you right now, Montana," Dad says. He's stern and fatherly. He thinks I am insane. Especially in last night's clothes with last night's smells and today's headache.

"Okay, well, we don't need to talk about me. I can do what I want," I say. I sound about ten. It's awful. And Bernardo looks mad too, like I'm supposed to jump up and down and stand up for our love in the face of all this judgment and all these pastries. "It's not even the issue. The issue is Karissa. She's why we're leaving!"

"She's not why we're leaving," Bernardo says in his small, hurt voice.

"Leaving?" Arizona says, and Roxanne shakes her head at me like it is definitely time for me to shut the eff up.

"Why are you doing this?" I ask Karissa. I try to think of ways to tell them about her lies where I don't sound like I'm trying to get some messed-up kind of revenge.

"We're together, Montana," Karissa says. "Your father and I. I can't keep secrets from him like that. I'm not like you and Natasha and all these other women, keeping secrets, being half in the relationship and half out. He's going to be my family. That means something real to me. I value him. And our family."

Arizona winces at the name Natasha and turns away from me, so far in the other direction that she's facing the wall. I wonder if I've lost her.

"But you haven't been honest! Oh my God, this is insane! She made up everything about her family. I am not the liar here. I'm not the big ugly secret keeper!"

"Show me your hand," Dad says again. His voice is louder.

"Show him," Karissa says, like I'm going to listen to her instead of him. She puts her hand in his and tilts her head and assumes this motherly stance that is absolute bullshit.

"She lets us drink," I say. "It's probably illegal." Now I'm desperate. If the Big Things won't resonate, maybe I can make them believe the smaller things. The little hiccups that have been adding up all summer so far.

"Montana, I'm not fucking around right now," Dad says. His face is severe. He's loud and spitting. I show him my hand. The one with the tattoo. It's funny that he finds it so surprising, given that he clearly knew it was there. "You didn't do this," he says.

"We're in love," I say.

But then I'm crying too. Because this isn't really how it's supposed to be. This is more like Dad telling me and Arizona about his latest wife in the diner and not at all like the celebration and romance Bernardo and I wanted. This isn't special and ours. This, too, is like the painting of the person with the painting of the person with the painting. A repeat of a repeat of a repeat.

"Did you think I would like this?" Dad says. His voice drops, and he's talking only to me now. Arizona stomps out of the room, and Roxanne follows her with a sigh of relief. I look to Bernardo, but he's staying still. Steady. He's not leaving me with this. He pours himself a coffee and keeps an eye on Karissa, like she might jump one or both of us. Like she's an explosive.

"It has nothing to do with you," I say. "You need to worry about who you're marrying. She's not who she says—"

"I thought you didn't believe in marriage," Dad says. It does sound like something I would have said in the diner or on the stoop or right here, over coffee, wishing I could smoke in front of my father.

"I don't believe in *your* marriages," I say.

"You're a kid. You don't know what you need or want. Or what you believe in."

I have lost the ability to speak.

"You're going to change," Dad says. "A million times over." It sounds more like a hope of his than a fact. And it stings, since I've seen a photograph detailing all the ways he'd like me to change.

"Montana doesn't want to change for you," Bernardo says.

"Well, what the hell do you think she's doing with you?" Karissa says.

Bernardo pretends not to have heard her. But I heard her.

"This is all me," I say. I mean the hair and the eyebrow ring and the tattoo and the being in love with Bernardo. But I also mean it in comparison to Karissa, and even Arizona, who are both part plastic and faking it. "You've always wanted me to change," I say to my father, the most honest I've ever been to him, the most direct. "You gave me that stupid gift certificate and told me I'd never be good enough and you sit there waiting for me to improve, and sorry, but this is who I'm going to be."

"Gift certificate?" Dad asks.

I wonder if there has been a single day I haven't thought about the plastic surgery gift certificate promise in my drawer. It's like my mother—a thing that is haunting me and changing everything. A thing I wish weren't true.

"You and Natasha. Our thirteenth birthdays. The promise of plastic surgery," I say, thinking we're family and I can use shorthand, but Dad looks full-on befuddled.

"That was a long time ago," Dad says. "A lifetime ago. I don't remember everything single thing that happened when—"

I wish Arizona were hearing this with me.

"You don't remember," I say. I knew. But I didn't really know.

"I'm sure there's all kinds of things we both remember differently," he says.

"It's in my bedroom. It's a thing you did to me. It's *the* thing you did to me," I say. "It wasn't a lifetime ago. None of it was. It's all part of my lifetime. All of it." I look him right in the eye. I say it clearly, the way we rarely talk to each other.

Dad doesn't look down or up or anywhere else.

He furrows his brow and tries to remember. Seeing him try to remember is almost as good as him remembering. I think he's about to apologize. Or tell me he remembers. Or tell me that he believes me, that it happened and that it mattered and that it changed everything.

"We'll work through this," Karissa says, "as a family. We can go to family counseling. We'll talk about it. Okay? We can consider it. Bernardo is a really nice guy. So now we're all on the same page, and I think we can all agree that Montana shouldn't be seeing this Natasha woman, and then everything will be fine and she can make a nice, clearheaded choice with her family."

Karissa's voice sounds so different. Unnatural. Like a cartoon version of a mother. Swinging and singing and old.

Bullshit.

Even my dad feels it. He clears his throat.

Maybe he even pauses to hear the things I've been saying in this kitchen, about her lies. About not knowing who she actually is.

Maybe he sees how much he's chosen not to see over the years.

He shuffles his feet and looks from me to Bernardo to Karissa and back around again. He pours himself a coffee and lets Bernardo pass him the milk. We all listen to the endless racket of the city outside the window. The noises we don't usually even notice because we're so used to them, but sometimes, at the most important times, we hear them like strangers would. Like tourists in a strange land, we finally see where we live and who we are.

It's the eye of a storm, but I don't know what's on the other side of it. I'm no meteorologist.

"That's not actually right, Karissa," he says. He clears his throat again, and I wonder if he'll be able to get the words out at all. I'm stunned into silence. "This is between me and my daughter." It's a squeaky sound. And sad.

"Our daughter," Karissa says. I don't even recognize her. I squint, to see if that will help, but she's not a girl I know anymore. She's grasping.

She was never the girl I thought I knew. She is only an invented person. It's terrifying me still, the casual way she lied about something so large. And now she's lying here too. Calling me her daughter. Changing her face. Pretending to be someone else.

I wonder what we'll look like in her retelling of this part of her life. Because I know now, with a fierce certainty, that she will retell this to someone in five years or ten and it will be entirely changed. Resculpted for her purposes. More dramatic or tragic or beautiful than it really is.

She has a lot in common with my father, in some ways. They both reimagine reality to be something different. My father creating people anew just as Karissa creates her life anew.

"No," Dad says, his voice growing louder. It feels like a door has opened between us. "She's not your daughter at all. In any way. She's mine." He's talking to Karissa the way he's talked to me and Arizona in the past. Deliberate and sure. Inarguable.

Karissa slams down her coffee mug and storms upstairs.

"You should go too," Dad says to Bernardo. For sure Bernardo's adjusting his body into the shape of an anchor so that he can stay, but Dad taking a sudden stand makes me want to follow suit. I have to do the same.

"I'll meet you later," I say.

"I don't want to leave you with this," he says, and rubs his tattoo like it's a genie's bottle that will grant him the wish of staying with me, but I don't want anything but to stand in the moment where my father declared me to be his family over Karissa.

"I'm okay," I say. "I promise." He leans in to kiss me, but I'm so afraid of wrecking what's happened that I only let him kiss my cheek. This moment is made of glass. It is not a durable thing.

And like that, it's me and my dad drinking coffee in the kitchen. Like fathers and daughters do.

July 17

The List of Things to Be Grateful For

1 Showing up at our bench at the park to discover Arizona and Roxanne are there even though we didn't talk about coming. The way they shove over to make room for me. Remove their purses. Recross their legs.

2 The fact of Bernardo at his bench, with his friends, like we could take it all back and do it all over and it would be just as magical but maybe different too.

3 Staying at our own benches. Talking with our own friends. Making eyes at each other. The romance of saying nothing.

forty-four

There are two bridesmaid dresses laid out on my bed three days later—one for me and one for Arizona. There's a note from Karissa about being sorry but also proud and on a quest to do the right thing.

It tells me not to drive a wedge between her and my father.

It tells me to be careful.

It tells me she hopes I like the dress.

I promised my father we'd come to the wedding when I sat with him in the kitchen the other day.

"Karissa's family didn't die in a car crash," I said, and watched his face for signs of horror.

He nodded. "If that's true, it's quite shocking," he said.

"Like, scary, Dad," I said. I wanted more of an impact. I wanted to see myself reflected in him—the crazed feelings I had in the club coming to the surface on his face, in his words. "You can't be with someone like that."

"I said this was different," he said. "I love her. I love all of her, no matter what. I'm working on it. That's what you girls want, right? For me to love someone without wanting to change them?" He looked heartbroken—the down-turned mouth of someone who keeps failing even when they think they're succeeding.

"Not, like, unconditionally," I said. Dad sighed and rubbed his forehead. He ate some French toast pastries and poured another cup of coffee for himself, so full that it splashed out the top and singed his fingers and spotted his shirt. Normally he'd run upstairs and fix it, but he didn't this time. He stayed with me.

"I'm trying to do the unconditional loving thing," Dad said. "It's not going to be perfect. But I'm marrying this girl."

"You've already changed her," I said. I wanted to tell him that every time he changed her I took it as a sign that he wants me to change too. I wanted to tell him I'd seen the terrible picture in his desk and that I may never recover from that, either. I wanted to tell him how unnecessary and depressing it all is—these problems he'd created.

But he looked so sad and small, pouring syrup on the pastries and avoiding eye contact, that I couldn't.

"You know what your mom used to say?" he said at last. He picked up my hand, the one with the ring tattoo, and turned it over, looking at the mark.

"I have no idea, actually," I said. I gave him a strong look, like he needed a reminder that I don't really have a mom, not the way I'm supposed to.

"I'm not going to get it quite right," he said. "She had a way with words, your mother."

"I didn't know that either," I said. I sounded bitter without meaning to, but maybe that's simply what I was, about my mother. Bitter.

"She used to say something about love meaning that you can see something awful in someone and not want to change it. That's why she left me, she said. Because I didn't get that."

He twirled a piece of pastry around and around in the syrup, making sticky patterns.

"I probably didn't say it right," he said.

I wanted to hear her say it right. I wanted that bad.

And I wanted to be like my mother. This little bit. This one little bit.

Arizona's in her old room, lying on the bed and staring at the glow-in-the-dark stars she put on the ceiling a million years ago, when Mom sent some letter about how you can see so many stars when you're out of the city. Arizona wanted the city to be every bit as good as wherever Mom was. To prove her wrong.

"We have the dresses," I say. I hold them up so she can get a look at the bright-red color, the ribbon straps, the too-low necklines.

"We're not wearing them," Arizona says.

"On board. What are we gonna do? Jeans with bikinis? Our Halloween costumes from the year we were mice?"

"He doesn't want to marry her," Arizona says. "That's what you said, right? When he talked to her the other day, he told her she wasn't family?"

"Like, sort of," I say. I get out cigarettes and light one for each of us.

"You know I don't smoke," she says.

"This is a smoking conversation."

She takes it from me and inhales. It's weird to love something so stupid as smoking under fake stars with your sister, but I think I love it more than anything else I've done this summer.

"Maybe he won't go through with it," I say.

"That never happens," Arizona says. She's so much sadder than I realized. On her back her boobs stay pointed straight up to the sky, but the rest of her is drooping.

"Things change," I say, not totally sure if I believe it.

I tell her the things he said about our mother. She gets what I imagine is the same look on her face that I had—longing and hopefulness that there's a solution to all this. An explanation. A key.

"I want to look in the Closet of Forgotten Things," Arizona says.

"I've taken a lot from it recently," I say. I don't want her to go scrounging in there looking for the sweatband I took when I went to see Tess, or the cardigan I wore out with Karissa that first night at Dirty Versailles. Not that Arizona would ever notice any of these things, but I've made so many mistakes lately I don't want to risk it.

"I'm sorry," I say. It's maybe the first time I've ever said it out loud and without a caveat. An impossible thing that is probably true. I hold back the explanation about love and spontaneity and the need to be different from everyone else and let the words sit there, untouched.

Arizona nods.

"You shouldn't have had a whole thing with Natasha without me," she says. She holds out her fingers for another cig. We're in it. We're going for it. There's a desperate need for a cracked window, but we haven't done it yet. Almost as if we like being caught in a cloud of smoke and cancer and after-smell.

"You hated her," I say.

"Well, exactly."

"I didn't," I say.

"But you did. And if you didn't, you should have."

I let a huge sigh escape. "Do you hate them on behalf of Mom?" I say. "Because isn't she pretty hateable too?" It seems impossible, but this is now the most we've ever really talked about Mom. Not our feelings about her, at least. Not acknowledging that we want something from her. We've wondered where in the world she is and we've left postcards from her out on each other's dressers so that we can both see them, so that there are no secrets between us.

I've been awful, when I really think it through.

"I wish Dad had remembered exactly what Mom said. About being in love," Arizona says. "We should know things like that, don't you think?" The words are coming out slowly, and I think she's spent all summer avoiding this room and these fake stars while I've spent it falling in love. Historically speaking, we didn't used to do things separately. We lived different variations of the same life until right now. "Mom was so sad, before she left. When she started getting surgeries."

"To the closet!" I say. I'm not sure I'm ready for Arizona's revelations, and the air in her room is feeling very close and too humid. The girl needs an air conditioner in a desperate way.

"I've been sad," Arizona says. "Or maybe angry. I've been really angry. Going away makes everything seem bigger and smaller, both.

Clearer. All these strangers ask about your life and your family, and when you tell them . . . you see in their faces how fucked up it all is. I hated that about being in college." I'd thought she loved everything about being away from me and the people who know her best. "And you've changed. And Roxanne has a whole new life. And how am I the oldest but the least together? And why is Dad okay with marrying someone who clearly hates me? And did she really lie about her whole life and family? Shouldn't we be scared of that and not getting dressed up to celebrate it? And why are you so eager to do the things Dad does?"

"I don't have any of those answers," I say.

"Not even about you marrying Bernardo?"

I think I'm not so sure I'm marrying Bernardo.

I think that's not an answer I have anymore.

I think I have to tell Bernardo that I want a space between being so, so together and being apart. That I want that third thing. The slow love thing. The getting-to-know-someone thing. The loving-someone-no-matter-what thing, built over time.

But he might not want those things. He might get the Casey-look on his face.

"You know what was nice?" I say. Neither of us are addressing the other one's questions or comments. It's a funny way to have a conversation.

"Hm?"

"Being at the park. When he and I didn't speak. And he was the mysterious guy with the weird scarf and thick glasses and I was Montana and everything was undecided."

* * *

We head to the Closet of Forgotten Things, and unload it item by item. We play a sad version of our game, where we're both pretty depressed about the whole situation. Turning a snow globe of Cleveland upside down, I tear up.

"Beginning of the relationship," I say. "Cleveland could only be construed as romantic at the very beginning."

"Seems like something he would have done for Tess," Arizona says.

"No," I say, surprised that I remember something that Arizona doesn't. "It was for Mom. She collected them. Snow globes. You don't remember? At the end, though, he got her an Eiffel Tower one and an ice-skating one and one with little kids sledding with their mom. In the beginning he must have gotten her snow globes on even the stupidest trips, in the airports. Like, how much do you have to love someone to get them a snow globe of Cleveland?"

"And how much do you have to love someone to keep it?" Arizona says.

"But she didn't keep it," I say. "She forgot it."

I shake up the snow globe again. Mini Cleveland gets stuck in a hurricane of confetti-like snow.

"We should bring it to her," Arizona says. Fake snow is more mesmerizing than I would have thought, and I don't think I've heard her right.

"Hm?"

"Mom. We should bring her the things we think are hers." Next to Arizona there's a pile of other things that she must have been gathering when I was pretending to be in a Cleveland snowstorm. Some bangle-y bracelets. A Knicks hat. A pouch of crystals. "And we could find out what she said to Dad, about love and change and stuff. And I don't know, whatever else we need? We could do that."

"Okay," I say, because sometimes changing everything is really simple. "Let's go to California."

Arizona smiles, but I'm not kidding. I have the suitcase and the money saved up and the snap of interest that Bernardo caused when he started talking about running away together the other night. Without another pause, Arizona is on board. I can see it in her eyes and her shoulders that move back and down from their slumped-forward, sad position. We're going. Like that.

And that's what love is, I think. The automatic yes. The unthinking agreement.

The way people can be in two places one minute and one place the next. Like teleporting is possible.

Love is teleporting.

I'm totally figuring this all out.

forty-five

Arizona and I stay for the reception. Bernardo stands next to me in a black suit. He doesn't have his scarf on.

"It doesn't go with my tie," he says.

His tie is yellow and paisley and his father's, I'm sure. It's the first time I've seen him in something that isn't wholly his.

We dance to old Frank Sinatra songs that my dad loves, and Bernardo says he loves them too. "Oh," I say. "I don't."

He looks taken aback, like he didn't know I could have my own opinions on love songs. Or love in general.

"I love you in your dress," he says instead of discussing the relative merits of old-timey love songs. Arizona and I are both in pale sundresses instead of our bridesmaid gowns. It's better this way.

My dad looks so uncertain I wonder if he crossed his finger behind his back for the vows. I wonder if he's already contacted his divorce attorney, probably the busiest lawyer in the city given my dad's record, to discuss getting out of this whole thing ASAP.

He wasn't made for unconditional love, maybe. Maybe none of us are, really.

"Do you want cake?" Bernardo says. I keep not telling him I can't run away with him. I don't know how to tell him about the in-between place I want to be. The different kind of love I want to have.

If I were from a different family, I'd ask my dad about his uncertainty and what percentage of love is supposed to be about doubt and what percentage about sureness. But we are not that family, and my dad can take a half step closer to being what I need him to be, but in his tux and red tie and red boutonniere and shiny gold wedding band, he is still mostly the old dad.

And he's given me all the answers I need.

"I hate wedding cake," I say.

If he loves me the way I want to be loved, I can make a mistake and be a different girl from the one he imagined, from the ideal one in his head. If he loves me the way I need him to, it will be okay that I'm not running away with him, that I'm going away with Arizona.

And if he doesn't, that's okay too.

forty-six

"Bernardo and I were going to go on the train too," I say.

"Romantic," Arizona says. She has a duffel bag and I have the tiny wheel-y suitcase Tess left behind. We brought them to the wedding and stored them in the special room at the Ritz that Karissa got ready in.

She didn't even notice them. Or us at all.

We'd clinked champagne glasses, and Karissa said she hoped we could all move forward as a family. I conducted some kind of physics experiment with the glass flute. How hard could I squeeze it without it shattering?

Karissa looked pretty but not good.

"You're next!" she said, filling our glasses and making us toast again. I think some small part of each of us, Karissa, Arizona, and me, thought this wasn't going to happen after the last few days. So it felt more like a dream than a wedding, and we weren't really there at all, in some ways. We were already on the train, across the country, trying to fix the broken parts of ourselves.

"We'll come back, right?" I say, watching the city behind us from the train. Because New York City can't possibly continue on without us. We are the ones keeping it alive, I think. With our cigarettes and dyed hair and cursing and stoop sitting and coffee inhaling, aren't we the very essence of the city?

There's no reason to say any of that to Arizona, who doesn't smoke enough cigarettes or have cool enough hair to count. But she's New York too, with her little heels and perfect outfits and sturdy boobs and sad eyes.

"Don't think about next," Arizona says, "when we're still doing now."

It's possible she's a prophet or a Buddha or something truly special and Important. But it's also possible that she's a little drunk from the open bar at the wedding and the promise-making shots we took and the champagne with Karissa, who I guess I don't really know at all, and the way adventure feels when it's moving through your veins.

I write down one more List of Things to Be Grateful For, to send to Bernardo.

"Do you think Mom will look like me or you?" Arizona says, like those are the only two options. We're on the train, side by side in a sleeper car, and I sort of can't wait for night to fall so we can go to sleep to the shaky, grumbling movements.

I shrug. Maybe I don't care who she looks like. What she looks like.

I don't want to be my mother, but I want to be a little like her. I don't want to be my father. But I want to be a little like him too. And a little of Arizona. And a little of something else.

I don't know exactly what I want.

I want Bernardo, but not the way it's been.

I take out my eyebrow ring but decide to keep my hair pink. I hope he keeps the parts of what we did together that he likes best too.

I hope that includes keeping me.

Bernardo's initial is on my finger, and I wonder what else it could stand for. I want us to be together, but not engaged. I want us to be something but not everything.

Beautiful.

Branded.

Bystander.

Breathe.

Blip.

Becoming.

Or maybe it stands for the summer I fell in love so hard my whole world changed. Maybe that's enough, even if it doesn't end in forever.

Belong.

It doesn't mean what I thought it did.

July 17

The List of Things to Be Grateful For: The For Bernardo
Edition

1 The way the city looks when you are holding hands with
someone versus the way it looks when you are not. That
it is beautiful either way. That it changes but doesn't
change.

2 How much can shift when you go from dirty blond to dirty
pink. The space between being pretty and being loved,
and not having to know which you actually are.

3 The things that didn't happen. The words I didn't say. The
promises I didn't keep. The undone. The things I didn't
hold on to. The things I'll never know. The person I didn't
become for you.

Acknowledgments

Thank you as always to my agent, Victoria Marini, and my editor, Anica Rissi, for making me feel understood, heard, capable, and strong. And for brilliantly locating the hearts of my books long before they are even books. I am so lucky to have you both in my life.

Thank you of course to my family—especially to Ellie and Amy for giving me adorable writing breaks with their video chats.

Thank you to Caela Carter, Alyson Gerber, Amy Ewing, and Alison Cherry for your amazing insights, the care you take with my characters, and all the little and big ways you make book-writing (and person-being) more possible.

Thank you Brandy Colbert for the way you understand my words, listen to my fears, share my joys, and push me to be better. Also for being an excellent Life Twin.

Special thank-yous to lovely, smart, and patient superstar and pal Alexandra Arnold, to Katherine Tegen, Rosanne Romanello, Valerie Shea, Bethany Reis, Amy Ryan, Erin Fitzsimmons, and the rest of the

Katherine Tegen Books team, who have all been so supportive of my books and me. I am incredibly proud to call Katherine Tegen Books my home.

Thank you to booksellers and librarians, who have been wonderful these past few years.

Thank you Julia Furlan for helping with this book, but more importantly, helping with every other aspect of my life. And to Anna Bridgforth, Honora Javier, and Pallavi Yetur for Being There.

Thank you Frank Scallon for listening to a lot of writer-talk, a lot of book-talk, and for being the best.

I have been blessed with so many amazing writer-friends who are now also friend-friends. Thank you for making this journey legitimately fun even when it is also terrifying. Most especially Jess Verdi, Mary Thompson, Kristen Kittscher, Lindsay Ribar, Mindy Raf, Dahlia Adler and Caroline Carlson.

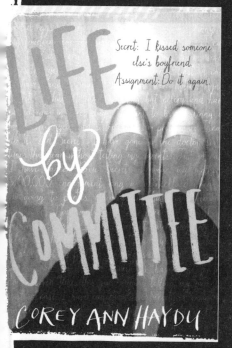
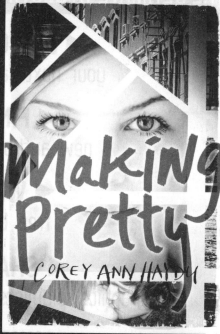